This book belongs to:

Juanita and
Nannette Smith

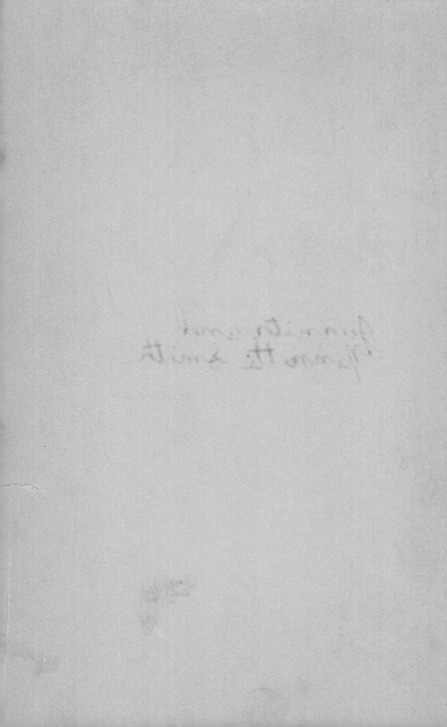

Good Housekeeping's
Best Book of
Mystery Stories

Good Housekeeping's
Best Book of
Mystery Stories

Edited by
PAULINE RUSH EVANS

Illustrated by
IRV DOKTOR

GOOD HOUSEKEEPING MAGAZINE

Distributed by
PRENTICE-HALL, INC. Englewood Cliffs, N. J.

Acknowledgements

Thanks are due to the following authors, publishers, publications and agents for permission to use the material indicated.

The Bodley Head for "The Open Window" from THE SHORT STORIES OF SAKI by Saki (H. H. Munro). George T. Bye and Company for "The Mystery in Four-and-a-Half Street" by Louise and Donald Peattie, copyright Louise and Donald Peattie. Mrs. George Curry for "Miss Hinch" by Henry Sydnor Harrison. Curtis Brown, Ltd. for "Nearly Perfect" by A. A. Milne, © 1950, by The Hearst Corporation, with the permission of the Author's Estate. Dodd, Mead & Company, Inc. for "The Fenchurch Street Mystery" from THE OLD MAN IN THE CORNER by Baroness Orczy, copyright © 1909 by Dodd, Mead & Company, Inc., copyright renewal 1937 by Baroness Orczy; for "The Blast of the Book" from THE SCANDAL OF FATHER BROWN by G. K. Chesterton, copyright © 1935 by G. K. Chesterton. Doubleday & Company, Inc. for "The Adventure at the Toll Bridge" from NIGHT BOAT AND OTHER TOD MORAN MYSTERIES by Howard Pease, copyright 1936 by Sprague Publications, Inc. McIntosh and Otis, Inc. for "The Dead Run" by W. J. Wallace, copyright © 1953 by W. J. Wallace, originally published in *Collier's*. Harold Ober Associates for "The Case of the Perfect Maid" by Agatha Christie, copyright © 1942 by Agatha Christie. Paul Reynolds & Son for "The Owl Hoots Twice" by Sax Rohmer, copyright, 1948, by the Crowell-Collier Publishing Company. Story Parade, Inc. for "Forgotten Island" by Elizabeth Coatsworth, copyright 1942 by Story Parade, Inc. The Viking Press, Inc. for "The Open Window" from THE SHORT STORIES OF SAKI by H. H. Munro, copyright 1930 by The Viking Press, Inc., N. Y.

The editor and publisher have made diligent efforts to trace the ownership of all copyrighted material in this volume, and believe that all necessary permissions have been secured. If any errors have inadvertently been made, proper corrections will gladly be made in future editions.

Introduction

Mystery stories come in all sizes and shapes, all types and kinds. There are folk legends and modern "whodunits"—stories of suspense, detective stories, and tales of the supernatural. But different as they may be, all real mysteries have one thing in common: they present a problem—a puzzle that is interesting to solve.

A good mystery always asks a question. Sometimes it's "Who did it?" as in the story by Agatha Christie about the too perfect maid who came to help out the old ladies. Sometimes it's "*Why* did they do it?" as in *The Dead Run*, W. J. Wallace's fine story of a hair-raising chase through the rugged countryside of Scotland. And sometimes the question is "What was done?" and you are left with the mystery still partly unsolved. A good example of this is *The Rescue at Sea*. I don't think you will be perfectly sure of what really happened when you finish reading the story, any more than I was. (But if you are, I wish you'd let me in on the secret.)

There are sixteen stories in this collection, and I'm not sure which is my favorite. Two which I like equally well are quite different: *The Purloined Letter* by Edgar

Allan Poe, father of the detective story, and *Nearly Perfect,* that delightfully witty tale by none other than A. A. Milne, best known for a completely different kind of story—*Winnie-the-Pooh.*

And naturally I can't guess which you will like best. But one thing at least I *do* know. You'll have an exciting time finding out!

Danbury, Conn.   P. R. E.

Contents

Good Housekeeping's
Best Book of
Mystery Stories

HOWARD PEASE

The Adventure at the Toll Bridge

Fog hazed across the low country that night as Tod Moran, with the utmost caution, drove his little car along the levee road. This was not a tule mist, he told himself as he peered past the windshield wiper, this was a real sea fog which sometimes crept upriver from San Francisco Bay. It made driving mighty slow. And at midnight he must be at the tollhouse on Bridge No. 3 to take over the graveyard watch.

When the levee road fell away behind and he glimpsed the white rails curving to the left, he breathed easier. Steadily the old Ford climbed in a sweeping curve until it was high above the river, then the roadway straightened out for its mile-long span across the San Joaquin. From the gloom ahead soon emerged the lights of the little toll office.

Buck Collinson stuck his head out the Dutch door.

"About time you're here, young feller," he called. "Two minutes to midnight."

"Well, I made it, didn't I?" Tod retorted. He swung his car out onto the narrow parking space opposite the office. "How's business?"

"Rotten." Buck opened the office door for him to enter. "I guess you'll have plenty of time to get your studies done. What's it tonight? Math again?"

"No such luck. History. Feudal age."

"Huh!" Buck Collinson snorted in disgust as he buttoned his suède jacket across his chest. "I can't see how studyin' about tripe like that'll get you anywhere these days."

Tod wholeheartedly agreed. He opened the cash drawer, counted the money with a practiced hand, and signed a paper showing he had received one hundred and forty-odd dollars from the four-to-twelve shift. "What's in these envelopes, Buck? Bills paid?"

"Yep. Some o' the trucks dropped 'em off when they crossed tonight. Three hundred and two dollars in checks and currency. Count it. Better watch that drawer careful too. We don't want to be left without change like we was after that holdup last month."

Tod grinned as he closed the money drawer. "Don't worry. This boy knows how to use a pistol."

"That so?" Buck Collinson's dark face showed concern. "Listen, brother. If any tough birds come along asking you to hand over that cash I'd advise you to do

"Tripe like that won't get you any place."

it. I ain't too keen about taking flowers to you in the hospital—or to your funeral either."

"Right you are, Buck. I'll watch my step." Tod nodded slowly, his gray eyes thoughtful. "It's No. 2 those guys have been after lately, isn't it? More money there."

"Yep—but more lonesome here." Buck opened the door with a quick movement. "See you later."

Buck's small red coupé disappeared into the fog toward the mainland. Tod stood at the door until the sound of the motor receded into the distance. For eight hours now he would be alone. Even the cars and trucks that passed during the night would be relatively few, for Toll Bridge No. 3 was no longer on the main artery of travel between Sacramento and the Bay. And on a foggy night there would be even less traffic. Pulling up his coat collar, he listened. No car was coming. Time now to make his rounds.

He plunged into the dripping grayness and turned toward the mainland. A few yards brought him to the safety barrier. He pulled down the long black-and-white arm, noting with satisfaction that its red light instantly went on. He pushed it up again and the light winked out.

Back he went to the tollhouse, crossed the checking bar and the weighing scales, and came to the end of the concrete roadway. Before him lay the steel section which was raised vertically in the manner of a lift whenever a steamer passed through. His shoes rang loudly as he advanced to the middle of the lift and leaned over the rail, facing upriver. The tide was on the ebb. He could hear far below him the current washing softly against the steel and masonry foundations of the towers. Through the fog the colored lights were dimly visible. The gray obscurity closed about the red and the green lamps as if bent upon shutting out all sense of direction for oncoming ships. But Tod was not worried. The telephone always announced the approach of a steamer from No. 2 downstream or from the smaller drawbridge that spanned the San Joaquin several miles up its course. When word reached No. 3 on a thick night, there was plenty of time to switch on the foghorns.

Crossing to the downriver side, he found the lights there even more obscured. No matter. Toll Bridge No. 3 had never yet been the scene of an accident with any seagoing freighter from the Bay.

A heavy truck, roaring up the incline from Marsh Island half a mile away, sent him hurrying on to the other safety barrier beyond the lift. The signal was in perfect working order. He waited for the truck to emerge from the mist and then jumped upon the step and rode back to the office. The truck, carrying a load of asparagus, was on its way to the mainland and the early market in San Francisco. He weighed it quickly, had the driver sign the slip, and then listened to its departing rumble. Silence once more pressed close about him.

Time now for a little real work. Slamming shut the upper half of the door, he turned to the high desk and opened his history. *The feudal system,* he read, *was the direct outgrowth of a need for protection in a world not yet civilized.* He read slowly, intently, just as he always did when alone on the graveyard shift.

Tod Moran worked for three nights every week end on Toll Bridge No. 3. As relief man he allowed the three regular men to get their weekly day off. It was a good job, Tod knew, and paid his expenses at college. Moreover, he usually had some time for study.

Yet tonight, for some unknown reason, he didn't seem able to concentrate. Maybe it was because Buck Collinson's jibe still echoed in his mind. Buck was right, too, Tod decided. There was no connection between the old feudal age in Europe and this modern machine age in America. Reading this stuff was not only boring; it was useless as well. But an outline had to be ready for his history instructor on Monday. Once the blamed thing was finished he could proceed to forget what it was all about.

Again he turned to his book. *When a runner announced the coming of an enemy to the lord of the castle* . . . Settling himself on the stool, Tod hunched his shoulders. This was better. He read with mounting interest. The only sound in the little office was the soft purr of the electric stove at his feet.

Interrupted only twice during the next hour, he was deep in his outline of the Carolingian age when he abruptly rubbed his eyes. His pencil, poised over the word *vassal,* dropped to the desk. The bridge lights winked once—twice! Darkness surrounded him.

Without misgivings he waited for them to flash on again. He wasn't concerned—not yet. Over at the substation across the delta islands the night engineer always switched the bridge onto another line when anything like this occurred. But always before, he suddenly recalled, the juice had gone off when a storm was raging in the Sierras and sweeping down into the valley. On a still night with only fog hanging over the river country any interruption in the service was unusual.

When he noticed the glowing units of the electric stove gradually grow dim and entirely disappear he became slightly uneasy. Maybe he'd better telephone the substation. Often during the small hours of the morning he had to raise the lift to allow a seagoing cargo-carrier to pass through on its way to the port of Stockton. Before he phoned, however, he'd better see if the line which served the motor was also out of order.

He flung open the office door, and at once the fog swirled in. Diving across in the darkness, he made his way more slowly into the motor shed. He lighted a match and pulled down the big switch. The motor began its shining whir. He was relieved. It was only the lights then.

Back in the office again, he felt for the telephone book. Several matches aided him in finding the number. He lifted the receiver from its hook.

"Hello," he said in a voice that rang loud in the confined space. "Operator!"

No answer. Not even a faint buzz sounded over the wire. He suddenly felt his heart turn cold. The line was dead.

Seated perfectly rigid on his stool, he tried to collect his thoughts. If the electric lights alone had gone off he wouldn't have felt so apprehensive. But the telephone too! It couldn't possibly be a coincidence. Something was up.

On the instant he slid off the stool. He took a step toward the little drawer at one end of the desk. When his fingers came in contact with cold steel and his hand closed round the butt of a pistol he gained new courage. Funny thing though, he hadn't heard any car.

Cautiously he turned to the door, leaned out the upper section, and listened. The fog seemed to blot out any sound. Yet he suspected that from either the island shore or the mainland someone would be coming quickly, intent upon gaining possession of the money in the drawer. The money! He whirled, opened the cash drawer, and felt around in the back until he found a soft cotton bag. This he hurriedly filled. He'd leave only ten or fifteen dollars in the till.

A moment later he was at the door. He had decided where he would hide the money. He ran for a short distance toward the Marsh Island end of the bridge and drew to a stop in the center of the steel roadway. Here on the lift would be a safe place. Feeling his way to the rail, he dropped the bag at his feet. On a thick night like this it would be overlooked here. As he turned away his hand felt for the revolver in his pocket. He drew it out and examined it in the darkness. It was loaded.

To his ears at that moment came the muffled sound of a car approaching from Marsh Island. He could hear the motor as it sped up the incline. Was it a casual fare—or did the car contain an enemy?

An enemy . . . Through his mind flashed a sentence he had read an hour before. *When a runner announced the coming of an enemy to the lord of the castle the first order given was to raise the drawbridge.* As though impelled by an urgent command Tod turned and raced for the motor shed. If he raised the great steel lift between him and the approaching car he could cut off the enemy.

In the shed he struck a match and pulled down the heavy switch. A steady whine came from the motor. At once he took a firm hold on a second switch and pressed it up into place. A loud rumble reached his ears. The steel section of the bridge was slowly lifting.

The next moment a thought struck him like a blow. Suppose it was merely an unsuspecting fare coming across the bridge? While the safety barriers would drop the very instant the lift began rising, there would be no red glow to warn the oncoming car, which might break through the wooden pole and dive off the concrete into the river. In that deep channel, with the current sweeping down toward the bay, only one end could await the occupants—death. With a hand that trembled he reversed the switch. Slowly the lift descended.

He brought it to a stop, however, before it had settled into place on its foundations; then he rushed out to see how far above the roadway it rested. The night was so black that he had to stretch forth his hands. The lift had stopped nearly three feet above the road.

Taking a deep breath, he waited. The oncoming car, apparently unsuspecting, was still racing toward him from Marsh Island. He could hear its motor clearly now; it was almost up to the lift. An instant later he caught the muffled crash of breaking wood. The car had plunged through the safety barrier.

Tod stood utterly still. He heard the grinding of brakes and a curse that ripped through the fog. The car had come to a halt. Good. Friend or foe, there was now no danger of its catapulting into the river. Yet a man could easily hop up three feet to the lift and run across. A man? . . . He recalled that it had been two men who had held up Buck Collinson a month before. It had been a black sedan, Buck never tired of telling, that had driven up to the toll office; and, while the driver kept him covered with an automatic, a confederate had rifled the money drawer. Suppose, Tod reflected, the same two men were now across there in the darkness, jumping from their black sedan?

At the thought he made a dive for the shed. It took him only a moment to switch on the power. An instant later the steady grind of the lift sounded deep and prolonged as it rose like an immense elevator into the night. There was no need for him to remain here longer. When the lift reached the top of the towers it would automatically stop.

Outside he could see nothing. The damp fog, pressing about his face, beaded his eyelashes with moisture. High above him the lift was still slowly rising. No sound of any kind came from across the open river. He turned back toward the toll office. What if another car came from the mainland? He couldn't be sure it would mean only another broken safety barrier.

Quickly he felt his way across to the little parking space. He climbed into his Ford, started the motor, switched on the lights, and then drove the car out into the roadway. When the lowered barrier pole hung directly across his headlights he pulled up short and, leaving the lights on, jumped out. Above him he heard the lift stop; only a faint purr came from the shed. Yet in his ears was the steadily growing sound of another motor. He listened. From the mainland a car was coming.

Instinctively his hand went to his pocket. He drew out the revolver and, standing well back in the shadow of his car, faced the safety barrier. Now he was ready. Let them come.

Out of the fog emerged two headlights. The bumper and radiator of a car took form as it slowed down and drew to a stop directly in front of Tod's own lights shining wanly through the mist. The arriving car was new and black in color.

A voice rang out. "Steamer going through?"

"Yes." Tod's voice was firm. "Stay right where you are. I've got you covered."

There came a startled grunt, then the voice went on. "What's the big idea? I'm Dr. Grover—on my way to a patient on Marsh Island."

Tod had never heard of any Dr. Grover. "Where are you from?" he questioned.

"Brentwood. I took over Dr. Taylor's practice six weeks ago. I've got to get through to the island as quickly as possible."

"Serious?"

"I'm not sure. It's old Mrs. Jameson. Taylor told me she's always getting him out in the middle of the night. But she does pay her bills." He paused for a moment. "Anything wrong?"

Tod moved forward a step. "I think so."

The rays of the Ford's lights disclosed the head and shoulders of a middle-aged man leaning out of his car window. "You're not very complimentary, young man. Who do you take me for?"

He listened in silence as Tod briefly told him. Finally he nodded. "So the other car's opposite, eh? Then I can't get across?"

"Not a chance."

There was no hesitation in his reply. "What can I do to help?"

"Turn around and go back to the first house a hundred yards from the bridge. That's the Stevens' place. Ask Mrs. Stevens to phone Buck Collinson and have him get in touch with the sheriff. Tell him to phone the substation and the telephone company too."

"That all?" Dr. Grover was slightly sarcastic. "And how about my patient?"

"The quicker you make it the bigger chance you'll have to save her."

"Oh, I'm not worried." The doctor's head disappeared. His car backed away, turned, and a moment later its red taillights vanished into the fog.

Once more Tod was alone. Somewhat uncertainly he glanced over his shoulder. Not more than twenty feet behind him lay the abyss that dropped away to the river far below. He raised his eyes to the steel tower, and his heart missed a beat at what he saw.

High above on the upraised lift he could faintly make

out the beam of a small flashlight against the steel girders. By thunder, he had forgotten something! Ladders led up to the towers on each side of the lift. Someone from that other car had climbed up the ladder on the far tower, made his way across the lift, and was now coming down to the tollhouse. How many were coming? One man—two?

On quick feet Tod went past the motor shed to the base of the steel tower. Putting his ear against the ladder, he listened. Footsteps, clearly audible, were descending in the darkness.

Without hesitation he raised his revolver. Aiming at the sky, he pulled the trigger. A shot cracked out, loud and abrupt.

"Better not come down," he shouted up into the fog.

There was no answer to his challenge. There was nothing he could see as he peered upward. The beam of the flashlight had vanished.

Again he put his ear to the ladder. The footsteps were still descending. So the shot had not been enough of a warning! Maybe he'd better take aim and show that he meant business. He could just hit the steel somewhere, not really plug the fellow. But in this pitch darkness—

At that moment, from upriver and appallingly close, sounded the dull blare of a whistle. His body grew taut. A steamer! All thought of the man on the ladder dropped from his mind. Once more came the muffled blare of the whistle, closer this time.

*Without hesitation **he** raised his revolver.*

He knew that sound. This was no river steamer with a rear paddle wheel; this was one of the seagoing cargo carriers that loaded grain at Stockton for the East Coast. Of six or eight thousand tons, it would need every safety device on Bridge No. 3. And the lights were out! Were the foghorns still working?

He rushed into the shed, swung down the proper switch and, hardly daring to breathe, waited for the sound of that first long wail of warning. He was familiar with them—the north horn loud and deep, the south one shrill and more abrupt. But no sound broke the stillness. The foghorns, too, were dead.

In a panic he swung about. That great deep-sea freighter was in danger. Bridge No. 3 was in danger. Outside he flung an agonized glance about him. The headlights of his Ford caught his eye.

Instantly he raced across to the open door of his car. Flinging himself into the seat, he started the motor, swung her into gear, turned, and drove with perilous speed past the dark little office straight for the void where the road dropped away. He put on his brake and stopped the car within two feet of the edge. Then he switched on his foglights in the desperate hope that their gleam, pouring downward, would be seen by the approaching ship. At the same time his other hand went into action. Under the intermittent pressure of his fingers the horn punctuated the stillness with steady notes of warning.

Would the captain and the river pilot aboard that big freighter realize that something was wrong on No. 3? When they heard the shrill horn sounding would they order full speed astern and stop to investigate? Between sounds he listened. He caught the faint clang of a bell, the steady throb of the steamer's engines. Upstream and almost level with himself he discerned a red light slowly approaching. It was the port light on the ship's navigation bridge shining warmly through the mist. Then, below it, portholes suddenly came into view. But the great ship was losing headway. He breathed easier.

Far below him the lookout on the forecastle head suddenly raised his voice. "Bridge twenty feet off starboard bow!" Almost at once a powerful searchlight on the navigation bridge flung its rays through the fog. The cone of light leaped down to the starboard, then swung back in a wide arc to port.

Abruptly Tod started. Something blunt and hard was pressing against his ribs. He turned his head. The shadowy figure of a man leaned over the car door. His face was muffled, his hat pulled low over his eyes. "Where's the coin, buddy?"

"In the office." In vain Tod tried to keep his voice steady.

"Twelve bucks? Come clean, buddy, if yer don't want to find yourself floating belly up. Where's the rest?"

The money. How unimportant it had suddenly become. The only thing that counted now was to get this steamer through in safety. "I put the money in a bag," Tod said quickly.

"Well, hand it across."

"You'll find it against the rail on the upstream side of the lift. Somewhere near the center of the span."

"Is this straight?"

"Yes. Can't you see all I want is to get this freighter through?"

"Okay. If I don't find it"—the pressure against Tod's side increased for a second—"I'll be back."

He was gone. His husky voice was only a memory that somehow didn't quite seem real.

From the river came the clang of a bell. Tod craned far out, gazing down to one side past his windshield. The blurred outline of the ship's wheelhouse drifted slowly by. Then a lifeboat hanging from its davits swam vaguely past. The low murmur of voices reached his ears. Two portholes of a lighted cabin came into view, drew abreast, and disappeared downstream. The big freighter had passed through Bridge No. 3.

On legs that were strangely weak Tod crawled from his car. Sweat stood out on the palms of his hands. By thunder, that was a close call. The money? It didn't matter.

He looked up in the darkness. Nothing but blackness met his gaze. Crossing to the motor shed, he leaned against the door. A low blare came from downstream.

The steamer was reaching the point where the San Joaquin joined the Sacramento.

Suddenly he raised his head. Across the open span a motor was starting. Well, what of it? Let it go. He heard the car turn and speed away toward Marsh Island. The man must have found the bag all right. Oh, why had he told him just where it was? Why hadn't he said the opposite rail? It was too late now. There'd be a nice little report for him to write up in the morning.

Slowly on tired feet he entered the motor shed, pulled down the switch, and heard the low rumble of the lift as it descended. There was nothing he could do but wait for Dr. Grover to return.

The doctor came back fifteen minutes later. "Everything all right? Good. Mrs. Stevens helped me do all the telephoning. Buck Collinson wasn't home yet, but I left word with his landlady. Now may I cross to my patient?"

"Thanks a million, Dr. Grover." Tod's voice was low, tired. "I'll get along okay now."

"How about the car that brought the men? They didn't get the money, did they?"

"Yes."

"Too bad. Well, I'll see you in about an hour."

Soon afterwards the sheriff arrived with a deputy, and almost on his heels followed a telephone linesman and a troubleshooter from the electric-light company. While the deputy went back to town to broadcast the alarm the sheriff plied Tod with questions. "About four hundred and fifty dollars, you say? How much in checks?"

"More than a hundred."

"They won't be cashed. The radio cars will soon be scouring this whole delta country. They'll pick up every black sedan on the roads."

Tod was once more his old self. "But how can we be sure it was a black sedan? I didn't even see it." He paused. "Let me have your flash, Sheriff, will you?"

"Okay."

Tod took it, entered the dark office, sat down upon his stool, and flung open his history text.

Behind him he heard a grunt of amazement. "What in thunder are you doing?" The sheriff stared down at the book. "Say, has this holdup driven you wacky? Or are you just a cool one? What you doing—studying?"

The office was suddenly flooded with light as the electricity came on. The foghorns began sounding, low and mournful.

"Shut off the horns, will you please, Sheriff?"

"I suppose they're bothering your studying, eh?" The sheriff stomped out in disgust.

Swiftly Tod searched in his history for a passage he vaguely remembered. Something was hammering in the back of his mind, something he could not put into words; but he knew that if he could only find the clue this half-formed idea would flash crystal clear. He read a page quickly, then turned to the next. Of a sudden he sat up straight. He had it. *With the drawbridge raised the castle would be safe for weeks, even months. It was only when there lurked an enemy—*

For some time he remained seated at his desk in silence. Finally he looked up to stare unseeingly out a window. At length he jumped from his stool, took the pistol from his rear pocket, and went out.

The sheriff met him by the motor shed. "Well, I turned 'em off. I don't suppose you even noticed."

"No," Tod told him, "I didn't."

The sheriff stared. Tod raised the revolver, pointed it aloft at one of the steel girders mistily visible in the light, took aim, and fired.

"You're a rotten shot, Moran. But what's the big idea?"

"I just wanted to see if my hand still shook."

"Well, it musta shook plenty to make you miss at this distance." The sheriff turned away.

Tod called after him. "Where are you going?"

"I'm going to take your little car if you don't mind and make a beeline for the Sacramento River. I've a hunch those birds might find their way blocked and turn back."

"Don't go yet." Tod spoke in all seriousness. "How long does it take a car to go upstream along the levee road, cross on the little drawbridge up there, and swing back along the mainland?"

"You mean to drive in a circle and come back to this point? About fifty minutes. In this fog, longer."

Tod took out his watch. "Then stay here. In half an hour the car you're hunting will be coming back to this bridge."

"Are you cuckoo?"

"No." Tod threw him a friendly grin. "Like you, I've a hunch; that's all."

"Well, I won't stay—see? If you're scared you can phone my office for another deputy when the line's fixed."

"Wouldn't you rather pick up this car yourself?" Tod urged.

"Baloney!" The sheriff regarded him with a puzzled frown. He moved off toward the parked Ford, hesitated, then sat down on the running board. "I'll stay just thirty minutes," he said.

The half-hour had almost dragged by when Dr. Grover pulled up on his way home from Marsh Island. "She was asleep when I arrived. Everybody sleeps but a doctor."

Three minutes later an empty truck rumbled up from the mainland. When it had disappeared toward the island shore the telephone rang. "Hi, Sheriff," Tod called. "She's working again."

For five minutes the sheriff kept the line hot. At last he swung about to Tod. "They've picked up five black sedans."

"But it isn't a black sedan we want," Tod insisted.

"I suppose," the sheriff remarked with heavy sarcasm, "you lamped a yellow limousine with pink stripes and forgot to mention it to me."

Tod had his head out the Dutch door, listening intently. His eyes flashed with sudden fire. "Get ready, Sheriff. Here comes a car. I think it's the one we want."

From the direction of the mainland an automobile was coming across Toll Bridge No. 3. Soon two headlights broke through the curtain of fog. The car slowed down and drew to a stop at the narrow parking space opposite the office. It was a smart red coupé.

"That's your man, Sheriff." Tod's voice was tense. "Take no chances."

Buck Collinson flung himself out the door. "Say, what's doing?" he called. "My landlady said Dr. Grover left word for me to come."

The Sheriff dropped his automatic to his side. "Rot! It's only Buck."

Tod reached for the sheriff's pistol. "I'll trade with you," he said quickly. He raised the automatic and pointed it directly at the man who worked the four-to-twelve shift. "We've got you, Buck."

Buck Collinson's dark face flushed. "What's the idea?"

"Stand right where you are," Tod commanded.

The sheriff looked across at Tod. "Do you mean,

Moran," he asked in a low tone, "you recognized the man who held you up tonight? You can swear it was Buck Collinson?"

Tod shook his head. "No, I didn't recognize him—or his voice either. But it was Buck just the same."

"What's the idea?"

"He's gone nuts, Sheriff." Buck's voice broke on laughter that was far from steady.

"Oh no, I haven't, Buck." Tod's hand never wavered as he faced the man in the suede jacket. "You made one mistake, Buck. Remember you told me that reading about the feudal age was just so much tripe? Well, it wasn't. It gave me an idea."

"Yeah?" Buck's low tone was filled with angry insolence. "An' what was this sweet little idea you got?"

Tod spoke with vibrant intensity. "You weren't held up last month, Buck. You took the money yourself and told a tall tale about it. And tonight you cut the wires —and came near wrecking a steamer. Furthermore, you substituted blank cartridges for the ones in the company's pistol."

"Bilge!" The word came forth with an oath, but Tod caught a glimpse of sudden fright in the man's dark eyes.

"We'll prove it. Sheriff, give that revolver of mine the once-over."

The sheriff at length looked up with amazement. "You're right, Moran. These are all blanks."

"Don't you see," Tod hurriedly explained. "Buck kept coming down that ladder after I fired because he knew there was no real danger from my revolver. He planned to change these blanks again when he came on duty at four this afternoon."

"You lie!" Buck challenged hoarsely.

Tod never took his gaze from the man's face. "Did you have time to hide the money? You needn't answer. Sheriff, maybe you'd better search his car. I wouldn't be surprised if the blamed fool didn't feel so sure of himself that he brought the loot along with him. The bag's got the company's name on it."

Tod heard the sheriff cross to the small red car and throw open the door. After a short while came his comment, "Nothing here." Then the rumble seat was opened. A moment later a grunt of surprise greeted Tod and his prisoner. "Moran, here's the bag—and it's full!"

Even as the sheriff spoke Buck Collinson made a swift dart forward and flung himself at Tod's legs. The youth went down to the pavement. But the sheriff was at his side in an instant, and when Tod finally rose it was to find Buck with handcuffs locked round his wrists.

The sheriff's face was grim. "It's a good thing I stayed with you, Moran. I apologize for saying maybe you were afraid."

"Maybe I was—a little," Tod admitted.

The sheriff grinned. "I thought you'd gone nuts. Honest I did. I thought you were studying that history book." He paused and dropped his voice low. "Just what were you up to?"

"Reading about the feudal age, Sheriff. Look, I'll show you." Tod entered the office and came back with the book. "I'll read you the lines. *With the drawbridge raised, the castle would be safe for weeks, even months. It was only when there lurked an enemy within the gates that imminent danger threatened.*" Tod stopped and looked across at the sheriff's prisoner. "You were the enemy within the gates, Buck Collinson."

"Hmm!" The sheriff nodded thoughtfully. "It strikes me, young feller, that the world hasn't changed so much after all. Maybe we can learn a thing or two from reading history."

WILHELM HAUFF

The Spectral Ship

My father occupied a little shop in Balsora. He was neither very poor, nor very rich, and was one of those persons who venture nothing, without great deliberation, for fear of losing the little they possess. He brought me up plainly and honestly, and it was not long before I was of considerable assistance to him. When I was eighteen years old, and just at the time when he had made his first really great speculation, he died, probably from anxiety at having entrusted so large a sum as a thousand gold-pieces to the treachery of the ocean. The result compelled me, not long after, to regard him as happy in his death; for a few weeks afterwards the news came that the ship, in which my father had ventured his goods, had gone to the bottom. But this misfortune could not break my youthful courage. I turned everything which my father had possessed into money. and set forth to try my fortune among strangers, accompanied by only one aged servant, who, from old associations, refused to separate himself from my destinies.

We embarked at Balsora, with favorable winds. The ship I had selected was bound for India. We had been sailing for fifteen days on the usual course, when the captain gave us notice of the approach of a tempest. He wore an air of great uneasiness, and confessed that, in this locality, he was not well enough acquainted with the true course to encounter a storm with indifference. He took in all the sails, and we ploughed along very slowly. The night had come on, clear and cold, and the captain was already beginning to think that he had been deceived in his anticipations, when suddenly a ship, which we had not seen till now, came on close by us with great speed. Wild shouts and frantic revelry sounded from her deck. The captain at my side was as pale as a ghost. "My ship is lost!" he cried; "for there sails Death!" Before I had time to inquire the meaning of his strange exclamation, the ship's crew rushed up, shrieking and howling. "Did you see him?" they shouted. "Our end has come at last!"

The captain ordered passages from the Koran to be read aloud, and took the helm himself. In vain; the storm visibly increased, and, before an hour had passed, the ship began to settle in the waves. The boats were hoisted out, and scarcely had the last man time to quit the wreck, when the vessel sank before our eyes, and I was floating beggared on the open sea. But our suffer-

Suddenly a ship came on close by us.

ings were not yet over. The tempest raged with increasing fury, and the boat soon became unmanageable. I flung my arms round my old servant, and we promised never to leave one another. Day broke at last. But just as the earliest rays of morning shone in the east, the wind caught our boat, and we were overturned. I have never seen any of the ship's company since.

The shock stunned me; and, when I awoke, I found myself in the arms of my old, faithful servant, who had saved himself on the overturned boat, and had drawn me up after him. The storm had subsided. Nothing was to be seen of our ship; but we discovered not far from us another vessel, towards which we were being driven by the waves. As we came nearer, I recognized the same ship which had rushed by us the previous night, and which had filled our captain with such intense terror. I felt a strange horror at its sight. The captain's exclamation of foreboding, so fearfully verified; the decayed look of the ship itself, on which, near as we were, and loud as we shouted, no living thing was to be seen, terrified me. But it was our only means of rescue, and we glorified the Prophet, who had watched so wonderfully over our safety.

A long rope hung from the bow of the vessel. We guided our boat towards it with hands and feet, to bring it within reach, and at last succeeded. But, although I exerted my voice to its utmost pitch, everything remained profoundly silent aboard the ship. At length we resolved to climb on board,—I, as the younger, going first. But, O horror! what a sight met my eye when I stepped upon the deck! The floor was red with blood, and twenty or thirty corpses, in Turkish clothes, lay extended on the planks, while at the mainmast stood a man, richly dressed, and with a sabre in his hand; his face pale and distorted, and through his temples went a long nail, fastening him to the mast. He was stone dead.

Such was my horror that I scarcely dared to breathe. Meanwhile my old servant had succeeded in following me. He, too, stood aghast at the sight of the deck, peopled solely by so many frightful corpses. We ventured at last, after calming somewhat the anguish of our souls by prayers to the Prophet, to advance farther into the ship. At every step we looked for some fresh and more dreadful horror to present itself to our gaze. But there was no further change; far and wide, no living creatures but ourselves, and the restless sea. We dared not speak above our breaths, lest the dead and transfixed master should turn his staring eyes upon us, or one of the dead bodies lift its ghastly head. At length we came to the stairs leading to the cabin. We halted involuntarily, and looked long at each other in silence, neither of us daring to express his thoughts aloud.

"O, master!" at length said my old servant, "some horrible deed has been committed here. But should the ship below be filled with murderers, I would rather

"At the mainmast stood a man . . ."

throw myself at once on their mercy, than remain a
moment longer among these frightful dead!" I shared
his feelings, and, plucking up a little courage, we descended to the cabin. Here, too, all was silent, and our
footsteps on the stairs were the only sounds we heard.
We halted at the cabin door. I held my breath and
listened; but no murmur came to our ears. I opened it.
The room was in the greatest disorder. Clothes, weapons
and other articles, lay scattered confusedly about. Nothing was in its place. The crew, or perhaps the captain,
had been carousing, to judge from appearances, only a
short time before the massacre. We went on, from
room to room, and everywhere we found scattered
about vast stores of silks, pearls, sugars and other valuable goods. I was beside myself with joy at all this; for,
as there was no one on board to claim them, I thought
I might fairly appropriate them to myself; but Ibrahim
called to my remembrance that we were still far from
land, and that without assistance from others we must
despair of reaching it.

We refreshed ourselves somewhat with the food and
wine, which we found at hand in great abundance, and
at length reascended to the deck. But here our flesh
crawled at the frightful appearance of the dead men,
and we resolved to throw them overboad, and relieve
ourselves of their presence. But imagine our sensations
when we found that not one of them could be lifted
from his position! They adhered so firmly to the deck,

that we should have been obliged to tear up the plank-
ing to remove them, and instruments to do this were
not at hand. Our attempts to release the captain from
the mast were equally unsuccessful; nor could we even
take away the sabre from his stark and rigid hand. We
spent the day in unhappy reflections over our situation,
and on the approach of night I permitted Ibrahim to lie
down to get some sleep; I myself remaining awake on
deck, to keep a look-out for means of escape or rescue.

But when the moon rose, and I judged by the stars
that it was about eleven o'clock, such an irresistible
torpor overpowered me, that I fell involuntarily to the
deck behind a cask which was standing near. Still my
condition more nearly resembled a stupefaction than a
sleep, for I could plainly hear the sea beating against
the sides of the vessel, and the sails creaking and groan-
ing in the wind. Suddenly I thought I heard voices and
men's footsteps on the deck. I tried to raise myself to
look, but an invisible power held me motionless, and I
could not move my eyes. Yet the voices came constantly
plainer to my ears; and it seemed as if a jovial ship's
company were hurrying to and fro about the deck. Now
and then, too, I thought I heard a master's powerful
voice, and the sound of ropes and sails drawn noisily
up and down. Gradually, however, my senses left me,
and I fell into a profound sleep, during which I thought
I could hear the clash of arms; and I did not wake till

the sun stood high in heaven, and was painfully burning my face. I looked about, confused and bewildered; the storm, the ship, the dead men, and the occurrences of the past night, coming before me like a dream. But, when I looked up, everything remained as it had been the previous day. Unmoved lay the bodies; the captain stood immovably at the mainmast. I laughed at my dream, and rose to seek my old servant.

I found him sitting sadly in the cabin. "O, master!" he exclaimed as I entered, "I would rather lie at the bottom of the ocean than spend another night on board this ship."

I inquired the cause of his distress, and he answered: "After sleeping some hours, I awoke, hearing people running up and down over my head. I thought at first it was you pacing the deck; but instantly perceived my mistake, for there were twenty or thirty moving over my head, and orders shouted in a stentorian voice struck hideously on my ear. At last heavy footsteps descended the stairs. I knew nothing further for some time; but, consciousness at length returning for a few moments, I saw the man who is nailed to the mast overhead sitting at this table, drinking and carousing, and him whose body, dressed in a suit of crimson, lies nearest to the captain, sitting here also, and sharing in his revels."

You may easily imagine, my friends, the effect this statement had on me. It had been, then, no vision of an excited fancy which had disturbed my slumbers, but a stern and terrible reality.

Meanwhile Ibrahim had been deep in thought. "I have it!" he exclaimed, at length. A stanza had occurred to his memory, which had been taught him by his grandfather, and which was of potent efficacy in exorcising apparitions; and he hoped by its aid, and by fervent prayers from the Koran, to keep away during the coming night the torpor which had overpowered our senses the evening before.

The old man's suggestion pleased me; and we waited in gloomy expectation the approach of night. There was a little apartment, opening out of the cabin, in which we resolved to take refuge. We bored several holes in the door, large enough to enable us to overlook the whole cabin, and then fastened the door on the inside as well as we could, while Ibrahim wrote the name of the Prophet in the four corners. Thus prepared, we waited for the horrors of the coming night.

About eleven o'clock a strong inclination to sleep came over me; but my companion begged me to recite prayers from the Koran, and I did so, with marked effect. All at once everything over our heads became replete with life; the ropes creaked, steps moved up and down on deck, and several voices could be plainly heard. We sat several minutes in intense anxiety, when we heard some one descending the cabin stairs. Hearing this, my old servant commenced reciting the verse which his grandfather had given him as a protection against magic:

> *"Be ye spirits of upper air,*
> *Or haunt ye the depths of the sea?*
> *In loathsome tombs do ye have your lair,*
> *Or come ye from fire to me?*
> *Remember Allah, your God and Lord;*
> *All wand'ring souls obey his word."*

I am free to confess I felt little confidence in this stanza; and, when the door opened, my hair stood on end. The same tall, handsome man, whom I had seen nailed to the mainmast, entered the cabin. The nail still pierced his forehead, but he had returned his sword to its sheath; and behind him came another man, less richly clad than his leader, whom I had also seen lying dead on deck. The captain, for such he undoubtedly was, had a livid face, a large black beard, and a pair of fierce, rolling eyes, with which he searched every corner of the cabin. I saw him with great distinctness as he passed our little chamber; but he seemed to take no notice of the door behind which we were concealed. Both took their seats at the table in the middle of the cabin, and conversed with each other in loud, harsh tones, and in an unknown tongue. Their voices grew louder and harsher, until at last the captain brought down his clenched fist on the table with such force that the whole room shook. The other sprang up, with a wild burst of laughter, and signed to the captain to fol-

He had a livid face, a black beard, and fierce eyes.

low him. The latter rose from his seat, tore his sabre from its sheath, and both left the apartment.

We breathed more freely after they had left us; but our terror was far from being at an end. The uproar on deck grew louder and louder. We could hear them running rapidly to and fro overhead, shouting, laughing, and yelling. At last a hellish noise was heard, mingled with yells and the clash of arms; then came a sudden silence.

When we ventured to return to the deck, many hours after, we found everything as we had left it the day before. Not one of the bodies had changed its posture, and all were as stiff as if carved in wood.

Thus passed many days on the ship. We drove constantly towards the east, where, according to my reckoning, land was surely to be reached at last. But though by day we traversed many miles, we seemed to return to our previous position during the night, for we found ourselves, when the sun rose, invariably in the same place. We could not explain this, otherwise than by supposing that the dead men steered their ship back every night with the trade wind. To prevent this we took in all the sails before night, and secured them by the same means we had employed with the cabin door; we wrote the name of the Prophet on parchment, together with the above-mentioned stanza, and fastened the talismans to the lowered sails. We waited in our state-room for the result, in intense anxiety. That night, magic seemed to be working with increased fury; but, O joy! the next morning the sails were still furled as we had left them the evening before. Henceforth, we spread during the day only so much sail as was needed to urge the ship moderately forward; and in this way in five days we advanced a considerable distance on our voyage.

At length, on the sixth day, we discovered land on the horizon, and gave thanks to Allah and his Prophet for our wonderful preservation. All this day and the following night we drove onward towards the coast, and on the seventh morning thought we discovered a city at no great distance. With great difficulty we hove over an anchor into the sea, and launching a small boat, which stood on the deck, rowed with all our strength towards the city. In half an hour we ran into the mouth of a stream which discharged into the ocean, and landed on the shore. Proceeding on foot to the city, we inquired its name at the gates, and learned that it was an Indian city, at no great distance from my original place of destination. We took lodgings at a caravansary; and, after refreshing our strength, which had been exhausted by our perilous voyage, I made inquiries for a man of wisdom and learning, giving our landlord to understand that I should prefer one somewhat acquainted with magic. He took me to a retired street, and knocked at an obscure house, giving me directions to inquire for Muley.

As I entered, an old, diminutive man, with a gray beard and a long nose, came towards me, and demanded my business. On my replying that I was in search of Muley the Wise, he told me it was himself. I asked him for advice as to what I should do with the dead bodies, and what measures I should adopt to get them out of the ship. He replied, that the people in the vessel had probably been bewitched because of some great crime perpetrated on the sea. He thought this witchcraft could be exorcised if they could be brought on shore; but that this was impossible, unless the planks on which they lay were taken up; that by all the laws of God and justice, the ship and all she contained belonged to me, but that I must keep profoundly silent in regard to it; and, if I would present to him a small portion of my surplus wealth, that he would bring his own slaves to help me in disposing of the bodies. I promised to reward him handsomely; and we set out for the ship, with five slaves, provided with saw and hatchets. While on our way, the magician could not sufficiently compliment the wisdom of our plan of guarding the sails with quotations from the Koran. He declared that this was the sole means by which we could have been saved.

It was still early in the morning when we reached the ship. We went zealously to work, and in an hour's time had placed four of the bodies in the skiff. Some of the slaves were ordered to row them ashore and bury them. They declared, when they came back, that the dead

men had saved them the trouble of burial, for no sooner
had they been laid on the ground than they had
crumbled into dust. We continued to remove the
corpses, and before evening every one of them had been
carried to the land. No one was left but the man whom
we had found nailed to the mainmast. We tried in vain
to draw out the nail. No exercise of strength seemed to
start it a hair's breadth. I was at a loss what to do next;
for it was out of the question to cut down the
mast in order to take him ashore. But Muley helped us
out of this embarrassment. He directed a slave to row
quickly to the shore, and bring away a basket of earth.
When this had been done the magician uttered some
mysterious words, and sprinkled the earth on the dead
man's head. The latter instantly opened his eyes, drew
a deep breath, and the wound made by the nail in his
brow began to bleed. We now drew the spike out without difficulty, and the body fell into the arms of one of
our slaves.

"Who has brought me here?" he asked. Muley
pointed to me, and I stepped closer. "Thanks, unknown
stranger," said he. "You have released me from long
torments. For fifteen years my body has been sailing on
these waters, and my soul been condemned to revisit
it at night. But now earth has rested on my head, and
I can go to my fathers, forgiven."

I begged him to let us know how he had merited this
fearful punishment, and he went on:

"Fifteen years ago I was a powerful and distinguished man, and lived in Algiers. A thirst for gain induced me to fit out a ship and take to piracy. I had practiced this mode of life for some time, when one day I took on board at Zante a dervish, who wished to travel free of expense. I and my crew were fierce people, and paid no regard to the sanctity of our passenger, but, on the contrary, made him the object of our ridicule. But on one occasion, when, in his holy zeal, he had rebuked my sinful course of life, my anger, which was more easily excited as I had been drinking deeply, obtained complete mastery over me. Furious at hearing from a dervish what I would not have endured tamely from the sultan himself, I plunged my dagger in his heart. With his dying breath he cursed my crew and me, condemning us to an existence of neither life nor death till we had laid our heads upon the earth.

The dervish died, and we threw him into the sea, laughing at his imprecations; but that very night his sentence was fulfilled. A part of my crew mutinied. We fought with dreadful fury till my adherents were all slain, and I nailed to the mast. But the mutineers also perished of their wounds, and soon my ship was merely one vast grave. My sight left me, my breath failed, and I awaited death. But it was only a torpor which had overpowered me. On the next night, at the same hour in which we had thrown the dervish into the sea, I and all my crew awoke to life; existence had returned to us again, but we could do nothing, say nothing, but what we had said and done that dreadful night. Thus we have sailed for fifteen years, unable to live, unable to die. We have spread every sail to the tempest with frantic joy, hoping to be dashed at last upon some friendly cliff, and lay our weary heads at rest. It was denied to us. But now I can die. Once more, my unknown savior, I thank you; and, if you value treasures, take my ship and its contents in token of my gratitude."

The captain let his head fall upon his breast, and, like his companions in suffering, crumbled into dust. We collected his ashes in a box, and buried them on the beach; and I obtained workmen from the city, who soon put my vessel in repair. After I had bartered away, at a great profit, the goods which I had found on board, I hired seamen, remunerated richly my friend Muley, and sailed for my native country. I took a circuitous route, visiting many countries and islands, and disposing of my goods. The Prophet blessed my undertaking. At the end of nine months I returned to Balsora twice as rich as the dying captain's bequest had made me. My fellow-citizens were surprised at my wealth and good fortune, and would not believe but that I had found the Valley of Diamonds of the famous voyager, Sindbad. I left them to their belief; and my example tempted all the youths of Balsora to go out into the world, in order, like me, to make their fortunes.

I lived calmly and at peace, and have made, every five years since then, a journey to Mecca, that I might thank God, in his holy place, for all his blessings, and pray for the captain and his crew, that He would receive them into Paradise.

ELIZABETH COATSWORTH

Forgotten Island

The fortuneteller told them both the same fortune. Jane went into the tent first and sat there with her hand held out across a table covered with an Oriental cloth. She felt a little scared as the woman in the bright-colored skirt and white waist, earrings, and a handkerchief about her head, looked at her palm for a while. Then the fortuneteller said, "There is adventure ahead of you. I see it soon, and yet the adventure is connected with something from far away and long ago."

The fortuneteller said some other things, too, unimportant things that didn't stick in Jane's mind after the sound had left her ears. She paid her quarter and slipped out. John was waiting for her.

"Any good?" he asked.

"I'm not sure," said Jane. "I don't suppose she's a real gypsy."

"The money goes to charity anyhow. I'd better see what she tells me," John said, and he went in.

"What did she tell you?" Jane asked as he came out a few minutes later.

"Oh, a lot of stuff about school, and being on the football team if I only believed I could make it. A lot of stuff like that. And then she said I was to have an adventure, soon, and that it was connected with a faraway place and things that had happened a long time ago."

Jane's gray eyes flashed indignantly.

"I bet she says that to everyone! That's just what she told me. I feel like going in and asking for my quarter back."

"Hold on." John was more logical than Jane. "Maybe we might be going to have it together."

They stuck around the tent. It was part of a church affair on Mrs. Sumner's lawn, and it was made up mostly of flower and needlework booths and things like that, with a pony they felt they were too big to ride, and a grab-bag filled mostly with rubber dolls and rubber balls. After getting themselves another bag of brownies, they had plenty of time to question some of their friends who had had their fortunes told.

"Hi, there! Bill, what did she tell you?"

They must have asked five or six children, but to none of them had there been promised an adventure of any kind. It kept them making guesses.

"I bet she means our going up to the cabin. That's an adventure, right on Green Pond, in the woods and everything," Jane said. But John, who was two years older, twelve going on thirteen, shook his head.

"It couldn't be that, Jane," he argued. "The cabin's new. Dad just had it built last winter. And it's on land where nothing has ever been before. That couldn't be it. We'll have to wait."

"I can't bear to wait!" Jane cried.

John grinned at her.

"Don't know what you'll do about it," he said. "Come on, I've got five cents left. That'll get us a piece of fudge, anyhow."

Two weeks later the Lane family were climbing out of their car at the end of a rough Maine wood-road. For a moment they all four stood still, feeling happy. Then Mr. Lane unlocked the back of the car, and they began to carry suitcases and blankets into the new log cabin which stood a little back from the edge of the water. They were as busy as four chipmunks during acorn season.

No one but Mr. Lane had ever seen the place. It was his surprise. He had been traveling up to Maine every week or two since last fall, superintending the building of the cabin. It was made of peeled logs, oiled to make them stay clean and shining. It had a big living room with a boulder fireplace with a fire already laid, which Mother immediately lighted as a house warming. There was a small kitchen, too, with a sink and a new pump painted red under the window, and three bedrooms in a row opening from the big room. Out of John's room went a stair leading up into the loft where cots could be placed when the Lanes had friends in.

"James," exclaimed Mrs. Lane. "You've thought of *everything*."

"You're pleased, Janet?" he asked anxiously, "it's the way you thought it would be?"

"Only much nicer!" said Mother.

The Lanes were a family that had very good times together. They loved to go camping together and they could all paddle and fish and swim and build a fire outdoors and flap pancakes on a skillet. So it had seemed perfect when Father found this land on a secluded cove on Green Pond and began having a cabin built. Now that he was a senior member in his law firm, he seemed able to get away from his offices a good deal in summer.

"People don't feel so quarrelsome in warm weather," he used to say—though that was probably a joke. "They get crotchety in the fall and begin to go to law about things after the first hard frosts."

Anyhow, whether he was joking or not as to the reason, Father managed to get away a good deal in the summer. Now they had a place of their own, and he and Mother were happy all day long working on the finishing touches. John and Jane tried to help, and did, too, but there were times when there was no need for them. Then they were likely to get into their bathing suits, pack a light lunch, and take to the canoe to go exploring.

They had named the canoe *The Adventure* because of the church-fair prophecies, but for a long time their excursions were of a quiet character. Green Pond was about ten miles long, but its shoreline was very uneven. Now the pond was a mile or two wide, now it narrowed to a few hundred feet, only to widen once more. Long coves indented its wooded shores, and here and there an island lay like a frigate becalmed. There were farms along the slopes in many places, but only occasionally did their hayfields stretch down to the water. More often there lay a fringe of woods or rough pastures along the lake. Sometimes, these woods were very thick, extending into the wilderness which covers Maine, the great central wilderness on which the farmlands lie like scattered patches, hardly noticeable to the eagle flying high overhead against the whiteness of the summer clouds.

There were no towns on Green Pond, no summer cottages except their own, no camps. Paddling along with silent paddles the children came upon many things, a deer drinking, or a fox slipping off into the underbrush, or a fish hawk rising, its prey catching the sunlight as it dangled in those fierce claws.

They heard voices calling at the farms, usually hidden from sight, and sometimes came upon a farmer fishing toward evening after the milking was done. But the

Paddling along, the children saw many things.

sounds which they heard most constantly were the clank-clank of cow bells and the slow notes of the thrushes. Less often, they heard sheep bells. And of course there were other birds, too, the warblers and white-throated sparrows and, above all, the big loons which seemed to like them and often appeared floating near them, uttering their lonely cries. But when the children paddled too close, the loons would dive and when they reappeared, it would be a long way off, to teach the young humans that they must keep their distance.

One day as they were eating their lunch on a flat rock under a pine at the opening of a small bay, a curious sound began vibrating through the air. It was hard to tell where it came from. It filled the bay and echoed back from the slopes above the trees, all the time growing louder and more and more insistent.

Jane stopped eating her sandwich.

"What's that?" she asked in a low voice. "It sort of scares me."

John squinted his eyes across the glint of water.

"It must be an outboard motor," he said. "It sounds near. We ought to see it."

But they saw nothing that day.

In the weeks which followed, however, they became acquainted with that sound. Sometimes they heard it at night, waking up to raise their heads from their pillows to listen to its passing; it sounded then as though it

circled in front of their cabin, like an animal circling a
fire. Sometimes they heard it by day, in the distance,
and once, in a thick fog which had come in from the
sea, it passed very close to them. They saw the outlines
of a boat and of a figure in an old slouch hat at the
stern. They waved but there was no gesture from the
boat, and in a moment it was gone again. Only the
coughing of the engine and the rank smell of gasoline
fumes were left to stain the ghostly silver of the day.

"There's something queer about that man," said
Jane. "Why don't we ever see him? And why didn't he
wave to us?"

John sent the canoe ahead with a powerful stroke of
his paddle.

"He probably didn't see us," he said. "I suppose he
goes fishing. We just don't happen to come across
him."

Jane still had her paddle trailing.

"No," she said, "it's a feeling. It's as though he were
always sneaking around the lake. Whenever I hear him
it scares me, but when the engine stops, it's worse.
Then you don't know *where* he is or *what* he's doing.
But I know he's up to no good."

"That's just because his outboard motor's old and
has that stumbling sound," insisted John. "He's probably a farmer at one of the farms trying to get some
bass for supper."

"He chooses very queer hours to go fishing then,"

Jane said, unconvinced. "And I don't know when he gets his farm work done, either. You know as well as I do that there's something queer about him, John, so don't pretend there isn't."

"Have it your own way, Jen," John said, not admitting anything, but a queer little cold feeling came over him, too, whenever he heard that choking splutter across the water. He, too, felt relieved when several days would go by and no sound of the outboard motor would come.

Often the children would explore the woods along the shore, following little paths or wood-roads when they saw them. One afternoon toward dusk they were going single file along a trail so faint that they were not sure it was a trail at all. Perhaps the deer used it, or a cow coming down to the pondside to drink. And, yet, here and there a twig seemed to have been broken off as though by a human hand.

It was hot in the woods and the mosquitoes bothered them. Jane picked a couple of big fern leaves, and they wore them upside down over their heads like caps, the green fringes protecting their necks, but even so they had to keep slapping.

"I vote we go back," said Jane at last, stopping. But John peered over her shoulder.

"There's a little cliff ahead," he said. "Let's just go that far, and then we'll go back." It seemed wrong to turn around until they'd reached some sort of landmark.

So Jane brandished her pine twigs over her shoulders, slapped a mosquito on her bare knee, and started ahead.

The cliff was very pretty, its seams filled with ferns, while funguses which they called "elephants' ears" seemed to be peeling in great green-and-gray scales from the granite surfaces.

But the children had no eyes for the woods at that moment. Around the faint bend of the trail something was hanging from a high branch. Jane gave a little scream of surprise and then stood staring. For it was the carcass of a sheep, such as she had sometimes seen in a butcher's shop, but strange and terrifying to come upon here in the midst of the woods.

For once the children said nothing. They stared and stared and then turned, and John made room for Jane to pass him and go first, while he brought up the rear with one horrified look over his shoulder. They crashed through the woods like two runaway colts and never stopped until *The Adventure* was well out from shore.

Then Jane heaved a great sigh. "Well!" she said.

"Well!" said John.

Their father was quite matter-of-fact about their tale.

"Probably a farmer has killed one of his sheep and didn't have any way of getting it up to the icehouse just then. So he may have hung it high out of reach of foxes until he can bring down a horse or a wheelbarrow for it."

"Dad, a horse or a wheelbarrow couldn't get to that

place, and it wasn't near any sheep pasture, either," John said.

"It's the man with the outboard motor!" cried Jane.

"You're jumping to conclusions, Jen," her father declared. "You haven't an iota of evidence that would stand in court."

But after a day or two of inquiry, they heard from the postmaster at the little postoffice, a mile or two away on the crossroads, that several sheep and heifers had disappeared in the neighborhood during the spring and summer. Some people thought that maybe a bear had come down from the north, or worse still, a lynx. If dogs had been ruining the stock, there would probably have been more noise. People inclined to think that the killer was a bear. There had been one seen for a while four or five years ago.

"A bear doesn't butcher his meat and hang it up in a tree," said Father, and told the postmaster where the children had seen the carcass. They felt very important for a little while and would have gone on discussing the affair, if something had not happened to put it altogether out of their minds.

About three miles from the Lane's cabin, across the pond, there was a cove lying between low marshy banks, where the swamp maples stood thick, with now and then a few pines on a knoll. The cove, too, was very shallow, choked with water plants of all sorts. Water lilies, both yellow and white, lay along the outskirts in archipelagoes of broad leaves and floating flowers. Beyond grew the pickerel weeds with their thin arrow-shaped leaves and their spikes of purple flowerlets, and there were bulrushes and joint-stem grasses through which the big-eyed dragonflies flew, like splinters of sunlight.

Several times John and Jane had forced their way for a few yards into this marine flower garden, but the canoe moved very slowly. John had to use his paddle for poling while Jane peered ahead, alert for the old submerged logs which here and there lay on the shallow bottom, the bark long since peeled away, but the white stubs of branches still thrust out to rake against the bottom of a passing boat.

They had soon turned back, until one day, when pushing in as usual among the reeds, they came upon a sort of channel leading up into the cove.

"It almost looks as though it had been made," said John, "anyhow, let's go up it."

If the channel had actually been cleared, it must have been done a long time ago, for here and there it was completely grown over, and once more the reeds would close about *The Adventure*, scraping its sides with their rubbery touch. Yet by standing upright for a moment in the bow, Jane was always able to see clear water ahead, and they would push forward into a new opening.

The cove was much longer and wider than they had dreamed. They seemed to be moving in a small separate

pond surrounded by maple-covered shores; all view of
Green Pond was lost now, with its slopes of farmlands
and woodlands and the Canton hills along the west.
The breeze was lost, too. It was very hot among the
reeds, and still. There was a secret feeling, moving
slowly along these hidden channels, while the dragonflies darted silently in and out among the leaves.

Deeper and deeper they went into this mysterious
place, and as they went they grew more and more quiet.
A voice sounded out of place in this silence. First, they
spoke in whispers and then scarcely spoke at all, and
Jane, balancing herself at the bow when the passage
was blocked, merely pointed to the clear water ahead,
shading her eyes against the sun.

It seemed only natural that they should come upon
something wonderful, so that they were excited but
not surprised when they saw an island ahead of them.
It, too, was larger than one would have expected, and
rockier. There were pines on it and tumbled ledges ten
or fifteen feet high. The channel led to a cove where a
small beach lay between low horns of rock. At a distance it would have seemed merely another knoll in
the swamplands, but it was a real island, with the water
lying all about it, and the shore of the mainland still
some distance away.

It seemed only part of the enchantment of the place
that a house should stand above the beach, an old-
fashioned house with fretwork scrolls ornamenting its

eaves, and an elaborate veranda. Time had been at work here, and it was hard to say whether the walls had been brown or red. One or two of the windows had been broken by falling branches or blundering birds, and the door stood open into the darkness of a hall.

The children exchanged one glance of awed agreement, and in a moment the bow of *The Adventure* grated on the sand. Jane jumped to the shore and turned to pull the canoe further up the beach.

Still in silence they ran up the rotting steps, and with a last glance backward into the sunlight, stepped through the gaping door into the house.

"You never saw anything like it in your life. It was all dusty and spooky with cobwebs over everything!" said Jane.

"And the swallows flew out and nearly scared us to death. They had their nests on the top bookcase shelves —" added John.

"One of them flew straight at my head! I thought it was a bat and would get into my hair."

"And there were footstools made of elephants' feet stuffed with straw, but the rats had got at them, and—"

"You've forgotten about the chairs and table made of horns, John—"

"You mean I haven't had a chance to tell about them! And there was a crocodile made of ebony inlaid with ivory—"

They stepped through the gaping door.

"Hold on! Hold on, children! Is this a dream or a new game, or what?" Father demanded.

"It's all real as real as real!" the children cried. "It's the island we discovered."

"They couldn't make up a house like that," Mother said. "You know they couldn't, Jim. What else was there, children?"

"Well," began John, "there had been lion skins and zebra skins on the floor, but they were pretty well eaten up, and on each end of the mantel there was a big bronze head—"

"Of a Negro girl," interrupted Jane. "John thinks they might have been boys because their hair was short, but they looked like girls, and they had necklaces around their neck, and their heads were held high—"

"And there were ivory tusks coming out of their heads. They were holders for the tusks. You'd like them, Mother. And there was another statue standing in an opening in the bookcase, about three feet high, a chief or a god or something with eyes made of sea shells, and hollow."

"Yes, and tell what was written over the mantel in queer letters—you remember we learned it—'Oh, the Bight of' what was it, John?"

> *"Oh, the Bight of Benin,*
> *The Bight of Benin,*
> *One comes out*
> *Where three goes in."*

"That settles it," said Father. "You two haven't gone mad or been hypnotized or had a dream. Your evidence is too circumstantial. That's the beginning of an old sea-chanty of the African Gold Coast. What else was there in this house?"

The children stared at him, their eloquence brought to a sudden stop.

"That's about all, Dad," John said, wrinkling his forehead, trying to bring back that strange interior with its smell of dust and mice and the stirrings overhead of loose boards. How could he describe how he and Jane had clung together, their hearts hammering, tiptoeing from room to room, ready to run at a moment's notice?

They hadn't gone upstairs. Upstairs had seemed too far from the open door. No one knew where they were. There might be some mysterious person living in this house, after all. They might come face to face with him at any moment. There were ashes in the fireplace. How long would ashes last? And in the dark kitchen into which they had peered for a breathless moment, John had seen fish bones on the sink-drain and an old knife. How long would fish bones last? Who had been using that knife and how long ago?

A sudden squawk from a heron outside had raised the hair on their heads. They had catapulted toward the door and then tiptoed back into what had been the living room.

"Do you think we might take the crocodile?" Jane

asked wistfully. "The rats will eat it if we leave it here."

But John had a very strong sense of law.

"We don't know who owns the house," he said. "It would just be stealing. And if the rats haven't eaten it by now, they won't eat it before we can get back."

For hours the Lanes sat before their own fireplace, talking over the mysterious house and making guesses about it.

It grew darker and darker outside, but Mother forgot to start supper on the stove and everyone forgot to be hungry. Over and over the children described just where they had found the house in its own lost and secluded cove. Then they went over what they had found inside. Now and then Mother asked a question, but Father hardly said anything but sat looking into the fire, smoking his pipe. It kept going out, and had to be refilled and relighted every few minutes, so the children knew he must be very interested.

"Far away and long ago," said Jane suddenly. "This is our adventure, John."

John was about to answer when the old droning squeal of the outboard motor sounded from the darkness of the lake. Once again it moved nearer and nearer them, and once more it seemed to pass the lights of their windows only to turn and pass them again.

"There's that same fisherman," Mother said, a little uneasily.

Father went to the door.

"Ahoy, friend!" he called into the darkness. "Ahoy! Won't you come ashore and have a visit?"

The engine seemed to check for a minute as though someone were listening. Then it began to sputter and drone again with its sawmill-wheel violence and, after apparently circling them once or twice more, whined off down the pond and at last merged into silence.

"I guess he couldn't hear me, that old outboard of his makes such a racket," Father said as he came back from the open doorway. "Anyway, it's of no importance. It's your island that interests me. Now all I can say is that there are several little ports of the Maine coast which once carried on a regular trade with the Gold Coast in the sailing-ship days. Take Round Pond —that's only about twenty miles from here. Fifty years ago, they say it used to be full of monkeys and parrots and African gimcracks brought back by the sailors. But your house has things too fine for any ordinary sailor to bring home. And why should he build a house on an island in a pond, and then desert it, with everything in it? If he was a captain, why didn't he build a house in a seaport, the way most of them did?"

"Maybe he didn't want people to know where he had gone," Jane suggested.

"Maybe that's it," agreed Father. "But don't you think that's a little too blood-and-thundery? He probably was just a nice old gentleman whose nephew had been on a hunting trip to Africa and brought back a few trophies for his eccentric old uncle. He kept them round for a few years, and then got tired of the place, and went out to California to visit his married sister. He liked it so well that he decided to buy a house, and never bothered to send for the African stuff, which he was tired of anyhow."

John looked at his Father indignantly.

"That might be it, Dad," he exclaimed. "But how about his writing 'Oh, the Bight of Benin, the Bight of Benin'?"

" 'One comes out where three goes in,' " Jane finished the quotation softly.

Father looked thoughtfully into the fire.

"Yes," he agreed, "that has the voice of adventure in it. Maybe it wasn't anyone's eccentric old uncle after all. We'll find out soon enough."

"How?" the children cried, all awake and excited once more.

"We'll go to the town clerk and see who owns the house."

"Tomorrow?" begged the children.

"Tomorrow, rain or shine," said Father.

"And now," said Mother, "what about some scrambled eggs and stewed tomatoes? It's after nine o'clock."

It took old Mr. Tobin over an hour and two pairs of glasses before he found the record of the ownership of the island.

"Here it is," he said at last in some triumph. "A man named E. R. Johnson bought it from old man Deering —the Deerings still own the farm back there on the east shore—paid two hundred dollars for it. That was on April 7, 1867. I remember there was talk about him when I was a boy. But he didn't stay more than two or three years, and I thought the place had burned down or fell down long ago."

He licked his thumb and turned over more pages.

"Let's see, here's the assessment for 1877, thirty dollars—that must have been after the house was built, of course. Paid. Here's 1878, paid too, and 1879. After that it's all unpaid. In 1883 they dropped the assessment to five dollars—guess they thought the house weren't worth much by then."

He went on turning pages with interest, while the Lanes sat about him on kitchen chairs watching his every motion.

"Here's 1890. I can't find any record of an assessment at all. I guess they thought a swamp island which didn't belong to anyone weren't worth carrying in the books. Kind of forgot about her. Yes, here's 1891. No sign of her in this, either. Well, let's figure her up. Three years at thirty dollars is ninety. And seven years at five is thirty-five, add ninety, and it makes one hundred and twenty-five dollars back taxes.

"Anyone wanted to pay one hundred and twenty-five dollars would own the island."

Father rose and shook hands with Mr. Tobin and thanked him for his trouble.

"We'll talk it over," he said mildly. "Nice weather we're having, but we need rain."

"My peas aren't filling out," said Mr. Tobin, "just yellowing on the vine. If we don't get a thundershower soon all the gardens in Maine won't be worth cussing at."

Mother couldn't stand it.

"Aren't we going to buy the island, Jim?" she asked.

But Father only looked absent-minded.

"Have to talk it over," he repeated vaguely. "Come, children, in we get. We ought to drive to town and get provisions. Thank you, Mr. Tobin. See you later—maybe."

In the car all the Lanes began chattering at once.

"*Can* we have it?"

"*Are* you going to buy it?"

"Oh, Father, how wonderful!"

"Look here," said Father severely. "You people don't know how to act about forgotten islands. You want to keep them forgotten. Raise as little talk as you can, slip in quietly, buy them quietly, don't start a ripple on the water. You'll spoil it all if you get the whole country-side sight-seeing and carrying off souvenirs. So long as Mr. Tobin just thinks you kids have run across an old ruined cottage on an island, which you'd like as a camp-

ing place, he'll hardly give it a thought, but you musn't
start his curiosity working."

"But you *will* buy it?" Jane begged.

"Of course, I will. What's more I'll buy it for you and
John. You found it and it's going to be yours. What'll
you name it? Adventure Island?"

"No," said John, "I like Forgotten Island better. It
seems more like the Bight of Benin."

"What *is* a bight?" Jane asked. "I like Forgotten Island, too. Forgotten Island, Forgotten Island. It makes
me feel sad and wonderful."

"A bight," said her Father patiently, "is a very large
bay. Benin was a great city up the river from the Gold
Coast. Those bronzes must have come from there, for
the Negroes of Benin were famous for their bronze
work. They used to trade in slaves and were very cruel.
It was an unhealthy coast for whites. They died from
fever and all sorts of tropic diseases."

It was not until late afternoon that the children paddled their parents over to see Forgotten Island. All was
as it had been the day before, except that the thunder-
heads were crowding along the sky to the northwest
and there was a little breeze, even across the acres of the
water garden. They were lucky in finding the channel
again and in managing to keep to it, with Jane as look-
out. Once *The Adventure* rasped over a flat stone, and
for a second they all thought they might be stuck there,

but after a moment or two, they pushed the canoe side-ways and were able to go on.

But today there was a different feeling in the air. There was a continual rustling among the maples as though they were preparing for a storm. A big turtle slid off a rock at the edge of the shore and raised its head to stare at them as they went by. It thought itself hidden among the reeds, but they could see its horny nose and the two small beadlike eyes which watched them as intruders from its hiding-place. Even the house had a more secret air about it. The door still stood open, but Jane suddenly thought of a trap, and even with her father and mother there, hung back a little before going in.

However, this curious antagonism, which all felt but no one mentioned, was not strong enough to drown their interest, once the Lanes had stepped across the threshold. All that the children had remembered was true and more still. There were carvings in wood, which they had forgotten, split and stained with age. They found chief's stools upheld by grinning squat figures shaped from solid logs, and hangings of curious woven cloths on the walls. Father and Mother were as excited as the children.

"I can't believe my own eyes," Mother kept exclaiming.

Father said more than once, "Now who the dickens

was this man Johnson, and where did he come from, and where did he go to?"

This day they went upstairs, testing each step carefully to make sure that it would hold. There were three bedrooms on the second floor, only one fully furnished, and it did not seem to go with the rest of the house. It had a set of heavy walnut furniture and a photograph of a mountain in a gold frame. The matting on the floor smelled of mold and damp, and a hornet's nest hung papery and lovely from one corner of the ceiling. Not a thing in the room suggested Africa.

The rats and squirrels had wrecked the old mattress for a hundred nests of their own.

"It's as though Mr. Johnson hadn't wanted to think of Africa when he went to bed," Mother said, quietly, as she looked about. "Perhaps the Bight of Benin was something he preferred to think about by daylight."

Jane was standing near the window, and happened to look out. She had a distinct feeling of seeing something move behind the bushes along the shore. But though she thought "It's a man," she really wasn't sure. Things move sometimes in the corner of your glance, half out of sight. This glimpse she had was at the very edge of her vision.

Lightning flashed in the sky, silent, without thunder, and the trees shook their leaves and shivered down all their branches. She could see nothing now but the whitening leaves. Their motion must have been what had caught her attention. She said nothing, but she was ready to go back to the new cabin, which they had built themselves, about which there was no mystery.

The lightning flashed again, brighter this time.

"Goodness!" exclaimed Mother. "I suppose we'd better be getting back before it rains. But I feel as though we were leaving a foreign land. I expect to see giraffes staring at us when we push off."

Halfway out of the cove a sound began at some distance.

"Thunder?" Father asked, cocking his head, but the children knew, without waiting to hear it again, that it was the sound of an old outboard motor going about its secret business.

The next day Father bought the island for back taxes and had the deed made out to John Lane and Jane Lane. The children signed it with a sense of awe.

"Now you'll have a place you can call your own," Father said, for Mr. Tobin's benefit. "You can camp there, if you're able to find a spot where the roof doesn't leak."

"Yes, Dad," the children exclaimed dutifully, but their eyes were wild with excitement. Forgotten Island was theirs; they owned its remoteness and its mystery, or it owned them. Anyway, they were bound together for all time.

For two days the words had been going through Jane's head, day and night:

"Oh, the Bight of Benin,
The Bight of Benin,
One comes out
Where three goes in!"

She woke up with the verse ringing through her mind like the echoes of a gong. It had rained during the night and the air was bright and clear this morning. She was ashamed of the oppression which had overtaken her the afternoon before on the island. The coming storm had set her to shivering like the trees, she thought, and with no more reason. Why had she imagined they were being spied on? If anyone else knew about the island, wouldn't he have taken away the things long ago?

Mr. Tobin saw them to his door.

"Jo Taylor, down the pond Canton way, has lost another heifer. He went out to the pasture lot to give them their salt, and he says only four came for it. He had a look around but couldn't find a sign of her. He's going to report it. There's a man calls himself Trip Anderson came in here last March and built himself a shack on the lake. Jo's suspicious of him, but it's pretty hard to get proof."

"Has Trip Anderson got an outboard motor?" John asked, thinking of the stranger.

"Yes," said Mr. Tobin, "so they say. They don't know where it came from, either. He's taken the old boat Eb Carson used to have before he died and patched it up. Mrs. Carson says she don't grudge him the boat; it was just rotting down by the willows. No one's missed an outboard round here."

"We've been all round the lake," said Jane, "and we've never seen his shack."

"I haven't either," Mr. Tobin agreed. "Don't get down to the pond much these days, though when I was a boy I was there most of my spare time. I'm not sure as anyone's seen his place, but they know it must be there, probably back a piece from the water. He's worked some for people. Told them he was planning to bring his wife and little girl when he got settled. A lot of people think he's all right, and that if anyone's stealing stock, it's likely to be that second Grimes boy who's always been wild, or there's old Nat Graham. He'd as soon take a thing as look at it—vegetables, anyhow."

That afternoon the children spent a rapturous two or three hours on Forgotten Island. Once more the place had its quiet, enchanted air. Even the house seemed to welcome them in as its owners. The swallows had left their nests and with their young were flying about outside.

Jane had brought a broom and begun the task of sweeping the living room, tying her hair up in her sweater when she saw what clouds of dust she raised. John carried out the more torn and bedraggled skins. One of the hangings on the wall was in shreds, but another had held. A zebra skin, too, was in fairly good condition. They put it in front of the hearth, and John gathered enough dead wood outdoors to lay a new fire.

"I'll bring an ax next time," he said, "and we must have matches in a tin box. Jen, have you noticed? This room seems as though it belonged to an older building. It's built stronger for one thing, and the floor boards are nearly two feet wide and the ceiling is lower. I think Mr. Johnson added on the rest of the house to something which was already here."

They went about examining the place and decided that John's guess was right. The windows in the living room had many panes, and in the other rooms they were only divided down the middle in a bleak way, and the thin boarded floors swayed under the children's weight.

"Perhaps we might get the rest torn down some day and have this for the house, with a low shingled roof. We could cook over the open fire."

"And we could have a long window seat built along one wall which we could use for cots—"

"And we'd keep the African things—"

They got very excited making their plans. All the time they were talking they worked, and by mid-afternoon the room looked very thrilling. They had rifled the other rooms for anything sound and strong, and now the old part of the house had the aspect of the sitting room of some African trader.

It was John who found the old well, while gathering

deadwood for a fire. "We'll bring over a new pail and a rope," he planned. "I think the water looks perfectly good."

They had never been so excited or so happy in their lives. They could not bear to go away from their new possession and kept returning to put a last touch here or there. At last the sun had gone down, and they knew they must go home. But just then Jane discovered a mass of old rubbish behind the bronze figure standing in a sort of niche in the bookcase. It was about three feet high and not as heavy as she had supposed. She dragged at it, but she put too much strength into the effort, and the thing toppled over and fell with a terrifying clang.

"Oh, dear!" cried Jane. "I hope it hasn't been dented! But wait, John, till I sweep up behind him. Then you can help me get him back in place."

The statue lay on its side where it had fallen, and they could see that it was hollow. It had one hand raised above its head. Perhaps it was from inside this hand, or from some corner of the inside of the head, that the things had been jarred which they found on the floor when they started to pick it up.

Gold is gold, and does not rust, no matter how long it may lay hidden. The ring, the crude little crocodile, the bird, the thing that looked like a dwarf—all were of soft virgin gold, almost warm to the children's stroking fingers.

"Look," murmured Jane, "there's gold dust on the floor, too."

The pale light faintly glittered on a haze of gold. Looking at the feet of the statue they could see now that once they must have been sealed over with metal. Someone had pried them open a long time ago, and found the statue filled with gold dust and, perhaps, other treasures like these small ones which had lain concealed.

The children looked and handled and exclaimed, scarcely able to believe their own good fortune. This was "far away and long ago" with a vengeance.

"It's getting late," John's conscience reminded him. "Mother and Dad will be sending out a search party for us soon. Let's put the treasure back where we found it and bring them over tomorrow and surprise them."

"Oh, let's take it back with us!" protested Jane. "You know, John, I've had the queerest feeling twice that we were being watched? Yesterday, when we were all here, and today after the statue fell. Something seemed to be at that window, over there behind me."

"What sort of thing, Jen?"

"I couldn't see. When I turned it was gone. I went over to the window and I couldn't see anything, either."

"Why didn't you tell me?"

"I didn't want you to call me a silly."

John went out quickly and looked under the window

which Jane had pointed to. There was a rank growth of nettles there, and not one had been broken.

"You've been seeing things, Jen," he declared cheerfully as he came back. "No one could have been at the window. Now be a good girl and give me the things. Good, those ought to stay put. I've used my handkerchief to help stuff them back in place. Now give me a hand at setting Mumbo Jumbo on his feet again."

All the time she was helping, Jane was protesting and arguing under her breath, but John was the leader and what he said usually went. She felt rather silly, anyway, about the things which she kept imagining that she saw.

"If they've been here safe since 1879, they can stay here a day or two longer," John declared. "Wait till you see Father's face! We'll invite them here for a picnic tomorrow and end up with the treasure."

Next day, however, it rained hard, and the children had to swallow their impatience. They wanted their party to be perfect in every way. In the late afternoon the rain changed into a fog with a little sunlight coming through.

"Can't we go over to the island?" Jane asked.

Father went out and looked at the sky.

"The fog banks are still blowing in," he said. "Smell that sea smell that comes with them! It's likely to rain again in an hour or two."

"Well, can't John and I take a picnic lunch now and just go to Oak Point around the corner?"

"We'd better let them," said Mother. "I've never known you children to be so restless. Perhaps a little paddling and picnicking will help you."

They had almost reached the point, moving through the fog so silently that they startled their friends the loons by coming upon them before they could dive; they had almost reached the point—when they found the man with the outboard motor. Everything about the picture was gray, a shabby gray coat, and a wiry shabby figure working over the motor at the stern, with the fog dripping from the broken rim of an old hat.

"Good evening," John hailed. "Can we help you?"

The man straightened and stared at them.

"No, thanks," he said then, "I'll be all right," and he bent again to his work. The children paddled on and reached the point. They had already on another day built a fireplace of big stones there, and John had brought kindling in his knapsack, so that soon the fire was crackling and the smell of frying bacon filled the air.

Jane felt uncomfortable. "He looks so kind of hungry," she whispered to John. "Go on, ask him if he won't come and eat with us."

"But—" began John.

"I don't care!" Jane broke in. "I don't care what people say. Ask him or I will."

The man who called himself Trip Anderson hesitated and then finally paddled his boat into shore with a crudely whittled-down board which seemed to be his

A shabby figure working over the motor.

only oar. He ate at the children's fire hungrily, but re-
membering his manners. He seemed like anyone who
was rather down on his luck, except for the way in which
he met a person's glance, staring back hard, showing a
thin rim of white all around the bright blue iris of his
eyes. They all talked a little about the pond and the
weather. The man knew a lot about fish. It was interesting, but the children were glad when supper was over
and the rain began again.

"Guess we've got to go," they said, and he stared at
them with his fixed eyes which he never allowed to shift
the least bit.

"Much obliged, kids," he said. "I'll do something for
you some day."

They told their father and mother that evening who
had been their guest, and their elders approved, within
reason.

During the night the wind shifted to the northwest
and the day came bright and perfect. The greatest excitement reigned in the cabin until 10:30 when *The
Adventure*, laden with passengers, baskets, and extra
supplies for Forgotten Island, put out into a pond that
rippled delightfully.

Father and Mother were much impressed by the
changes one afternoon's hard work had made in the
living room. John showed Father what the original
house must have been like, and he caught their enthu-
siasm immediately.

"It wouldn't be much of a job tearing off the 1870 part," he said. "We might be able to sell it for old wood, or if we can't, it could be burned on the rocks. Then this would be a wonderful little place. Nothing like it anywhere in the country."

The picnic was eaten in state around the table whose legs were made of horns, while a small unneeded fire crackled in the fireplace to give an added welcome. After the baskets were packed again and the room in order, Father brought out his pipe, while Mother began to knit.

This was the moment for which the children had been waiting for nearly two days.

"Want to see something else we found?" John asked with elaborate carelessness.

Jane bounded forward to help him.

They tugged out the statue and laid it on its back, and John reached far up its depths into the hollow arm, while everyone waited breathlessly.

Jane saw the look of shock and surprise come to his face and knew what had happened before he spoke.

"Why," he said rather blankly. "They're gone, the gold things are gone. There isn't even my handkerchief there.

"Sorry, Jane," he muttered to her when she ran forward to help search the crevices of the statue, and she squeezed his hand hard.

"It doesn't matter a bit," she cried, bravely blinking the tears out of her eyes. "Think of all we have left."

They didn't talk any more about the treasure. John felt too badly about it to bear any mention of it. Jane felt badly, too, of course, but it wasn't half so hard for her as for John, who had left the things just where they had found them.

They all paddled home to the cabin, making occasional conversation about nothing much, and that evening Father brought out *Huckleberry Finn* and read for hours, not saying once that his voice was getting tired.

Mother had glanced once or twice at the clock, when they heard a car come down their road and a moment later a knock sounded at the door.

It was late for visiting in the country, and everyone looked at each other in surprise as Father went to the door. Two men stood there whom they didn't know, one of them in uniform.

"Come in," said Father. "I'm James Lane. Did you want to see me?"

The older man shook hands first. "I'm Will Deering, Mr. Lane," he explained, "from over across the pond, and this is Mr. Dexter, of the State Police."

Mr. Lane shook hands with Mr. Dexter and introduced them both to the family.

"Mr. Dexter has come up here on business," Mr. Deering explained. "There've been complaints about a man who calls himself Trip Anderson. One man's lost two heifers and another man, who has a camp over on Muscongus Pond, missed an outboard motor from his boat. They brought Mr. Dexter to me because I know the lake pretty well and had an idea of where his shanty was. I took Mr. Dexter there while he was away, and we searched it and found proof he'd been doing a lot of thieving hereabouts. Proof wasn't needed, because when this Anderson came back, Mr. Dexter recognized him as a fellow who'd broken jail at Thomaston a year or so ago."

"His real name is Tom Jennings," the other man broke in. "He was serving a term for armed robbery. No, he ain't got a wife nor kids. That was just cover. He's been in and out of jail since he was sixteen."

Mother looked worried, thinking that the children had been having a picnic with such a man only the evening before. But Father knew that, somehow or other, the business must concern them, or these two men wouldn't have knocked at their door at ten o'clock at night.

"Did you wish me to identify him?" he asked, but Mr. Dexter shook his head.

"He don't need identifying," he remarked, pulling out his watch and looking at it. "By now, he's at Thomaston. But just before we took him away he said he had some things he wanted to return. He had them hidden in the flour tin. Said he'd been using the island you've bought, but never took any of the big things because they could be spotted too easy. When you kids began to go there, he kept an eye on you. He's good at that, moves like an Indian. One day when he was hanging round he heard a crash and looked in and saw you find the gold stuff. That was more up his alley. He could melt it down, and no one could ever prove anything against him."

The State Policeman fished again in his vest pocket and brought out first the dwarf, and then the bird, and then the crocodile. The ring came last. He poured them all into Jane's hand, and she quickly brought them to John.

"Think of his giving them back!" she exclaimed. "Oh, thank you for bringing them! We were so bothered when we found they were gone."

"Jennings said you were good kids and had asked him to eat with you."

"Do you want to see the things?" John asked eagerly. He took them about so that everyone might examine the little objects close at hand.

Mr. Deering held up the crocodile.

"We have one at home like this," he said, "in the old teapot, I think it is. My grandfather used to say Johnson gave it to him for boarding his horse, after he'd run out of the gold-dust quills he used to get his money from. The day he gave grandfather the crocodile and drove off was the last time he was ever seen around here. 'I took one image from that African temple that was chuck full of gold,' he told Grandfather. 'It stands to reason the other images have gold in them. Anyway, I aim to go and see.'

"But he never came back," continued Mr. Deering. "I figure he could play a trick on the temple priests once, maybe, but next time they'd get him. We never knew where he came from, nor what vessel he took for Africa, but it wouldn't be hard to find one in those days, when there was still a good trade there. Grandfather said he had the bearing of a captain. Probably no one else ever knew that the idol he'd stolen had gold in it, and he came away here, on the quiet, where no one ever *would* know it: But he was a reckless spender, Grandfather said. Money just poured out of his hands while he had it, and then he started back to get more. Anyhow, he never came back."

Everyone had been listening with breathless interest.

"Why didn't your grandfather use the house on the island, or sell it?" Mr. Lane asked.

"It wasn't his," the farmer replied. "Johnson had bought the island out and out. And Grandma didn't want any of that African stuff around the place. She called it outlandish, and my mother didn't like it either. We just minded our own business, and no one else but us had had direct dealings with him or knew much about the place. Every year the cove filled up more and more with pickerel weed and, pretty soon, the island and Johnson were kind of forgotten—"

"That's what we call it—Forgotten Island!" the children cried.

Mr. Deering looked at them and smiled.

"Well, it's yours now," he said. "It's nice to have neighbors on it again. Glad we found you all at home."

Everyone got up to see their visitors to the door. Mr. Deering stepped out first and, as Mr. Dexter turned to say good-bye, Jane asked, "Is there anything we can do for Trip Anderson?"

The officer shook his head.

"He's all right," he said. "Don't worry about him. I guess he was getting pretty tired of his freedom. He said he'd be glad to be back where he'd be taken care of. I'll tell him you inquired."

Then the door closed behind the strangers and, a moment later, there came the roar of a self-starter. Little by little the sound receded up the road and silence settled again in the woods, and, after a while, even the Lanes' cabin was dark and still, and the Lanes, too, were asleep. But on the mantel, in the silence broken only by the occasional calling of the loons, watched the four talismans of gold, keeping guard—the treasure of Forgotten Island, made by dark hands far away and long ago.

SAKI

The Open Window

"My aunt will be down presently, Mr. Nuttel,"
said a very self-possessed young lady of fifteen; "in the
meantime you must try and put up with me."

Framton Nuttel endeavoured to say the correct something which should duly flatter the niece of the moment
without unduly discounting the aunt that was to come.
Privately he doubted more than ever whether these for-
mal visits on a succession of total strangers would do
much towards helping the nerve cure which he was supposed to be undergoing.

"I know how it will be," his sister had said when he
was preparing to migrate to this rural retreat; "you will
bury yourself down there and not speak to a living soul,
and your nerves will be worse than ever from moping.
I shall just give you letters of introduction to all the people I know there. Some of them, as far as I can remember, were quite nice."

Framton wondered whether Mrs. Sappleton, the lady

to whom he was presenting one of the letters of introduction, came into the nice division.

"Do you know many of the people round here?"
asked the niece, when she judged that they had had sufficient silent communion.

"Hardly a soul," said Framton. "My sister was stay-
ing here, at the rectory, you know, some four years ago,
and she gave me letters of introduction to some of the
people here."

He made the last statement in a tone of distinct re-
gret.

"Then you know practically nothing about my aunt?"
pursued the self-possessed young lady.

"Only her name and address," admitted the caller.
He was wondering whether Mrs. Sappleton was in the
married or widowed state. An undefinable something
about the room seemed to suggest masculine habita-
tion.

"Her great tragedy happened just three years ago,"
said the child; "that would be since your sister's time."

"Her tragedy?" asked Framton; somehow in this rest-
ful country spot tragedies seemed out of place.

"You may wonder why we keep that window wide
open on an October afternoon," said the niece, indicat-
ing a large French window that opened on to a lawn.

"It is quite warm for the time of the year," said
Framton; "but has that window got anything to do with
the tragedy?"

"Out through that window, three years ago to a day, her husband and her two young brothers went off for their day's shooting. They never came back. In crossing the moor to their favourite snipe-shooting ground they were all three engulfed in a treacherous piece of bog. It had been that dreadful wet summer, you know, and places that were safe in other years gave way suddenly without warning. Their bodies were never recovered. That was the dreadful part of it." Here the child's voice lost its self-possessed note and became falteringly human. "Poor aunt always thinks that they will come back some day, they and the little brown spaniel that was lost with them, and walk in at that window just as they used to do. That is why the window is kept open every evening till it is quite dusk. Poor dear aunt, she has often told me how they went out, her husband with his white waterproof coat over his arm, and Ronnie, her youngest brother, singing, 'Bertie, why do you bound?' as he always did to tease her, because she said it got on her nerves. Do you know, sometimes on still, quiet evenings like this, I almost get a creepy feeling that they will all walk in through that window—"

She broke off with a little shudder. It was a relief to Framton when the aunt bustled into the room with a whirl of apologies for being late in making her appearance.

"I hope Vera has been amusing you?" she said.

"She has been very interesting," said Framton.

"I hope you don't mind the open window," said Mrs. Sappleton briskly; "my husband and brothers will be home directly from shooting, and they always come in this way. They've been out for snipe in the marshes today, so they'll make a fine mess over my poor carpets. So like you men-folk, isn't it?"

She rattled on cheerfully about the shooting and the scarcity of birds, and the prospects for duck in the winter. To Framton it was all purely horrible. He made a desperate but only partially successful effort to turn the talk on to a less ghastly topic; he was conscious that his hostess was giving him only a fragment of her attention, and her eyes were constantly straying past him to the open window and the lawn beyond. It was certainly an unfortunate coincidence that he should have paid his visit on this tragic anniversary.

"The doctors agree in ordering me complete rest, an absence of mental excitement, and avoidance of anything in the nature of violent physical exercise," announced Framton, who laboured under the tolerably wide-spread delusion that total strangers and chance acquaintances are hungry for the least detail of one's ailments and infirmities, their cause and cure. "On the matter of diet they are not so much in agreement," he continued.

"No?" said Mrs. Sappleton, in a voice which only replaced a yawn at the last moment. Then she suddenly

She rattled on cheerfully.

brightened into alert attention—but not to what Framton was saying.

"Here they are at last!" she cried. "Just in time for tea, and don't they look as if they were muddy up to the eyes!"

Framton shivered slightly and turned towards the niece with a look intended to convey sympathetic comprehension. The child was staring out through the open window with dazed horror in her eyes. In a chill shock of nameless fear Framton swung round in his seat and looked in the same direction.

In the deepening twilight three figures were walking across the lawn towards the window; they all carried guns under their arms, and one of them was additionally burdened with a white coat hung over his shoulders. A tired brown spaniel kept close at their heels. Noiselessly they neared the house, and then a hoarse young voice chanted out of the dusk: "I said, Bertie, why do you bound?"

Framton grabbed wildly at his stick and hat; the hall-door, the gravel-drive, and the front gate were dimly noted stages in his headlong retreat. A cyclist coming along the road had to run into the hedge to avoid imminent collision.

"Here we are, my dear," said the bearer of the white mackintosh, coming in through the window; "fairly muddy, but most of it's dry. Who was that who bolted out as we came up?"

Frampton swung round in his seat and looked.

"A most extraordinary man, a Mr. Nuttel," said Mrs. Sappleton; "could only talk about his illnesses, and dashed off without a word of good-bye or apology when you arrived. One would think he had seen a ghost."

"I expect it was the spaniel," said the niece calmly; "he told me he had a horror of dogs. He was once hunted into a cemetery somewhere on the banks of the Ganges by a pack of pariah dogs, and had to spend the night in a newly dug grave with the creatures snarling and grinning and foaming just above him. Enough to make any one lose their nerve."

Romance at short notice was her specialty.

HENRY SYDNOR HARRISON

Miss Hinch

In going from a given point on 126th Street to the subway station at 125th, it is not usual to begin by circling the block to 127th Street, especially in sleet, darkness, and deadly cold. When two people pursue so unusual a course at the same time, moving unobtrusively on opposite sides of the street, in the nature of things the coincidence is likely to attract the attention of one or the other of them.

In the bright light of the entrance to the tube they came almost face to face, and the clergyman took a good look at her. Certainly she was a decent-looking old body, if any woman was: white-haired, wrinkled, spectacled, and stooped. A thoroughly respectable domestic servant of the upper class she looked, in her old black hat, wispy veil, and blue shawl. Nevertheless, the reverend gentleman, going more slowly down the drafty steps, continued to study her from behind with a singular intentness.

An express train was just thundering in, which the clergyman, handicapped as he was by his clubfoot and stout cane, was barely in time to catch. He entered the same car with the woman and chanced to take a seat directly across from her. It must have been then after half-past eleven o'clock, and the wildness of the weather was discouraging to travel. The car was almost deserted. Even in this underground retreat the bitter breath of the night blew and bit, and the old woman shivered under her shawl. At last, her teeth chattering, she got up in an apologetic sort of way and moved toward the better protected rear of the car, feeling the empty seats as she went, in a palpable search for hot

pipes. The clergyman's eyes followed her candidly, and he watched her sink down, presently, into a seat on his own side of the car. A young couple sat between them now; he could no longer see the woman, beyond occasional glimpses of her black knees and her ancient bonnet, skewered on with a long steel hatpin.

Nothing could have seemed more trivial than this change of seats on the part of a thin-blooded and half-frozen passenger. But it happened to be a time of mutual doubt and mistrust in the metropolis, of alert suspicions and hair-trigger watchfulness, when men looked

He took a seat directly across from her.

askance into every strange face and the most infini-
tesimal incidents were likely to take on a hysterical importance. Through days of fruitless searching for a fu-
gitive outlaw of extraordinary gifts, the nerve of the city
had been slowly strained to the breaking point. All
jumped, now, when anybody cried "Boo!" and the hue
and cry went up false twenty times a day.

The clergyman pondered; mechanically he turned up
his coat collar and fell to stamping his icy feet. He was
an Episcopal clergyman, by his garb—rather short, very
full-bodied, not to say fat, bearded, and somewhat puffy-
faced, with heavy cheeks cut by deep creases. Well-lined
against the cold though he was, he, too, began to suffer
visibly, and presently was forced to retreat in his turn,
seeking out a new place where the heating apparatus
gave a better account of itself. He found one only two
seats beyond the old serving woman, limped into it, and
soon relapsed into his own thoughts.

The young couple, now half the car-length away, were
very thoroughly absorbed in each other's society. The
fifth traveler, a withered old gentleman sitting across
the aisle, napped fitfully upon his cane. The woman in
the hat and shawl sat in a sad kind of silence; and the
train hurled itself roaringly through the tube. After a
time, she glanced timidly at the meditating clergyman,
and her look fell swiftly from his face to the discarded
"ten-o'clock extra" lying by his side. She removed her
dim gaze and let it travel casually about the car; but

before long it returned again, pointedly, to the news-paper. Then, with some obvious hesitation, she bent forward and said,—

"Excuse me, Father, but would you please let me look at your paper a minute, sir?"

The clergyman came out of his reverie instantly and looked up with almost an eager smile.

"Certainly. Keep it if you like; I am quite through with it. But," he said, in a pleasant deep voice, "I am an Episcopal minister, not a priest."

"Oh, sir—I beg your pardon; I thought—"

He dismissed the apology with a smile and a good-natured wave of the hand.

The woman opened the paper with decent cotton-gloved fingers. The garish headlines told the story at a glance: "Earth Opened and Swallowed Miss Hinch—Headquarters Virtually Abandons Case—Even Jessie Dark"—so the black capitals ran on—"Seems Stumped." Below the spread was a luridly written but flimsy narrative, marked "By Jessie Dark," which at once confirmed the odd implication of the caption. Jessie Dark, it was manifest, was one of those most extra-ordinary of the products of yellow journalism, a woman "crime expert," now in action. More than this, she was a crime expert to be taken seriously, it seemed—no mere office-desk sleuth, but an actual performer with, unexpectedly enough, a somewhat formidable list of notches on her gun. So much, at least, was to be gathered from her own newspaper's loud display of "Jessie Dark's Triumphs":

March 2, 1901. Caught Julia Victorian, alias Gregory, the brains of the "Healey Ring" kidnapers.

October 7-29, 1903. Found Mrs. Trotwood and secured the letter that convicted her of the murder of her lover, Ellis E. Swan.

December 17, 1903. Ran down Charles Bartsch in a Newark laundry and trapped a confession from him.

July 4, 1904. Caught Mary Calloran and recovered the Stratford jewels.

And so on—nine "triumphs" in all; and nearly every one of them, as even the least observant reader could hardly fail to notice, involved the capture of a woman.

Nevertheless, it could not be pretended that the "snappy" paragraphs in this evening's extra seemed to foreshadow a new or tenth triumph on the part of Jessie Dark at an early date; and the old serving-woman in the car presently laid down the newspaper with an irrepressible sigh.

The clergyman glanced toward her kindly. The sigh was so audible that it seemed to be almost an invitation; besides, public interest in the great case was so tense that conversation between total strangers was the rule wherever two or three were gathered together.

"You were reading about this strange mystery, per-haps?"

The woman, with a sharp intake of breath, answered: "Yes, sir. Oh, sir, it seems as if I couldn't think of any-thing else."

"Ah?" he said, without surprise. "It certainly appears to be a remarkable affair."

Remarkable indeed the affair seemed. In a tiny little room within ten steps of Broadway, at half-past nine o'clock on a fine evening, Miss Hinch had killed John Catherwood with the light sword she used in her well-known representation of the Father of his Country. Catherwood, it was known, had come to tell her of his approaching marriage; and ten thousand amateur de-tectives, athirst for rewards, had required no further "motive" of a creature so notorious for fierce jealousy. So far the tragedy was commonplace enough. What had given it extraordinary interest was the amazing faculty of the woman, which had made her famous while she was still in her teens. Coarse, violent, utterly unmoral she might be; but she happened also to be the most astonishing impersonator of her time. Her brilliant "act" consisted of a series of character changes, many of them done in full sight of the audience with the as-sistance only of a small table of properties half concealed under a net. Some of these transformations were so amazing as to be beyond belief, even after one had sat and watched them. Not her appearance only, but voice, speech, manner, carriage, all shifted incredibly to fit the new part; so that the woman appeared to have no permanent form or fashion of her own, but to be only so much plastic human material out of which her cunning could mold at will man, woman, or child.

With this strange skill, hitherto used only to enthrall huge audiences, the woman known as Miss Hinch—she appeared to be without a first name—was now fighting for her life somewhere against the police of the world. Without artifice, she was a tall, thin young woman with strongly marked features and considerable beauty of a bold sort. What she would look like at the present moment nobody could even venture a guess. Having stabbed John Catherwood in her dressing-room at the theater, she had put on her hat and coat, dropped two wigs and her make-up kit into a handbag, said good night to the doorman, and walked out into Broadway. Within ten minutes the dead body of Catherwood was found and the chase begun. That had been two weeks ago. Since then, no one had seen her. The earth, indeed, seemed to have opened and swallowed her. Yet her features were almost as well known as a president's.

"A very remarkable case," repeated the clergyman, rather absently; and his neighbor, the old woman, respectfully agreed that it was. After that she hesitated a moment, and then added, with sudden bitterness:

"Oh, they'll never catch her, sir—never! She's too smart for 'em all, Miss Hinch is."

Attracted by her tone, the divine inquired if she was particularly interested in the case.

"Yes, sir—I got reason to be. Jack Catherwood's mother and me was at school together, and great friends all our life long. Oh, sir," she went on, as if in answer to his look of faint surprise, "Jack was a fine gentleman, with manners and looks and all beyond his people. But he never grew away from his old mother, sir—no, sir, never! And I don't believe ever a Sunday passed that he didn't go up and set the afternoon away with her, talking and laughing just like he was a little boy again. Maybe he done things he hadn't ought, as high-spirited lads will, but he was a good boy in his heart. And it does seem hard for him to die like that—and that hussy free to go her way, ruinin' and killin'."

"My good woman," said the clergyman presently, "compose yourself. No matter how diabolical this woman's skill is, her sin will assuredly find her out."

The woman dutifully lowered her handkerchief and tried to compose herself, as bidden.

"But oh, sir, she's that clever—diabolical, just as ye say, sir. Through poor Jack we of course heard much gossip about her, and they do say that her best tricks was not done on the stage at all. They say, sir, that, sittin' around a table with her friends, she could begin

and twist her face so strange and terrible that they
would beg her to stop, and jump up and run from the
table—frightened out of their lives, sir, grown-up people. And let her only step behind her screen for a minute—for she kept her secrets well, Miss Hinch did—
and she'd come walking out to you, and you could go
right up to her in the full light and take her hand, and
still you couldn't make yourself believe that it was her."

"Yes," said the clergyman, "I have heard that she is
remarkably clever—though, as a stranger in this part of
the world, I never saw her act. It is all very interesting
and strange."

He turned his head and stared through the rear door
at the dark, flying walls. At the same moment the
woman turned her head and stared full at the clergyman. When he turned back, her gaze had gone off toward the front of the car, and he picked up the paper
thoughtfully.

"I'm a visitor in the city, from Denver, Colorado,"
he said presently, "and knew little or nothing about the
case until an evening or two ago, when I attended a
meeting of gentlemen here. The men's club of St. Mat-
thias' Church—perhaps you know the place? Upon my
word, they talked of nothing else. I confess they got me
quite interested in their gossip. So tonight I bought this
paper to see what this extraordinary woman detective it
employs had to say about it. We don't have such things

in the West, you know. But I must say I was disappointed, after all the talk about her."

"Yes, sir, indeed, and no wonder, for she's told Mrs. Catherwood herself that she's never made such a failure as this, so far. It seemed like she could always catch women, sir, up to this. It seemed like she knew in her own mind just what a woman would do, where she'd try to hide and all; and so she could find them time and time when the men detectives didn't know where to look. But oh, sir, she's never had to hunt for such a woman as Miss Hinch before!"

"No? I suppose not," said the clergyman. "Her story here in the paper certainly seems to me very poor."

"*Story*, sir! Bless my soul!" suddenly exploded the old gentleman across the aisle, to the surprise of both. "You don't suppose the clever little woman is going to show her hand in those stories, with Miss Hinch in the city and reading every line."

The approach to his station, it seemed, had roused him from his nap just in time to overhear the clergyman's criticism. Now he answered the looks of the old woman and the divine with an elderly cackle.

"Excuse my intrusion! I can't sit silent and hear anybody run down Jessie Dark. No, sir! Why there's a man at my boarding-place—astonishing young fellow named Hardy, Tom Hardy—who's known her for *years!* As to those stories, sir, I can assure you that she puts in them *exactly the opposite of what she really thinks!*"

"You don't tell me!" said the clergyman encouragingly.

"Yes, sir! Oh, she plays the game—yes, yes! She has her private ideas, her clues, her schemes. The woman doesn't live who is clever enough to hoodwink Jessie Dark. I look for developments any day—any day, sir!"

A new voice joined in. The young couple down the car had been frankly listening; and it was illustrative of the public mind at the moment that, as they now rose for their station, the young fellow felt perfectly free to offer his contribution:

"Tremendously dramatic situation, isn't it? Those two clever women pitted against each other in a life-and-death struggle, fighting it out silently in the underground somewhere—keen professional pride on one side and the fear of the electric chair on the other."

"Oh, yes! Oh, yes!" exclaimed the old gentleman rather testily. "But, my dear sir, it's not *professional pride* that makes Jessie Dark so resolute to win. It's feminine jealousy, if you follow me—no offense, madam. Yes, sir! Women never have the slightest respect for each other's abilities—not the slightest. No mercy for each other, either! I tell you, Jessie Dark'd be ashamed to be beaten by another woman. Read her stories between the lines, sir—as I do. Invincible determination—no weakening—no mercy! You catch my point, sir?"

"It sounds reasonable," answered the Colorado

clergyman, with his courteous smile. "All women, we are told, are natural rivals at heart."

"Oh, I'm for Jessie Dark every time!" the young fellow broke in eagerly—"especially since the police have practically laid down. But—"

"Why, she's told my young friend Hardy," the old gentleman rode him down, "that she'll find Hinch if it takes her a lifetime! Knows a thing or two about actresses, she says. Says the world isn't big enough for the creature to hide from her. Well! What do you think of that?"

"Tell them what we were just talking about, George," said the young wife, looking at her husband with admiring eyes.

"But oh, sir," began the old woman timidly, "Jack Catherwood's been dead two weeks now, and—and——"

"Two weeks, madam! And what is that, pray?" exploded the old gentleman, rising triumphantly. "A lifetime, if necessary! Oh, never fear! Miss Victorian was considered pretty clever, wasn't she? Remember what Jessie Dark did for her? Nan Parmalee, too—though the police did their best to steal Miss Dark's credit. She'll do just as much for Miss Hinch—you may take it from me!"

"But how's she going to make the capture, gentlemen?" cried the young fellow, getting his chance at last.

"That's the point my wife and I've been discussing. Assuming that she succeeds in spotting this woman-devil, what will she *do*? Now——"

"Do, sir! Yell for the police!" burst from the old gentleman at the door.

"And have Miss Hinch shoot her—and then herself, too?"

"Grand Central!" cried the guard; and the young fellow broke off reluctantly to find his pretty wife towing him strongly toward the door.

"Hope she nabs her soon, anyway," he called back to the clergyman over his shoulder. "The thing's getting on my nerves."

The door rolled shut behind him, and the train flung itself on its way. Within the car, a lengthy silence ensued. The clergyman stared thoughtfully at the floor, and the old woman fell back upon her borrowed paper. She appeared to be rereading the observations of Jessie Dark with considerable care. Presently she lowered the paper and began a quiet search for something under the folds of her shawl; at length, her hands emerging empty, she broke the silence with a timid request:

"Oh, sir—have you a pencil you could lend me, please? I'd like to mark something in the piece to send to Mrs. Catherwood. It's what she says here about the disguises, sir."

The kindly divine felt in his pockets, and after some

hunting produced a pencil—a fat white one with blue lead. She thanked him gratefully.

"How is Mrs. Catherwood bearing all this strain and anxiety?" he asked suddenly. "Have you seen her to-day?"

"Oh, yes, sir. I've been spending the evening with her since seven o'clock and am just back from there now. Oh, she's very much broke up, sir."

She looked at him hesitatingly. He stared straight in front of him, saying nothing, though he knew, in common with the rest of the reading world, that Jack Catherwood's mother lived, not on 126th Street, but on East Tenth. Presently he wondered if his silence had not been an error of judgment. Perhaps that misstatement had not been a slip, but something cleverer.

The woman went on with a certain eagerness: "Oh, sir, I only hope and pray those gentlemen may be right; but it does look to Mrs. Catherwood, and me too, that if Jessie Dark was going to catch her at all, she'd have done it before now. Look at those big, bold blue eyes Miss Hinch had, sir, with lashes an inch long, they say, and that terrible long chin. They do say she can change the color of her eyes, not forever of course, but put a few of her drops into them and make them look entirely different for a time. But that chin, sir, ye'd say——"

She broke off; for the clergyman had suddenly picked up his heavy stick and risen.

"Here we are at Fourteenth Street," he said, nodding pleasantly. "I must change here. Good night. Success to Jessie Dark, I say!"

He was watching the woman's faded face intently, and he saw just that look of respectful surprise break into it that he had expected.

"Fourteenth Street, sir! I'd no notion at all we'd come so far. It's where I get out too, sir, the expresses not stopping at my station."

"Ah?" said the clergyman, with the utmost dryness.

He led the way, limping and leaning on his stick. They emerged upon the chill and cheerless platform. The clergyman, after stumping along a few steps, stopped and turned. The woman had halted. Over the intervening space their eyes met.

"Come," said the man gently. "Come, let us walk about a little to keep warm."

"Oh, sir—it's too kind of you, sir," said the woman, coming forward.

From other cars two or three blue-nosed people had got off to make the change; one or two more came straggling in from the street; but, scattered over the bleak concrete expanse, they detracted little from the isolation that seemed to surround the woman and the clergyman. Step for step, the odd pair made their way to the extreme northern end of the platform.

"By the way," said the clergyman, halting abruptly, "may I see that paper again for a moment?"

"Oh, yes, sir—of course," said the woman, producing it from beneath her shawl. "If you want it back, sir——"

He said that he wanted only to glance at it for a moment; but he fell to looking through it page by page, with considerable care. The woman glanced at him several times with timid respect. Finally she said hesitatingly:

"I think, sir, I'll ask the ticket-chopper how long before the next train. I'm very late as it is, sir; and I still must stop to get something to eat before I go to bed."

"An excellent idea," said the clergyman.

He explained that he, too, was already an hour behind time, and was spending the night with cousins in Newark, to boot. Side by side, they retraced their steps down the platform, ascertained the schedule from the sleepy chopper, and, as by some tacit consent, started slowly back again. But, before they had gone very far, the woman all at once stopped short and, with a white face, leaned against the wall.

"Oh, sir, I'm afraid I'll just have to stop and get a bite somewhere before I go on. You'll think me foolish, sir; but I missed my supper entirely tonight, and there is quite a faint feeling coming over me."

The clergyman looked at her with apparent concern. "Do you know, my friend, you seem to anticipate all my own wants: Your mentioning something to eat just now reminded me that I myself was all but famishing."

He glanced at his watch, appearing to deliberate. "Yes, there is still time before my train. Come, we will find a modest eating-place together."

"Oh, sir," she stammered, "but—you wouldn't want to eat with a poor old woman like me, sir."

"And why not? Are we not all equal in the sight of God?"

They ascended the stairs together, like any prosperous parson and his poor parishioner, and, coming out into Fourteenth Street, started west. In the first block they came to a restaurant, a brilliantly lighted, tiled, and polished place of the quick lunch variety. But the woman timidly preferred not to stop here, saying that the glare of such places was very bad for her old eyes. The kindly divine accepted the objection without argument. Two blocks farther on they found on a corner a quieter eating-place, an unpretentious little restaurant which boasted a "Ladies' Entrance" down the side street.

They entered by the front door, and sat down at a table facing each other. The woman read the menu through, and finally, after much embarrassed uncertainty, ordered poached eggs on toast. The clergyman ordered the same. The simple meal was soon dispatched. Just as they were finishing it, the woman said apologetically:

"If you'll excuse me, sir—could I see the bill of fare a minute? I think I'd best take a little pot of tea to warm me up, if they do not charge too high."

"I haven't the bill of fare," said the clergyman.

They looked diligently for the cardboard strip, but it was nowhere to be seen. The waiter drew near.

"Yes, ma'am! I certainly left it there on the table when I took the order."

"I'm sure I can't imagine what's become of it," repeated the clergyman, rather insistently.

He looked hard at the woman and found that she was looking hard at him. Both pairs of eyes fell instantly.

The waiter brought another bill of fare; the woman ordered tea; the waiter came back with it. The clergyman paid for both orders with a dollar bill that looked hard-earned.

The tea proved to be very hot: it could not be drunk down at a gulp. The clergyman, watching the woman intently as she sipped, seemed to grow more and more restless. His fingers drummed the tablecloth; he could hardly sit still. All at once he said: "What is that calling in the street? It sounds like newsboys."

The woman put her old head on one side and listened. "Yes, sir. There seems to be an extra out."

"Upon my word," he said, after a pause, "I believe I'll go get one. Good gracious! Crime is a very interesting thing, to be sure!"

He rose slowly, took down his hat from the hanger near him, and grasping his heavy stick, limped to the door. Leaving it open behind him, much to the annoyance of the proprietor in the cashier's cage, he stood a moment in the little vestibule, looking up and down the street. Then he took a few slow steps eastward, beckoning with his hand as he went, and so passed out of sight of the woman at the table.

The eating-place was on the corner, and outside the clergyman paused for half a breath. North, east, south, and west he looked, and nowhere found what his flying glance sought. He turned the corner into the darker cross street, and began to walk, continually looking about him. Presently his pace quickened, quickened so that he no longer even stayed to use his stout cane. A newsboy thrust an extra under his very nose, and he did not even see it.

Far down the street, nearly two blocks away, a tall figure in a blue coat stood under a street light, stamping his feet in the freezing sleet; and the hurrying divine sped straight toward him. But he did not get very far. As he passed the side entrance at the extreme rear of the restaurant, a departing guest dashed out so recklessly as to run full into him, stopping him dead.

Without looking, he knew who it was. In fact, he did not look at her at all, but turned his head hurriedly east and west, sweeping the cross street with a swift eye. But the old woman, having drawn back with a sharp exclamation as they collided, rushed breathlessly into apologies:

"Oh, sir—excuse me, sir! A newsboy popped his head into the side door just after you went out, sir; and I ran

Presently his pace quickened.

to him to get you the paper. But he got away too quick for me, sir; and so I——"

"Exactly," said the clergyman in his quiet, deep voice. "That must have been the very boy I myself was after."

On the other side, two men had just turned into the street, well muffled against the night, talking cheerfully as they trudged along. Now the clergyman looked full at the woman, and she saw that there was a smile on his face.

"As he seems to have eluded us both, suppose we return to the subway?"

"Yes, sir; it's full time I——"

"The sidewalk is so slippery," he went on gently, "perhaps you had better take my arm."

The woman did as she was bidden.

Behind the pair in the restaurant, the waiter came forward to shut the door, and lingered to discuss with the proprietor the sudden departure of his two patrons. However, the bill had been paid in full, with a liberal tip for service; and so there was no especial complaint to make. After listening to some markedly unfavorable comments on the ways of the clergy, the waiter returned to his table to set it in order for the next customer.

On the floor in the carpeted aisle between tables lay a white rectangle of cardboard, which he readily recognized as one of their bills of fare, face downward. He stooped and picked it up. On the back of it was some scribbling, made with a blue lead pencil. The handwriting was very loose and irregular, as if the writer had had his eyes elsewhere while he wrote; and it was with some difficulty that the waiter deciphered this message:

Miss Hinch 14th St. subway. Get police quick.

The waiter carried this curious document to the proprietor, who read it over a number of times. He was a dull man, and had a dull man's suspiciousness of a practical joke. However, after a good deal of irresolute discussion, he put on his overcoat and went out for a policeman. He turned west, and halfway up the block met an elderly bluecoat sauntering east. The policeman looked at the scribbling, and dismissed it profanely as a wag's foolishness of the sort that was bothering the life out of him a dozen times a day. He walked along with the proprietor; and as they drew near to the latter's place of business, both became aware at the same moment of footsteps thudding nearer up the cross street from the south. As they looked up, two young policemen, accompanied by a man in a uniform like a streetcar conductor's, swept around the corner and dashed straight into the restaurant.

The first policeman and the proprietor ran in after them, and found them staring about rather vacantly. One of the breathless arms of the law demanded if any suspicious characters had been seen about the place, and the dull proprietor said no. The officers, looking rather flat, explained their errand. It seemed that a few moments before, the third man, who was a ticket-chopper at the subway station, had found a mysterious message lying on the floor by his box. Whence it had come, how long it had lain there, he had not the slightest idea. However, there it was. The policeman exhibited a crumpled white scrap torn from a newspaper, on which was scrawled in blue pencil:

Miss Hinch Miller's Restaurant. Get police quick.

The first policeman, who was both the oldest and the fattest of the three, produced the message on the bill of fare, so utterly at odds with this. The dull proprietor, now bethinking himself, mentioned the clergyman and the old woman who had taken poached eggs and tea together, called for a second bill of fare, and departed so unexpectedly by different doors. The ticket-chopper recalled that he had seen the same pair at his station; they had come up, he remembered, and questioned him closely about trains. The three policemen were momentarily puzzled by this testimony. But it was soon plain to them that if either the woman or the clergyman really had any information about Miss Hinch—a highly improbable supposition in itself—they would never have stopped with peppering the neighborhood with silly little contradictory messages.

"They're a pair of old fools tryin' to have sport with

the police, and I'd like to run them in for it," growled the fattest of the officers; and this was the general verdict.

The little conference broke up. The dull proprietor returned to his cage, the waiter to his table; the subway man departed on the run for his choppingbox; the three policemen passed out into the bitter night. They walked together, grumbling, and their feet, perhaps by some subconscious impulse, turned eastward toward the subway. And in the middle of the next block a man came running up to them.

"Officer, look what I found on the sidewalk a minute ago. Read that scribble!"

He held up a white slab which proved to be a bill of fare from Miller's restaurant. On the back of it the three peering officers saw, almost illegibly scrawled in blue pencil:

Police! Miss Hinch 14th St. subw——

The hand trailed off on the *w* as though the writer had been suddenly interrupted.

The fat policeman swore and threatened arrests. But the second policeman, who was dark and wiry, raised his head from the bill of fare and said suddenly: "Tim, I believe there's something in this."

"There'd ought to be ten days on the Island in it for them," growled fat Tim.

"Suppose, now," said the other policeman, staring

intently at nothing, "the old woman was Miss Hinch herself, f'r instance, and the parson was shadowing her while pretendin' he never suspicioned her, and Miss Hinch not darin' to cut and run for it till she was sure she had a clean getaway. Well now, Tim, what better could he do——"

"That's right!" exclaimed the third policeman. "Specially when ye think that Hinch carries a gun, an'll use it, too! Why not have a look in at the subway station anyway, the three of us?"

This proposal carried the day. The three officers started for the subway, the citizen following. They walked at a good pace and without more talk. As the minds of the four men turned inward upon the odd behavior of the pair in Miller's Restaurant, the conviction that, after all, something important might be afoot grew and strengthened within each one of them. Unconsciously their pace quickened. It was the dark, wiry policeman who first broke into an open run, but the three other men had been for twenty paces on the verge of it.

However, these consultations and waverings had taken time. The stout clergyman and the poor old woman had five minutes' start on the officers of the law; and that, as it happened, was all that the occasion required. On Fourteenth Street, as they made their way arm in arm to the station, they were seen, and remembered, by a number of pedestrians. It was observed by more than one that the old woman lagged as if she were tired, while the club-footed divine, supporting her on his arm, steadily kept her up to his own brisk gait.

So walking, the pair descended the subway steps, came out upon the bare platform again, and presently stood once more at the extreme uptown end of it, just where they had waited half an hour before. Near by a careless porter had overturned a bucket of water, and a splotch of thin ice ran out and over the edge of the concrete. Two young men who were taking lively turns up and down distinctly heard the clergyman warn the woman to look out for this ice. Far away to the north was to be heard the faint roar of an approaching train.

The woman stood nearest the track, and the clergyman stood in front of her. In the vague light their looks met, and each was struck by the pallor of the other's face. In addition the woman was breathing hard, and her hands and feet betrayed some nervousness. It was difficult now to ignore the too patent fact that for an hour they had been clinging desperately to each other, at all costs; but the clergyman made a creditable effort to do so. He talked ramblingly, in a kind voice, for the most part of the deplorable weather and his train to Newark, for which he was now so late. And all the time both of them were incessantly turning their heads toward the station entrance, as if expecting some arrival.

As he talked, the clergyman kept his hands unobtrusively busy. From the bottom edge of his black coat he drew a pin and stuck it deep into the ball of his middle finger. He took out his handkerchief to dust the hard sleet from his broad hat, and under his overcoat he pressed the handkerchief against his bleeding finger. While making these small arrangements, he held the woman's eyes with his own, chatting kindly; and, still holding them, he suddenly broke off his random talk and peered at her cheek with concern.

"My good woman, you've scratched your cheek somehow! Why, bless me, it's bleeding quite badly."

"Never mind," said the woman, and looked hurriedly toward the entrance.

"But, good gracious, I must mind! The blood will fall on your shawl. If you will permit me—ah!"

Too quick for her, he leaned forward and, through the thin veil, swept her cheek hard with his handkerchief; and, removing it, held it up so that she might see the blood for herself. But she did not glance at the handkerchief, and neither did he. His gaze was riveted upon her cheek, which looked smooth and clear where he had smudged the clever wrinkles away.

Down the steps and upon the platform pounded the feet of three flying policemen. But it was quite evident now that the express would thunder in just ahead of them. The clergyman, standing close in front of the woman, took a firmer grip on his heavy stick and smiled full into her face.

"Miss Hinch, you are not so terribly clever, after all!"

The woman sprang back from him with an irrepressible exclamation, and in that moment her eye fell upon the police. Unluckily, her foot slipped upon the treacherous ice—or it may have tripped on the stout cane when the clergyman suddenly shifted its position. And in the next breath the express train roared past.

By one of those curious circumstances that sometimes refute all experience, the body of the woman was not mangled or mutilated in the least. There was a deep blue bruise on the left temple, and apparently that was all; even the ancient hat remained on her head, skewered fast by the long pin. It was the clergyman who found the body, huddled at the side of the track where the train had flung it—he who covered the still face and superintended the removal to the platform. Two eye-witnesses of the tragedy pointed out the ice on which the unfortunate woman had slipped, and described their horror as they saw her companion spring forward just too late to save her.

Not wishing to bring on a delirium of excitement among the half-dozen chance bystanders, two policemen drew the clergyman quietly aside and showed him the three mysterious messages. Apparently much affected by the woman's shocking end, he readily owned to having written them. He briefly recounted how the woman's strange movements on 126th Street had arrested his attention, and how, watching her closely on the car, he had finally detected that she wore a wig. Un-

fortunately, however, her suspicions appeared to have
been aroused by his interest in her; and thereafter a long
battle of wits had ensued between them—he trying to
call the police without her knowledge, she dogging him
close to prevent that, and at the same time watching
her chance to give him the slip. He rehearsed how, in
the restaurant, when he had invented an excuse to leave
her for an instant, she had made a bolt and narrowly
missed getting away; and finally how, having brought
her back to the subway and seeing the police at last
near, he had exposed her make-up and had spoken her
name, with unexpectedly shocking results.

"And now," he concluded in a shaken voice, "I am
naturally most anxious to know whether I am right—
or have made some terrible mistake. Will you look at
her, officer, and tell me if it is—she?"

But the fat policeman shook his head over the well-
known ability of Miss Hinch to look like everybody
else in the world but herself.

"It'll take God Almighty to tell ye that, sir—saving
your presence. I'll leave it f'r headquarters," he continued as if that were the same thing. "But, if it is her,
she's gone to her reward, sir."

"God pity her!" said the clergyman.

"Amen! Give me your name, sir. They may want
ye in the morning."

The clergyman gave it: Rev. Theodore Shaler, of
Denver; city address, 245 East 126th Street. Having

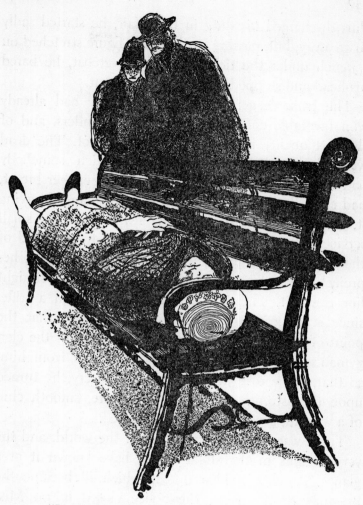

"*If it is her, she's gone to her reward, sir.*"

thus discharged his duty in the affair, he started sadly to go away; but, passing by the silent figure stretched on a bench under the ticket-chopper's overcoat, he bared his head and stopped for one last look at it.

The parson's gentleness and efficiency had already won favorable comments from the bystanders, and of the first quality he now gave a final proof. The dead woman's wadded-up handkerchief, which somebody had recovered from the track and laid upon her breast, had slipped to the floor; and the clergyman, observing it, stooped silently to restore it again. This last small service chanced to bring his head close to the head of the dead woman; and, as he straightened up again, her projecting hatpin struck his cheek and ripped a straight line down it. This in itself would have been a trifle, since scratches soon heal. But it happened that the point of the hatpin caught under the lining of the clergyman's perfect beard and ripped it clean from him; so that, as he rose with a sudden shrill cry, he turned upon the astonished onlookers the bare, smooth chin of a woman, curiously long and pointed.

There was only one such chin in the world, and the very urchins in the street would have known it at a glance. Amid a sudden uproar which ill became the presence of the dead, the police closed in on Miss Hinch and handcuffed her with violence, fearing suicide, if not some new witchery; and at the stationhouse an unemotional matron divested the famous imperson-

ator of the last and best of all her many disguises. This
much the police did. But it was quite distinctly understood that it was Jessie Dark who had really made the
capture, and the papers next morning printed pictures
of the unconquerable little woman and of the hatpin
with which she had reached back from another world
to bring her greatest adversary to justice.

WASHINGTON IRVING

Don Roderick and the Magic Tower

Now, so it happened, according to the legend, that as King Roderick was seated one day on his throne, surrounded by his nobles, in the ancient city of Toledo, two men of venerable appearance entered the hall of audience. Their snowy beards descended to their breasts, and their gray hairs were bound with ivy. They were arrayed in white garments of foreign or antiquated fashion, which swept the ground, and were cinctured with girdles, wrought with the signs of the zodiac, from which were suspended enormous bunches of keys of every variety of form. Having approached the throne and made obeisance,—"Know, O king," said one of the old men, "that in days of yore, when Hercules of Lybia, surnamed the Strong, had set up his pillars at the ocean strait, he erected a tower near to this ancient city of Toledo. He built it of prodigious strength, and finished it with magic art, shutting up within it a fearful secret, never to be penetrated without peril and disaster. To protect this terrible mystery he closed the entrance to the edifice with a ponderous door of iron, secured by a great lock of steel, and he left a command that every king who should succeed him should add another lock to the portal; denouncing woe and destruction on him who should eventually unfold the secret of the tower.

"The guardianship of the portal was given to our ancestors, and has continued in our family, from generation to generation, since the days of Hercules. Several kings, from time to time, have caused the gate to be thrown open, and have attempted to enter, but have paid dearly for their temerity. Some have perished within the threshold; others have been overwhelmed with horror at tremendous sounds, which shook the foundations of the earth, and have hastened to reclose the door and secure it with its thousand locks. Thus, since the days of Hercules, the inmost recesses of the pile have never been penetrated by mortal man, and a profound mystery continues to prevail over this great enchantment. This, O king, is all we have to relate; and our errand is to entreat thee to repair to the tower and affix thy lock to the portal, as has been done by all thy predecessors." Having thus said, the ancient men made a profound reverence and departed from the presence-chamber.

Don Roderick remained for some time lost in

thought after the departure of the men; he then dismissed all his court excepting the venerable Urbino, at that time archbishop of Toledo. The long white beard of this prelate bespoke his advanced age, and his overhanging eyebrows showed him a man full of wary counsel.

"Father," said the king, "I have an earnest desire to penetrate the mystery of this tower."

The worthy prelate shook his hoary head. "Beware, my son," said he; "there are secrets hidden from man for his good. Your predecessors for many generations have respected this mystery, and have increased in might and empire. A knowledge of it, therefore, is not material to the welfare of your kingdom. Seek not then to indulge a rash and unprofitable curiosity, which is interdicted under such awful menaces."

"Of what importance," cried the king, "are the menaces of Hercules the Libyan? Was he not a pagan? and can his enchantments have aught avail against a believer in our holy faith? Doubtless in this tower are locked up treasures of gold and jewels, amassed in days of old, the spoils of mighty kings, the riches of the pagan world. My coffers are exhausted; I have need of supply; and surely it would be an acceptable act in the eyes of Heaven to draw forth this wealth which lies buried under profane and necromantic spells, and consecrate it to religious purposes."

The venerable archbishop still continued to remon-

The worthy prelate shook his hoary head.

strate, but Don Roderick heeded not his counsel, for he was led on by his malignant star. "Father," said he, "it is in vain you attempt to dissuade me. My resolution is fixed. To-morrow I will explore the hidden mystery, or rather the hidden treasures, of this tower."

The morning sun shone brightly upon the cliff-built towers of Toledo, when King Roderick issued out of the gate of the city at the head of a numerous train of courtiers and cavaliers, and crossed the bridge that bestrides the deep rocky bed of the Tagus. The shining cavalcade wound up the road that leads among the mountains, and soon came in sight of the necromantic tower.

This singular tower was round and of great height and grandeur, erected upon a lofty rock, and surrounded by crags and precipices. The foundation was supported by four brazen lions, each taller than a cavalier on horseback. The walls were built of small pieces of jasper and various colored marbles, not larger than a man's hand; so subtilely joined, however, that, but for their different hues, they might be taken for one entire stone. They were arranged with marvelous cunning, so as to represent battles and warlike deeds of times and heroes long since passed away, and the whole surface was so admirably polished that the stones were as lustrous as glass, and reflected the rays of the sun with such resplendent brightness as to dazzle all beholders.

King Roderick and his courtiers arrived wondering and amazed at the foot of the rock. Here there was a narrow arched way cut through the living stone, the only entrance to the tower. It was closed by a massive iron gate, covered with rusty locks of divers workmanship, and in the fashion of different centuries, which had been affixed by the predecessors of Don Roderick. On either side of the portal stood the two ancient guardians of the tower, laden with the keys appertaining to the locks.

The king alighted, and approaching the portals ordered the guardians to unlock the gate. The hoary-headed men drew back with terror. "Alas!" cried they, "what is it Your Majesty requires of us? Would you have the mischiefs of this tower unbound, and let loose to shake the earth to its foundations?"

The venerable Archbishop Urbino likewise implored him not to disturb a mystery which had been held sacred from generation to generation within the memory of man, and which even Cæsar himself, when sovereign of Spain, had not ventured to invade. The youthful cavaliers, however, were eager to pursue the adventure, and encouraged him in his rash curiosity.

"Come what come may," exclaimed Don Roderick, "I am resolved to penetrate the mystery of this tower." So saying, he again commanded the guardians to unlock the portal. The ancient men obeyed with fear and trembling, but their hands shook with age, and when they applied the keys the locks were so rusted by time, or of such strange workmanship, that they resisted their feeble efforts, whereupon the young cavaliers pressed forward and lent their aid. Still the locks were so numerous and difficult, that with all their eagerness and strength a great part of the day was exhausted before the whole of them could be mastered.

When the last bolt had yielded to the key, the guardians and the reverend archbishop again entreated the king to pause and reflect. "Whatever is within this tower," said they, "is as yet harmless, and lies bound under a mighty spell; venture not then to open a door which may let forth a flood of evil upon the land." But the anger of the king was roused, and he ordered that the portal should instantly be thrown open. In vain, however, did one after another exert his strength, and equally in vain did the cavaliers unite their forces, and apply their shoulders to the gate; though there was neither bar nor bolt remaining, it was perfectly immovable.

The patience of the king was now exhausted, and he advanced to apply his hand; scarcely, however, did he touch the iron gate, when it swung slowly open, uttering, as it were, a dismal groan, as it turned reluctantly upon its hinges. A cold, damp wind issued forth, accompanied by a tempestuous sound. The hearts of the ancient guardians quaked within them, and their knees smote together; but several of the youthful cavaliers rushed in, eager to gratify their curiosity, or to signalize themselves in this redoubtable enterprise. They had scarcely advanced a few paces, however, when they recoiled, overcome by the baleful air, or by some fearful vision. Upon this, the king ordered that fires should be kindled to dispel the darkness, and to correct the noxious and long-imprisoned air; he then led the way into the interior; but, though stout of heart, he advanced with awe and hesitation.

After proceeding a short distance, he entered a hall

With a dismal groan it swung slowly open.

or antechamber, on the opposite side of which was a door and before it, on a pedestal, stood a gigantic figure, of the color of bronze and of a terrible aspect. It held a huge mace, which it whirled incessantly, giving such cruel and resounding blows upon the earth as to prevent all further entrance.

The king paused at sight of this appalling figure, for whether it were a living being, or a statue of magic artifice, he could not tell. On its breast was a scroll, whereon was inscribed, in large letters, "I do my duty." After a little while Roderick plucked up heart, and addressed it with great solemnity. "Whatever thou be," said he, "know that I come not to violate this sanctuary, but to inquire into the mystery it contains; I conjure thee, therefore, to let me pass in safety."

Upon this the figure paused with uplifted mace, and the king and his train passed unmolested through the door.

They now entered a vast chamber, of a rare and sumptuous architecture, difficult to be described. The walls were incrusted with the most precious gems, so joined together as to form one smooth and perfect surface. The lofty dome appeared to be self-supported, and was studded with gems, lustrous as the stars of the firmament. There was neither wood, nor any other common or base material to be seen throughout the edifice. There were no windows or other openings to admit the day, yet a radiant light was spread throughout the place which seemed to shine from the walls and to render every object distinctly visible.

In the centre of this hall stood a table of alabaster, of the rarest workmanship, on which was inscribed, in Greek characters, that Hercules Alcides, the Theban Greek, had founded this tower in the year of the world three thousand and six. Upon the table stood a golden casket, richly set round with precious stones, and closed with a lock of mother-of-pearl, and on the lid were inscribed the following words: —

"In this coffer is contained the mystery of the tower. The hand of none but a king can open it; but let him beware! for marvelous events will be revealed to him, which are to take place before his death."

King Roderick boldly seized upon the casket. The venerable archbishop laid his hand upon his arm, and made a last remonstrance. "Forbear, my son," said he; "desist while there is yet time. Look not into the mysterious decrees of Providence. God has hidden them in mercy from our sight, and it is impious to rend the veil by which they are concealed."

"What have I to dread from a knowledge of the future?" replied Roderick, with an air of haughty presumption. "If good be destined me, I shall enjoy it by anticipation; if evil, I shall arm myself to meet it." So saying, he rashly broke the lock.

Within the coffer he found nothing but a linen cloth, folded between two tablets of copper. On unfolding it,

he beheld painted on it figures of men on horseback, of
fierce demeanor, clad in turbans and robes of various
colors, after the fashion of the Arabs, with scimitars hanging from their necks, and cross-bows at their saddle-backs,
and they carried banners and pennons with divers devices.
Above them was inscribed, in Greek characters, "Rash
monarch! behold the men who are to hurl thee from thy
throne, and subdue thy kingdom!"

At sight of these things the king was troubled in spirit,
and dismay fell upon his attendants. While they were
yet regarding the paintings, it seemed as if the figures
began to move, and a faint sound of warlike tumult arose
from the cloth, with the clash of cymbal and bray of
trumpet, the neigh of steed and shout of army; but all
was heard indistinctly, as if afar off, or in a reverie or
dream. The more they gazed, the plainer became the
motion, and the louder the noise; and the linen cloth
rolled forth, and amplified, and spread out, as it were, a
mighty banner, and filled the hall, and mingled with
the air, until its texture was no longer visible, or appeared as a transparent cloud. And the shadowy figures
became all in motion, and the din and uproar became
fiercer and fiercer; and whether the whole were an animated picture, or a vision, or an array of embodied
spirits, conjured up by supernatural power, no one present could tell. They beheld before them a great field
of battle, where Christians and Moslems were engaged

in deadly conflict. They heard the rush and tramp of steeds, the blast of trump and clarion, the clash of cymbal, and the stormy din of a thousand drums. There was the clash of swords and maces and battle-axes, with the whistling of arrows and the hurtling of darts and lances.

The Christians quailed before the foe; the infidels pressed upon them and put them to utter rout; the standard of the cross was cast down, the banner of Spain was trodden under foot, the air resounded with shouts of triumph, with yells of fury, and with the groans of dying men. Amidst the flying squadrons King Roderick beheld a crowned warrior, whose back was towards him, but whose armor and device were his own, and who was mounted on a white steed that resembled his own war-horse Orelia. In the confusion of the flight, the warrior was dismounted and was no longer to be seen, and Orelia galloped wildly through the field of battle without a rider.

Roderick stayed to see no more, but rushed from the fatal hall, followed by his terrified attendants. They fled through the outer chamber, where the gigantic figure with the whirling mace had disappeared from his pedestal, and, on issuing into the open air, they found the two ancient guardians of the tower lying dead at the portal, as though they had been crushed by some mighty blow. All nature, which had been clear and serene, was now in wild uproar. The heavens were darkened by heavy clouds; loud bursts of thunder rent the air, and the earth was deluged with rain and rattling hail.

The king ordered that the iron portal should be closed, but the door was immovable, and the cavaliers were dismayed by the tremendous turmoil and the mingled shouts and groans that continued to prevail within. The king and his train hastened back to Toledo, pursued and pelted by the tempest. The mountains shook and echoed with the thunder, trees were uprooted and blown down, and the Tagus raged and roared and flowed above its banks. It seemed to the affrighted courtiers as if the phantom legions of the tower had issued forth and mingled with the storm; for amidst the claps of thunder and the howling of the wind, they fancied they heard the sound of the drums and trumpets, the shouts of armies, and the rush of steeds. Thus beaten by tempest and overwhelmed with horror, the king and his courtiers arrived at Toledo, clattering across the bridge of the Tagus, and entering the gate in headlong confusion, as though they had been pursued by an enemy.

In the morning the heavens were again serene, and all nature was restored to tranquillity. The king, therefore, issued forth with his cavaliers, and took the road to the tower, followed by a great multitude, for he was anxious once more to close the iron door, and shut up those evils that threatened to overwhelm the land. But

They hastened by, pursued and pelted by the tempest.

lo! on coming in sight of the tower, a new wonder met their eyes. An eagle appeared high in the air, seeming to descend from heaven. He bore in his beak a burning brand, and, lighting on the summit of the tower, fanned the fire with his wings. In a little while the edifice burst forth into a blaze, as though it had been built of rosin, and the flames mounted into the air with a brilliancy more dazzling than the sun; nor did they cease until every stone was consumed, and the whole was reduced to a heap of ashes.

Then there came a vast flight of birds, small of size and sable of hue, darkening the sky like a cloud; and they descended, and wheeled in circles round the ashes, causing so great a wind with their wings that the whole was borne up into the air, and scattered throughout all Spain, and wherever a particle of that ashes fell it was as a stain of blood. It is furthermore recorded by ancient men and writers of former days, that all those on whom this dust fell were afterwards slain in battle, when the country was conquered by the Arabs, and that the destruction of this necromantic tower was a sign and token of the approaching perdition of Spain.

The Case of the Perfect Maid

"Oh, if you please, M'am, could I speak to you a moment?"

Miss Marple said promptly, "Certainly, Edna; come in and shut the door. What is it?"

Obediently shutting the door, Miss Marple's little maid advanced into the room, pleated the corner of her apron between her fingers, and swallowed once or twice.

"Yes, Edna?" said Miss Marple encouragingly.

"Oh, please, M'am, it's my cousin Gladdie."

"Dear me," said Miss Marple, her mind leaping to the worst—and, alas, the most usual conclusion. "Not —not in *trouble*?"

Edna hastened to reassure her.

"Oh, no, M'am, nothing of *that* kind. It's just that she's upset. You see, she's lost her place."

"Dear me, I am sorry to hear that. She was at Old Hall, wasn't she, with the Miss—Miss—Skinners?"

"Yes, M'am, that's right, M'am. And Gladdie's very upset about it—very upset indeed."

"Gladys has changed places rather often before, though, hasn't she?"

"Oh, yes, M'am. She's always one for a change, Gladdie is. She never seems to get really *settled*, if you know what I mean. But she's always been the one to *give* the notice, you see!"

"And this time it's the other way round?" said Miss Marple dryly.

"Yes, M'am, and it's upset Gladdie something awful."

Miss Marple looked slightly surprised. Her recollection of Gladys, who had occasionally come to drink tea in the kitchen on her "days out," was of a stout, giggling girl of unshakably equable temperament.

Edna went on. "You see, M'am, it's the *way* it happened—the way Miss Skinner looked."

"How," inquired Miss Marple patiently, "did Miss Skinner look?"

This time Edna got well away with her news bulletin.

"Oh, M'am, it was ever such a shock to Gladdie. You see, one of Miss Emily's brooches was missing and such a hue and cry for it as never was, and, of course, nobody likes a thing like that to happen—it's upsetting, M'am, if you know what I mean. And Gladdie helped search *everywhere*, and there was Miss Lavinia saying she was going to the police about it, and then it turned up again, pushed right to the back of a drawer in the dressing-table, and *very* thankful Gladdie was. And the very next day as ever was a plate got broken, and Miss Lavinia she bounced out right away and told Gladdie to take a month's notice. And what Gladdie feels is it *couldn't* have been the plate, and that Miss Lavinia was just making an excuse of that, and that it must be because of the brooch, and they think as she took it and put it back when the police was mentioned, and Gladdie wouldn't do such a thing, and what she feels is as it will get round and tell against her, and it's a very serious thing for a girl, as you know, M'am."

Miss Marple nodded.

Edna said wistfully, "I suppose, M'am, there isn't anything you could do about it? Gladdie's in ever such a state."

"Tell her not to be silly," said Miss Marple crisply. "If she didn't take the brooch—which I'm sure she didn't—then she has no cause to be upset."

"It'll get about," said Edna dismally.

"I—er—am going up that way this afternoon," said Miss Marple. "I'll have a word with the Miss Skinners."

"Oh! *thank* you, M'am," said Edna.

Old Hall was a big Victorian house surrounded by woods and parkland. Since it had proved unlettable and unsalable as it was, an enterprising speculator had divided it into four flats with a central hot-water system, and the use of "the grounds" to be held in common by the tenants.

The experiment had been satisfactory. A rich and eccentric old lady and her maid occupied one flat. The old lady had a passion for birds and entertained a feathered gathering to meals every day. A retired Indian judge and his wife rented a second flat. A very young couple, recently married, occupied the third, and the fourth had been taken only two months ago by two maiden ladies of the name of Skinner.

The four sets of tenants were only on the most distant terms with each other, since none of them had anything in common. The landlord had been heard to say that this was an excellent thing. What he dreaded were friendships followed by estrangements and subsequent complaints to him.

Miss Marple was acquainted with all the tenants, though she knew none of them well. The elder Miss Skinner, Miss Lavinia, was what might be termed the working member of the firm. Miss Emily, the younger, spent most of her time in bed suffering from various complaints which, in the opinion of St. Mary Mead, were largely imaginary. Only Miss Lavinia believed devoutly in her sister's martyrdom and patience under affliction, and willingly ran errands and trotted up and down to the village for things that "my sister had suddenly fancied."

It was the view of St. Mary Mead that if Miss Emily

suffered half as much as she said she did, she would have
sent for Doctor Haydock long ago. But Miss Emily,
when this was hinted to her, shut her eyes in a superior
way and murmured that her case was not a simple one
—the best specialists in London had been baffled by
it—and that a wonderful new man had put her on a
most revolutionary course of treatment and that she
really hoped her health would improve under it. No
humdrum G.P. could *possibly* understand her case.

"And it's my opinion," said the outspoken Miss
Hartnell, "that she's very wise not to send for him. Dear
Doctor Haydock would tell her that there was nothing
the matter with her and to get up and not make a fuss.
Do her a lot of good!"

Failing such arbitrary treatment, however, Miss
Emily continued to lie on sofas, to surround herself with
strange little pill-boxes, and to reject nearly everything
that had been cooked for her and ask for something
else.

The door was opened to Miss Marple by Gladdie,
looking more depressed than Miss Marple had ever
thought possible. In the sitting-room Miss Lavinia rose
to greet Miss Marple.

Lavinia Skinner was a tall, gaunt, bony female of fifty.
She had a gruff voice and an abrupt manner.

"Nice to see you," she said. "Emily's lying down—
feeling low today, poor dear. Hope she'll see you, it
would cheer her up, but there are times when she

doesn't feel up to seeing *anybody*. Poor dear, she's wonderfully patient."

Miss Marple responded politely. Servants were the main topic of conversation in St. Mary Mead, so it was not difficult to lead the conversation in that direction. Miss Marple said she had heard that that nice girl, Gladys Holmes, was leaving.

Miss Lavinia nodded. "Wednesday week. Broke things, you know. Can't have that."

Miss Marple sighed and said we all had to put up with things nowadays. Did Miss Skinner really think it was wise to part with Gladys?

"Know it's difficult to get servants," admitted Miss Lavinia. "The Devereuxs haven't got *anybody*—but then I don't wonder—always quarreling, jazz on all night—meals any time. Then the Larkins have just lost *their* maid. Of course, what with the judge's Indian temper and his wanting Chota Hazri, as he calls it, at six in the morning, and Mrs. Larkin always fussing, I don't wonder at that, either. Mrs. Carmichael's Janet is a fixture, of course—though in my opinion she's the most disagreeable woman and absolutely *bullies* the old lady."

"Then don't you think you might reconsider your decision about Gladys? She really is a nice girl. I know all her family—very honest and superior."

Miss Lavinia shook her head.

Miss Marple murmured, "You missed a brooch, I understand——"

"Now who has been talking? I suppose the girl has. Quite frankly, I'm almost certain she took it. And then got frightened and put it back—but of course one can't say anything unless one is *sure*." She changed the subject. "Do come and see Miss Emily, Miss Marple. I'm sure it would do her good."

Miss Marple followed meekly to where Miss Lavinia knocked on a door, was bidden enter, and ushered her guest into the best room in the flat, most of the light of which was excluded by half-drawn blinds. Miss Emily was lying in bed.

The dim light showed her to be a thin, indecisive looking creature with a good deal of grayish-yellow hair untidily wound round her head and erupting into curls —the whole thing looking like a bird's nest of which no self-respecting bird could be proud. There was a smell in the room of eau-de-cologne, stale biscuits, and camphor.

With half-closed eyes and in a thin, weak voice Emily Skinner explained that this was one of her *bad* days.

"The worst of ill health is," said Miss Emily in a melancholy tone, "that one knows what a *burden* one is to everyone around one."

"No, no, Emily dear, indeed that is not so," protested her sister.

"Lavinia is very good to me," said Miss Emily. "Lavvie dear, I do so hate giving trouble, but if my hot-water bottle could only be filled in the way I like it—*too* full it weighs on me so; on the other hand, if it is not *sufficiently* filled, it gets *cold* immediately!"

"I'm sorry, dear. Give it to me. I will empty a little out."

"Perhaps, if you're doing that, it might be refilled. There are no rusks in the house, I suppose—no, no, it doesn't matter. I can do without. Some weak tea and a slice of lemon—no lemons? No, really, I couldn't drink tea without lemon—I think the milk was slightly turned this morning—it has put me right against milk in my tea. It doesn't matter. I can do without my tea. Only I do feel so weak. Oysters, they say, are nourishing —I wonder if I could fancy a few? No, no, too much bother to get hold of them so late in the day. I can fast until tomorrow."

Lavinia left the room, murmuring something incoherent about bicycling down to the village.

Miss Marple told Edna that evening that she was afraid her embassy had met with no success.

She was rather troubled to find that rumors as to Gladys's dishonesty were already going round the village.

In the Post Office Miss Wetherby tackled her. "My dear Jane, they gave her a written reference saying she

"I do so hate giving trouble."

was willing and sober and respectable, but saying nothing about *honesty*—that seems to me *most* significant! They'll find it most difficult to get anyone else. Girls simply *will not* go to Old Hall. You'll see, the Skinners won't find anyone else, and then perhaps that dreadful hypochondriac sister will *have* to get up and do something!"

Great was the chagrin of the village when it was made known that the Misses Skinner had engaged, from an agency, a new maid who, by all accounts, was a perfect paragon.

"A three years' reference recommending her most warmly; she *prefers* the country and actually asks less wages than Gladys. I really feel we have been *most* fortunate."

It then became the opinion of St. Mary Mead that the paragon would cry off at the last minute.

None of these prognostications came true, however, and the village was able to observe the domestic treasure, by name Mary Higgins, driving through the village in Reed's taxi to Old Hall. A most respectable looking woman, very neatly dressed.

When Miss Marple next visited Old Hall, on the occasion of recruiting stallholders for the Vicarage Fête, Mary Higgins opened the door. She was certainly a superior-looking maid, at a guess forty years of age, with neat black hair, rosy cheeks, a plump figure discreetly arrayed in black with a white apron and a cap—"quite the good, old-fashioned type of servant," as Miss Marple explained afterwards, and with the proper, inaudible, respectful voice.

Miss Lavinia was looking far less harassed than usual, and although she regretted that she could not take a stall owing to her preoccupation with her sister, she nevertheless tendered a handsome monetary contribution and promised to produce a consignment of penwipers and babies' socks.

Miss Marple commented on her air of well-being.

"I really feel I owe a great deal to Mary. I am so *thankful* I had the resolution to get rid of that other girl. Mary is really *invaluable*. Cooks nicely and waits beautifully and keeps our little flat scrupulously clean—mattresses turned *every day*. And she is really *wonderful* with Emily!"

Miss Marple hastily inquired after Emily.

"Oh, poor dear, she has been very much under the weather lately. She can't help it, of course, but it really makes things a little *difficult*, sometimes. Wanting certain things cooked and then, when they come, saying she can't eat now—and then wanting them again half an hour later. It makes, of course, a lot of work—but fortunately Mary does not seem to mind *at all*. She's been used to waiting on invalids, she says, and understands them. It is such a *comfort*."

"Dear me," said Miss Marple. "You *are* fortunate."

"Yes, indeed. I really feel Mary has been sent to us as an answer to *prayer*."

"She sounds to me," said Miss Marple, "almost too good to be true. I should—well, I should be a little careful if I were you."

Lavinia Skinner failed to perceive the point of this remark. She said, "Oh! I assure you I do all I can to make her comfortable. I don't know what I should do if she left."

"I don't expect she'll leave until she's ready to leave," said Miss Marple, and stared very hard at her hostess.

"If one has no domestic worries," said Miss Lavinia, "it takes such a load off one's mind, doesn't it? How is your little Edna shaping?"

"She's doing quite nicely. Not much *head*, of course. Not like your Mary. Still, I do know all about Edna, because she's a village girl."

Again she stared hard at Miss Lavinia; then sighed and changed the subject, asking if she should go in and see Miss Emily.

"Not today, I'm afraid," said Lavinia, shaking her head. "Poor Emily is quite unfit for visitors."

Miss Marple expressed polite sympathy and took her leave.

As she went out into the hall she heard the invalid's voice fretfully raised: "This compress has been allowed to get quite dry—Doctor Allerton particularly said moisture *continually* renewed. There, there, leave it. I want a cup of tea and a boiled egg—boiled only three minutes and a half, remember—and send Miss Lavinia to me."

The efficient Mary emerged from the bedroom, and saying to Lavinia, "Miss Emily is asking for you, Madam," proceeded to open the door for Miss Marple, helping her into her coat and handing her her umbrella.

Miss Marple took the umbrella, dropped it, tried to pick it up, and dropped her bag, which flew open. Mary politely retrieved various odds and ends—a handkerchief, an engagement book, an old-fashioned leather purse, two shillings, three pennies, and a striped piece of peppermint rock.

Miss Marple received the last with some signs of confusion.

"Oh, *dear*, that must have been Mrs. Clement's little boy. He *was* sucking it, I remember, and he took my bag to play with. He must have put it inside. It's terribly sticky, isn't it?"

"Shall I take it, Madam?"

"Oh! would you? Thank you so much."

Mary stooped to retrieve the last item, a small mirror, upon recovering which Miss Marple exclaimed fervently, "How lucky now that that isn't broken!"

She thereupon departed, Mary standing politely by the door holding a piece of striped rock with a completely expressionless face.

She stooped to retrieve a small mirror.

For ten days longer St. Mary Mead had to endure hearing of the excellencies of Miss Lavinia's and Miss Emily's treasure. On the eleventh day, the village awoke to its big thrill.

Mary, the paragon, was missing. Her bed had not been slept in and the front door was found ajar. She had slipped out quietly during the night.

And not Mary alone was missing! Two brooches and five rings of Miss Lavinia's; three rings, a pendant, a bracelet, and four brooches of Miss Emily's were missing also!

It was the beginning of a chapter of catastrophe.

Young Mrs. Devereux had lost her diamonds which she kept in an unlocked drawer, and also some valuable furs given to her as a wedding present. The judge and his wife also had had jewelry taken and a certain amount of money. Mrs. Carmichael was the greatest sufferer. Not only had she some very valuable jewels but she also kept in the flat a large sum of money, which had gone. It had been Janet's evening out and her mistress was in the habit of walking round the gardens at dusk calling to the birds and scattering crumbs. It seemed clear that Mary, the perfect maid, had had keys to fit all the flats!

There was, it must be confessed, a certain amount of ill-natured pleasure in St. Mary Mead. Miss Lavinia had boasted so much of her marvelous Mary.

"And all the time, my dear, just a common *thief!*"

Interesting revelations followed. Not only had Mary

disappeared into the blue but the agency which had provided her and vouched for her credentials was alarmed to find that the Mary Higgins who had applied to them and whose references they had taken up had, to all intents and purposes, never existed. It was the name of a *bona fide* servant who had lived with the *bona fide* sister of a dean, but the real Mary Higgins was existing peacefully in a place in Cornwall.

"Damned clever, the whole thing," Inspector Slack was forced to admit. "And if you ask me, that woman works in with a gang. There was a case of much the same kind in Northumberland a year ago. Stuff was never traced and they never caught her. However, we'll do better than that in Much Benham!"

Nevertheless, weeks passed and Mary Higgins remained triumphantly at large. In vain Inspector Slack redoubled the energy that so belied his name.

Miss Lavinia remained tearful. Miss Emily was so upset, and felt so alarmed by her condition, that she actually sent for Doctor Haydock.

The whole of the village was terribly anxious to know what he thought of Miss Emily's claims to ill health, but naturally could not ask him.

Satisfactory data came to hand on the subject, however, through Mr. Meek, the chemist's assistant, who was walking out with Clara, Mrs. Price-Ridley's maid.

It was then known that Doctor Haydock had prescribed a mixture of asafœtida and valerian which, according to Mr. Meek, was the stock remedy for malingerers in the Army! It was felt that this settled the question of Miss Emily's health once and for all, and great admiration was felt for Doctor Haydock's masterly handling of the case.

Soon afterwards it was learned that Miss Emily, not relishing the medical attention she had had, was declaring that in the state of her health she felt it her duty to be near the specialist in London who *understood* her case. It was, she said, only fair to Lavinia.

The flat was put up for sub-letting.

It was a few days after that that Miss Marple, rather pink and flustered, called at the police-station in Much Benham and asked for Inspector Slack.

Inspector Slack did not like Miss Marple. But he was aware that the Chief Constable, Colonel Melchett, did not share that feeling. Rather grudgingly, therefore, he received her.

"Good afternoon, Miss Marple; what can I do for you?"

"Oh, dear," said Miss Marple, "I'm afraid you're in a hurry."

"Lot of work on," said Inspector Slack, "but I can spare a few moments."

"Oh, dear," said Miss Marple, "I hope I shall be able

to put what I say properly. So difficult, you know, to explain oneself, don't you think? No, perhaps you don't. But you see, not having been educated in the modern style—just a governess, you know, who taught one the dates of the Kings of England and General Knowledge —Doctor Brewer—three kinds of diseases of wheat— blight, mildew—now what was the third—was it *smut?*"

"Do you want to talk about smut?" asked Inspector Slack, and then blushed.

"Oh, no, no. Just an *illustration*, you know. It's about Miss Skinner's maid. Gladys, you know."

"Mary Higgins," said Inspector Slack.

"Oh, yes, the *second* maid. But it's Gladys Holmes I mean—rather an impertinent girl and far too pleased with herself, but really strictly honest, and it's so important that that should be *recognized*."

"No charge against *her* so far as I know," said the Inspector.

"No, I know there isn't a charge—but that makes it worse. Because you see, people go on *thinking* things. Oh dear—I knew I should explain badly. What I really mean is that the important thing is to find Mary Higgins."

"Certainly," said Inspector Slack. "Have you any ideas on the subject?"

He grudgingly remembered that Miss Marple's ideas

had occasionally proved of use in the administration of justice.

"Well, as a matter of fact, I *have*," said Miss Marple. "May I ask you a question? Are fingerprints of no use to you?"

"Ah!" said Inspector Slack, "that's where she was a bit too artful for us. Did most of her work in rubber gloves or housemaid's gloves, it seems. And she'd been careful—wiped off everything in her bedroom and on the sink. Couldn't find a single fingerprint in the place!"

"If you did have her fingerprints, would it help?"

"It might, Madam; they may be known at the Yard. This isn't her first job, I'd say!"

Miss Marple nodded brightly. She opened her bag and extracted a small cardboard box. Inside it, wedged in cotton-wool, was a small mirror.

"From my handbag," said Miss Marple. "The maid's prints are on it. I *think* they should be satisfactory— she touched an extremely sticky substance a moment previously."

Inspector Slack stared. "Did you get her fingerprints on purpose?"

"Of course."

"You suspected her, then?"

"Well, you know, it did strike me that she was a little *too good to be true*. I practically told Miss Lavinia so —but she simply wouldn't take the hint! I'm afraid, you know, Inspector, that I don't believe in *paragons*. Most of us have our faults—and domestic service shows them up very quickly!"

"Well," said Inspector Slack, recovering his balance. "I'm obliged to you, I'm sure. We'll send these up to the Yard and see what they have to say."

He stopped. Miss Marple had put her head a little on one side and was regarding him with a good deal of meaning.

"You wouldn't consider, I suppose, Inspector, looking a little *nearer home?*"

"What do you mean, Miss Marple?"

"It's very difficult to explain, but when you come across a peculiar thing you notice it. Although, often, peculiar things may be the merest trifles. I've felt that all along, you know—I mean, about Gladys and the brooch. She's an honest girl, she didn't take that brooch —then *why did Miss Skinner think she did?* Miss Skinner's not a fool, far from it! Why was she so anxious to let a girl go who was a good servant, when servants are hard to get? It was *peculiar*, you know. So I wondered . . . I wondered a good deal. And I noticed another peculiar thing! Miss Emily's a hypochondriac —but she's the first hypochondriac who hasn't sent for some doctor or other at once. Hypochondriacs *love* doctors. Miss Emily didn't!"

"What are you suggesting, Miss Marple?" Inspector Slack was still quite fogged.

"The maid's prints are on it."

"Well, I'm suggesting, you know, that Miss Lavinia and Miss Emily are peculiar people. Miss Emily spends nearly all her time in a dark room. And if that hair of hers isn't a wig I—I'll eat my own back switch! And what I say is this—it's perfectly possible for a thin, pale, gray-haired, whining woman to be the same as a black-haired, rosy-cheeked, plump woman. And nobody that *I* can find ever *saw Miss Emily and Mary Higgins at one and the same time.* Plenty of time to get impressions of all the keys, plenty of time to find out all about the other tenants, and then—get rid of the local girl. Miss Emily takes a brisk walk across country one night and arrives at the station as Mary Higgins next day. And then, at the right moment, Mary Higgins disappears, and off goes the hue and cry after *her.*

"I'll tell you where you'll find her, Inspector. On Miss Emily Skinner's sofa! Get *her* fingerprints if you don't believe me, but you'll find I'm right! A couple of clever thieves, that's what the Skinners are—and no doubt in league with a clever post and rails, or fence, or whatever you call it. But they won't get away with it *this* time! I'm not going to have one of our village girl's character for honesty taken away like that! Gladys Holmes is as honest as the day and everybody's going to know it! Good afternoon!"

Miss Marple had stalked out before Inspector Slack had recovered.

"Whew!" he muttered. "I wonder if she's right?"

He soon found out that Miss Marple was right again. Colonel Melchett congratulated Slack on his efficiency, and Miss Marple arranged for Gladys to come to tea with Edna and spoke to her seriously on settling down in a good situation when she got one.

EDGAR ALLAN POE

The Purloined Letter

At Paris, just after dark one gusty evening in the autumn of 18—, I was enjoying the twofold luxury of meditation and a meerschaum, in company with my friend C. Auguste Dupin, in his little back library, or book-closet, *au troisième, No. 33, Rue Dunôt, Faubourg St. Germain*. For one hour at least we had maintained a profound silence; while each, to any casual observer, might have seemed intently and exclusively occupied with the curling eddies of smoke that oppressed the atmosphere of the chamber. For myself, however, I was mentally discussing certain topics which had formed matter for conversation between us at an earlier period of the evening; I mean the affair of the Rue Morgue, and the mystery attending the murder of Marie Rogêt. I looked upon it, therefore, as something of a coincidence, when the door of our apartment was thrown open and admitted our old acquaintance, Monsieur G——, the Prefect of the Parisian police.

We gave him a hearty welcome; for there was nearly half as much of the entertaining as of the contemptible about the man, and we had not seen him for several years. We had been sitting in the dark, and Dupin now arose for the purpose of lighting a lamp, but sat down again, without doing so, upon G——'s saying that he had called to consult us, or rather to ask the opinion of my friend, about some official business which had occasioned a great deal of trouble.

"If it is any point requiring reflection," observed Dupin, as he forebode to enkindle the wick, "we shall examine it to better purpose in the dark."

"That is another of your odd notions," said the Prefect, who had a fashion of calling everything "odd" that was beyond his comprehension, and thus lived amid an absolute legion of "oddities."

"Very true," said Dupin, as he supplied his visitor with a pipe, and rolled towards him a comfortable chair.

"And what is the difficulty now?" I asked. "Nothing more in the assassination way, I hope?"

"Oh no; nothing of that nature. The fact is, the business is *very* simple indeed, and I make no doubt that we can manage it sufficiently well ourselves; but then I thought Dupin would like to hear the details of it, because it is so excessively *odd*."

"Simple and odd," said Dupin.

"Why, yes; and not exactly that, either. The fact is,

we have all been a good deal puzzled because the affair *is* so simple, and yet baffles us altogether."

"Perhaps it is the very simplicity of the thing which puts you at fault," said my friend.

"What nonsense you *do* talk!" replied the Prefect, laughing heartily.

"Perhaps the mystery is a little *too* plain," said Dupin.

"Oh, good heavens! who ever heard of such an idea?"

"A little *too* self-evident."

"Ha! ha! ha!—ha! ha! ha!—ho! ho! ho!"—roared our visitor, profoundly amused, "oh, Dupin, you will be the death of me yet!"

"And what, after all, *is* the matter on hand?" I asked.

"Why, I will tell you," replied the Prefect, as he gave a long, steady, and contemplative puff, and settled himself in his chair. "I will tell you in a few words; but, before I begin, let me caution you that this is an affair demanding the greatest secrecy, and that I should most probably lose the position I now hold, were it known that I confided it to any one."

"Proceed," said I.

"Or not," said Dupin.

"Well, then; I have received personal information, from a very high quarter, that a certain document of the last importance, has been purloined from the royal apartments. The individual who purloined it is known; this beyond a doubt; he was seen to take it. It is known, also, that it still remains in his possession."

"Dupin, you will be the death of me."

"How is this known?" said Dupin.

"It is clearly inferred," replied the Prefect, "from the nature of the document, and from the non-appearance of certain results which would at once arise from its passing *out* of the robber's possession;—that is to say, from his employing it as he must design in the end to employ it."

"Be a little more explicit," I said.

"Well, I may venture so far as to say that the paper gives its holder a certain power in a certain quarter where such power is immensely valuable." The Prefect was fond of the cant of diplomacy.

"Still I do not quite understand," said Dupin.

"No? Well; the disclosure of the document to a third person, who shall be nameless, would bring in question the honor of a personage of most exalted station; and this fact gives the holder of the document an ascendancy over the illustrious personage whose honor and peace are so jeopardized."

"But this ascendancy," I interposed, "would depend upon the robber's knowledge of the loser's knowledge of the robber. Who would dare—"

"The thief," said G——, "is the Minister D——, who dares all things, those unbecoming as well as those becoming a man. The method of the theft was not less ingenious than bold. The document in question—a letter, to be frank—had been received by the personage robbed while alone in the royal *boudoir*. During its perusal she was suddenly interrupted by the entrance of the other exalted personage from whom especially it was her wish to conceal it. After a hurried and vain endeavor to thrust it in a drawer, she was forced to place it, open as it was, upon a table. The address, however, was uppermost, and, the contents thus unexposed, the letter escaped notice. At this juncture enters the Minister D——. His lynx eye immediately perceives the paper, recognizes the handwriting of the address, observes the confusion of the personage addressed, and fathoms her secret. After some business transactions, hurried through in his ordinary manner, he produces a letter somewhat similar to the one in question, opens it, pretends to read it, and then places it in close juxtaposition to the other. Again he converses, for some fifteen minutes, upon the public affairs. At length, in taking leave, he takes also from the table the letter to which he had no claim. Its rightful owner saw, but, of course, dared not call attention to the act, in the presence of the third personage who stood at her elbow. The Minister decamped; leaving his own letter—one of no importance —upon the table."

"Here, then," said Dupin to me, "you have precisely what you demand to make the ascendancy complete— the robber's knowledge of the loser's knowledge of the robber."

"Yes," replied the Prefect; "and the power thus attained has, for some months past, been wielded, for political purposes, to a very dangerous extent. The personage robbed is more thoroughly convinced, every day, of the necessity of reclaiming her letter. But this, of course, cannot be done openly. In fine, driven to despair, she has committed the matter to me."

"Than whom," said Dupin, amid a perfect whirl-
wind of smoke, "no more sagacious agent could, I suppose, be desired, or even imagined."

"You flatter me," replied the Prefect; "but it is possible that some such opinion may have been entertained."

"It is clear," said I, "as you observe, that the letter
is still in possession of the Minister; since it is this possession, and not any employment of the letter, which
bestows the power. With the employment the power
departs."

"True," said G——; "and upon this conviction I proceeded. My first care was to make thorough search of
the Minister's hotel; and here my chief embarrassment
lay in the necessity of searching without his knowledge.
Beyond all things, I have been warned of the danger
which would result from giving him reason to suspect
our design."

"But," said I, "you are quite *au fait* in these investigations. The Parisian police have done this thing often
before."

"O yes; and for this reason I did not despair. The
habits of the Minister gave me, too, a great advantage.
He is frequently absent from home all night. His servants
are by no means numerous. They sleep at a distance
from their master's apartment, and, being chiefly Nea-
politans, are readily made drunk. I have keys, as you
know, with which I can open any chamber or cabinet

in Paris. For three months a night has not passed, during the greater part of which I have not been engaged, personally, in ransacking the D—— Hôtel. My honor is interested, and, to mention a great secret, the reward is enormous. So I did not abandon the search until I had become fully satisfied that the thief is a more astute man than myself. I fancy that I have investigated every nook and corner of the premises in which it is possible that the paper can be concealed."

"But is it not possible," I suggested, "that although the letter may be in possession of the Minister, as it unquestionably is, he may have concealed it elsewhere than upon his own premises?"

"This is barely possible," said Dupin. "The present peculiar condition of affairs at court, and especially of those intrigues in which D—— is known to be involved, would render the instant availability of the document— its susceptibility of being produced at a moment's notice—a point of nearly equal importance with its possession."

"Its susceptibility of being produced?" said I.

"That is to say, of being *destroyed*," said Dupin.

"True," I observed; "the paper is clearly then upon the premises. As for its being upon the person of the Minister, we may consider that as out of the question."

"Entirely," said the Prefect. "He has been twice waylaid, as if by footpads, and his person rigorously searched under my own inspection."

"You might have spared yourself this trouble," said Dupin. "D——, I presume, is not altogether a fool, and, if not, must have anticipated these waylayings, as a matter of course."

"Not *altogether* a fool," said G——, "but then he's a poet, which I take to be only one remove from a fool."

"True," said Dupin, after a long and thoughtful whiff from his meerschaum, "although I have been guilty of certain doggerel myself."

"Suppose you detail," said I, "the particulars of your search."

"Why the fact is, we took our time, and we searched *everywhere*. I have had long experience in these affairs. I took the entire building, room by room; devoting the nights of a whole week to each. We examined, first, the furniture of each apartment. We opened every possible drawer; and I presume you know that, to a properly trained police agent, such a thing as a *secret* drawer is impossible. Any man is a dolt who permits a 'secret' drawer to escape him in a search of this kind. The thing is *so* plain. There is a certain amount of bulk—of space—to be accounted for in every cabinet. Then we have accurate rules. The fiftieth part of a line could not escape us. After the cabinets we took the chairs. The cushions we probed with the fine long needles you have seen me employ. From the tables we removed the tops."

"Why so?"

"Sometimes the top of a table, or other similarly arranged piece of furniture, is removed by the person wishing to conceal an article; then the leg is excavated, the article deposited within the cavity, and the top replaced. The bottoms and tops of bedposts are employed in the same way."

"But could not the cavity be detected by sounding?" I asked.

"By no means, if, when the article is deposited, a sufficient wadding of cotton be placed around it. Besides, in our case, we were obliged to proceed without noise."

"But you could not have removed—you could not have taken to pieces *all* articles of furniture in which it would have been possible to make a deposit in the manner you mention. A letter may be compressed into a thin spiral roll, not differing much in shape or bulk from a large knitting-needle, and in this form it might be inserted into the rung of a chair, for example. You did not take to pieces all the chairs?"

"Certainly not; but we did better—we examined the rungs of every chair in the hotel, and, indeed, the jointings of every description of furniture, by the aid of a most powerful microscope. Had there been any traces of recent disturbance we should not have failed to detect it instantly. A single grain of gimlet-dust, for ex-

ample, would have been as obvious as an apple. Any
disorder in the gluing—any unusual gaping in the joints
—would have sufficed to insure detection."

"I presume you looked to the mirrors, between the
boards and the plates, and you probed the beds and the
bedclothes, as well as the curtains and carpets."

"That of course; and when we had absolutely completed every particle of the furniture in this way, then
we examined the house itself. We divided its entire surface into compartments, which we numbered, so that
none might be missed; then we scrutinized each individual square inch throughout the premises, includ-
ing the two houses immediately adjoining, with the
microscope, as before."

"The two houses adjoining!" I exclaimed; "you must
have had a great deal of trouble."

"We had; but the reward offered is prodigious."

"You included the *grounds* about the houses?"

"All the grounds are paved with brick. They gave us
comparatively little trouble. We examined the moss between the bricks, and found it undisturbed."

"You looked among D——'s papers, of course, and
into the books of the library?"

"Certainly; we opened every package and parcel; we
not only opened every book, but we turned over every
leaf in each volume, not contenting ourselves with a
mere shake, according to the fashion of some of our
police officers. We also measured the thickness of every

book *cover,* with the most accurate admeasurement, and applied to each the most jealous scrutiny of the microscope. Had any of the bindings been recently meddled with, it would have been utterly impossible that the fact should have escaped observation. Some five or six volumes, just from the hands of the binder, we carefully probed, longitudinally, with the needles."

"You explored the floors beneath the carpets?"

"Beyond doubt. We removed every carpet, and examined the boards with the microscope."

"And the paper on the walls?"

"Yes."

"You looked into the cellars?"

"We did."

"Then," I said, "you have been making a miscalculation, and the letter is *not* upon the premises, as you suppose."

"I fear you are right there," said the Prefect. "And now, Dupin, what would you advise me to do?"

"To make a thorough re-search of the premises."

"That is absolutely needless," replied G——, "I am not more sure that I breathe than I am that the letter is not at the Hôtel."

"I have no better advice to give you," said Dupin. "You have, of course, an accurate description of the letter?"

"Oh yes."—And here the Prefect, producing a memorandum-book, proceeded to read aloud a minute ac-

count of the internal, and especially of the external appearance of the missing document. Soon after finishing the perusal of this description, he took his departure, more entirely depressed in spirits than I had ever
known the good gentleman before.

In about a month afterwards he paid us another visit,
and found us occupied very nearly as before. He took a
pipe and a chair and entered into some ordinary conversation. At length I said,—

"Well, but G——, what of the purloined letter? I
presume you have at last made up your mind that there
is no such thing as overreaching the Minister?"

"Confound him, say I—yes; I made the re-examina-
tion, however, as Dupin suggested—but it was all labor
lost, as I knew it would be."

"How much was the reward offered, did you say?"
asked Dupin.

"Why, a very great deal—a *very* liberal reward—I
don't like to say how much, precisely; but one thing I
will say, that I wouldn't mind giving my individual
check for fifty thousand francs to any one who could obtain me that letter. The fact is, it is becoming of more
and more importance every day; and the reward has
been lately doubled. If it were trebled, however, I could
do no more than I have done."

"Why, yes," said Dupin, drawlingly, between the
whiffs of his meerschaum, "I really—think, G——, you

have not exerted yourself—to the utmost in this matter. You might—do a little more, I think, eh?"

"How?—in what way?"

"Why—puff, puff—you might—puff, puff—employ counsel in the matter, eh?—puff, puff, puff. Do you remember the story they tell of Abernethy?"

"No; hang Abernethy!"

"To be sure! hang him and welcome. But, once upon a time, a certain rich miser conceived the design of sponging upon this Abernethy for a medical opinion. Getting up, for this purpose, an ordinary conversation in a private company, he insinuated his case to the physician, as that of an imaginary individual."

" 'We will suppose,' said the miser, 'that his symptoms are such and such; now, doctor, what would *you* have directed him to take?'

" 'Take!' said Abernethy, 'why, take *advice*, to be sure.' "

"But," said the Prefect, a little discomposed, "I am *perfectly* willing to take advice, and to pay for it. I would *really* give fifty thousand francs to anyone who would aid me in the matter."

"In that case," replied Dupin, opening a drawer, and producing a check-book, "you may as well fill me up a check for the amount mentioned. When you have signed it, I will hand you the letter."

I was astounded. The Prefect appeared absolutely

thunderstricken. For some minutes he remained speech-
less and motionless, looking incredulously at my friend
with open mouth, and eyes that seemed starting from
their sockets. Then, apparently recovering himself in
some measure, he seized a pen, and after several pauses
and vacant stares, finally filled up and signed a check
for fifty thousand francs, and handed it across the table
to Dupin. The latter examined it carefully and deposited it in his pocketbook; then, unlocking an *escri-
toire*, took thence a letter and gave it to the Prefect. This
functionary grasped it in a perfect agony of joy, opened
it with a trembling hand, cast a rapid glance at its contents, and then, scrambling and struggling to the door,
rushed at length unceremoniously from the room and
from the house, without having uttered a syllable since
Dupin had requested him to fill up the check.

When he had gone, my friend entered into some explanations.

"The Parisian police," he said, "are exceedingly able
in their way. They are persevering, ingenious, cunning,
and thoroughly versed in the knowledge which their
duties seem chiefly to demand. Thus, when G—— detailed to us his mode of searching the premises at the
Hôtel D——, I felt entire confidence in his having made
a satisfactory investigation—so far as his labors
extended."

"So far as his labors extended?" said I.

"Yes," said Dupin. "The measures adopted were **not**

Rushed unceremoniously from the room.

only the best of their kind, but carried out to absolute perfection. Had the letter been deposited within the range of their search, these fellows would, beyond a question, have found it."

I merely laughed—but he seemed quite serious in all that he said.

"The measures, then," he continued, "were good in their kind, and well executed; their defect lay in their being inapplicable to the case, and to the man. A certain set of highly ingenious resources are, with the Prefect, a sort of Procrustean bed, to which he forcibly adapts his designs. But he perpetually errs by being too deep or too shallow, for the matter in hand; and many a schoolboy is a better reasoner than he. I knew one about eight years of age, whose success at guessing in the game of 'even and odd' attracted univeral admiration. This game is simple, and is played with marbles. One player holds in his hand a number of these toys, and demand of another whether that number is even or odd. If the guess is right, the guesser wins one; if wrong, he loses one. The boy to whom I allude won all the marbles of the school. Of course he had some principle of guessing; and this lay in mere observation and admeasurement of the astuteness of his opponents. For example, an arrant simpleton is his opponent, and, holding up his closed hand, asks, 'are they even or odd?' Our schoolboy replies, 'odd,' and loses; but upon the second trial he wins, for he then says to himself, 'the simpleton had them even upon the first trial, and his amount of cunning is just sufficient to make him have them odd upon the second; I will therefore guess odd;'—he guesses odd, and wins.

Now, with a simpleton a degree above the first, he would have reasoned thus: "This fellow finds that in the first instance I guessed odd, and, in the second, he will propose to himself upon the first impulse, a simple variation from even to odd, as did the first simpleton; but then a second thought will suggest that this is too simple a variation, and finally he will decide upon putting it even as before. I will therefore guess even;'—he guesses even, and wins. Now this mode of reasoning in the schoolboy, whom his fellows termed 'lucky,'—what, in its last analysis, is it?"

"It is merely," I said, "an identification of the reasoner's intellect with that of his opponent."

"It is," said Dupin; "and, upon inquiring of the boy by what means he effected the *thorough* identification in which his success consisted, I received answer as follows: 'When I wish to find out how wise, or how stupid, or how good, or how wicked is any one, or what are his thoughts at the moment, I fashion the expression of my face, as accurately as possible, in accordance with the expression of his, and then wait to see what thoughts or sentiments arise in my mind or heart, as if to match or correspond with the expression.' This response of the schoolboy lies at the bottom of all the spurious profundity which has been attributed to Rochefoucauld, to La Bougive, to Machiavelli, and to Campanella."

"And the identification," I said, "of the reasoner's intellect with that of his opponent, depends, if I understand you aright, upon the accuracy with which the opponent's intellect is admeasured."

"For its practical value it depends upon this," replied Dupin; "and the Prefect and his cohort fail so frequently, first, by default of this identification, and, secondly, by ill-admeasurement, or rather through non-admeasurement, of the intellect with which they are engaged. They consider only their *own* ideas of ingenuity; and, in searching for anything hidden, advert only to the modes in which *they* would have hidden it. They are right in this much—that their own ingenuity is a faithful representative of that of *the mass*; but when the cunning of the individual felon is diverse in character from their own, the felon foils them, of course. This always happens when it is above their own, and very usually when it is below. They have no variation of principle in their investigations; at best, when urged by some unusual emergency—by some extraordinary reward—they extend or exaggerate their old modes of *practice*, without touching their principles.

What, for example, in this case of D——, has been done to vary the principle of action? What is all this boring and probing, and sounding, and scrutinizing with the microscope, and dividing the surface of the building into registered square inches—what is it all but an exaggeration *of the application* of the one principle or set of principles of search, which are based upon the one set of notions regarding human ingenuity, to which the Prefect, in the long routine of his duty, has been accustomed?

Do you not see he has taken it for granted that *all* men proceed to conceal a letter,—not exactly in a gimlet-hole bored in a chair-leg—but, at least, in *some* out-of-the-way hole or corner suggested by the same tenor of thought which would urge a man to secrete a letter in a gimlet-hole bored in a chair-leg? And do you not see also, that such *recherché* nooks for concealment are adapted only for ordinary occasions, and would be adopted only by ordinary intellects; for in all cases of concealment, a disposal of the article concealed —a disposal of it in this *recherché* manner,—is, in the very first instance, presumable and presumed; and thus its discovery depends, not at all upon the acumen, but altogether upon the mere care, patience, and determination of the seekers; and where the case is of importance—or, what amounts to the same thing in the policial eyes, when the reward is of magnitude,—the qualities in question have *never* been known to fail. You will now understand what I mean in suggesting that, had the purloined letter been hidden anywhere within the limits of the Prefect's examination—in other words, had the principle of its concealment been comprehended within the principles of the Prefect—its discovery would have been a matter altogether beyond question. This functionary, however, has been thoroughly mystified; and the remote source of his defeat lies in the supposition that the Minister is a fool, because he has acquired renown as a poet. All fools are poets; this the Prefect *feels*; and he is merely guilty of a *non distributio medii* in thence inferring that all poets are fools."

"But is this really the poet?" I asked. "There are two brothers, I know; and both have attained reputation in letters. The Minister I believe has written on the Differential Calculus. He is a mathematician, and no poet."

"You are mistaken; I know him well; he is both. As poet *and* mathematician, he would reason well; as mere mathematician, he could not have reasoned at all, and thus would have been at the mercy of the Prefect."

"You surprise me," I said, "by these opinions, which have been contradicted by the voice of the world. You do not mean to set at naught the well-digested idea of centuries. The mathematical reason has long been regarded as *the* reason *par excellence*."

"'*Il y a à parier*,'" replied Dupin, quoting from Cahmfort, "'*que toute idée publique, toute convention reçue, est une sottise, car elle a convenue au plus grand nombre.*' The mathematicians, I grant you, have done their best to promulgate the popular error to which you allude, and which is none the less an error for its promulgation as truth. With an art worthy a better cause, for example, they have insinuated the term 'analysis' into application to algebra. The French are the originators of this particular deception; but if a term is of any importance—if words derive any value from applicability—then 'analysis' conveys 'algebra' about as much as, in Latin, *'ambitus'* implies 'ambition,' *'religio'* 'religion,' or *'homines honesti,'* a set of *honorable men.*"

"You have a quarrel on hand, I see," said I, "with some of the algebraists of Paris; but proceed."

"I dispute the availability, and thus the value, of that reason which is cultivated in any especial form other than the abstractly logical. I dispute, in particular, the reason educed by mathematical study. The mathematics are the science of form and quantity; mathematical reasoning is merely logic applied to observation upon form and quantity. The great error lies in supposing that even the truths of what is called *pure* algebra, are abstract or general truths. And this error is so egregious that I am confounded at the universality with which it has been received. Mathematical axioms are *not* axioms of general truth. What is true of *relation*—of form and quantity—is often grossly false in regard to morals, for example. In this latter science it is very usually *untrue* that the aggregated parts are equal to the whole. In chemistry also the axiom fails. In the consideration of motive it fails; for two motives, each of a given value, have not, necessarily, a value when united, equal to the sum of their values apart.

There are numerous other mathematical truths which are only truths within the limit of *relation*. But the mathematician argues, from his *finite truths*, through habit, as if they were of an absolutely general applicability—as the world indeed imagines them to be. Bryant, in his very learned 'Mythology,' mentions an analogous source of error, when he says that 'although the Pagan fables are not believed, yet we forget ourselves continually, and make inferences from them as existing realities.' With the algebraists, however, who are Pagans themselves, the 'Pagan fables' *are* believed, and the inferences are made, not so much through lapse of memory, as through an unaccountable addling of the brains. In short, I never yet encountered the mere mathematician who could be trusted out of equal roots, or one who did not clandestinely hold it as a point of his faith that x^2+px is *not* altogether equal to q, and, having made him understand, get out of his reach as speedily as convenient, for, beyond doubt, he will endeavor to knock you down.

"I mean to say," continued Dupin, while I merely laughed at his last observations, "that if the Minister had been no more than a mathematician, the Prefect would have been under no necessity of giving me this check. I knew him, however, as both mathematician and poet, and my measures were adapted to his capacity, with reference to the circumstances by which he was surrounded. I knew him as a courtier, too, and as a bold *intrigant*. Such a man, I considered, could not fail to be aware of the ordinary policial modes of action. He could not have failed to anticipate—and events have proved that he did not fail to anticipate—the waylayings to which he was subjected. He must have foreseen, I reflected, the secret investigations of his premises. His frequent absences from home at night, which were hailed by the Prefect as certain aids to his success, I regarded only as *ruses*, to afford opportunity for thorough search to the police, and thus the sooner to impress them with the conviction to which G——, in fact, did finally arrive—the conviction that the letter was not upon the premises.

I felt, also, that the whole train of thought, which I was at some pains in detailing to you just now, concerning the invariable principle of policial action in searches for articles concealed—I felt that this whole train of thought would necessarily pass through the mind of the Minister. It would imperatively lead him to despise all the ordinary *nooks* of concealment. *He* could not, I reflected, be so weak as not to see that the most intricate and remote recess of his hotel would be as open as his commonest closets to the eyes, to the probes, to the gimlets, and to the microscopes of the Prefect. I saw, in fine, that he would be driven, as a matter of course, to *simplicity*, if not deliberately induced to it as a matter of choice. You will remember, perhaps, how desperately the Prefect laughed when I suggested, upon our first interview, that it was just possible this mystery troubled him so much on account of its being so *very* self-evident."

"Yes," said I, "I remember his merriment well. I really thought he would have fallen into convulsions."

"The material world," continued Dupin, "abounds with very strict analogies to the immaterial; and thus some color of truth has been given to the rhetorical dogma, that metaphor, or simile, may be made to strengthen an argument, as well as to embellish a description. The principle of the *vis inertiæ*, for example, seems to be identical in physics and metaphysics. It is not more true in the former, that a large body is with more difficulty set in motion than a smaller one, and that its subsequent *momentum* is commensurate with this difficulty, than it is, in the latter, that intellects of the vaster capacity, while more forcible, more constant, and more eventful in their movements than those of inferior grade, are yet the less readily moved, and more embarrassed and full of hesitation in the first few steps of their progress. Again: have you ever noticed which of the street signs, over the shop doors, are the most attractive of attention?"

"I have never given the matter a thought," I said.

"There is a game of puzzles," he resumed, "which is played upon a map. One party playing requires another to find a given word—the name of town, river, state or

empire—any word, in short, upon the motley and perplexed surface of the chart. A novice in the game generally seeks to embarrass his opponents by giving them
the most minutely lettered names; but the adept selects
such words as stretch, in large characters, from one end
of the chart to the other. These, like the over-largely
lettered signs and placards of the street, escape observation by dint of being excessively obvious; and here the
physical oversight is precisely analogous with the moral
inapprehension by which the intellect suffers to pass un-
noticed those considerations which are too obtrusively
and too palpably self-evident. But this is a point, it appears, somewhat above or beneath the understanding of
the Prefect. He never once thought it probable, or possible, that the Minister had deposited the letter immediately beneath the nose of the whole world, by way
of best preventing any portion of that world from perceiving it.

"But the more I reflected upon the daring, dashing,
and discriminating ingenuity of D——; upon the fact
that the document must always have been *at hand*, if he
intended to use it to good purpose; and upon the deci-
sive evidence, obtained by the Prefect, that it was not
hidden within the limits of that dignitary's ordinary
search—the more satisfied I became that, to conceal
this letter, the Minister had resorted to the compre-
hensive and sagacious expedient of not attempting to
conceal it at all.

"Full of these ideas, I prepared myself with a pair of green spectacles, and called one fine morning, quite by accident, at the Ministerial hotel. I found D—— at home, yawning, lounging, and dawdling, as usual, and pretending to be in the last extremity of *ennui*. He is, perhaps, the most really energetic human being now alive—but that is only when nobody sees him.

"To be even with him, I complained of my weak eyes, and lamented the necessity of the spectacles, under cover of which I cautiously and thoroughly surveyed the apartment, while seemingly intent only upon the conversation.

"I paid special attention to a large writing-table near which he sat, and upon which lay confusedly, some miscellaneous letters and other papers, with one or two musical instruments and a few books. Here, however, after a long and very deliberate scrutiny, I saw nothing to excite particular suspicion.

"At length my eyes, in going the circuit of the room, fell upon a trumpery filigree card-rack of paste-board, that hung dangling by a dirty blue ribbon, from a little brass knob just beneath the middle of the mantel-piece. In this rack, which had three or four compartments, were five or six visiting cards and a solitary letter. This last was much soiled and crumpled. It was torn nearly in two, across the middle—as if a design, in the first instance, to tear it entirely up as worthless, had been altered, or stayed, in the second. It had a large black seal, bearing the D—— cipher *very* conspicuously, and was addressed, in a diminutive female hand, to D——, the minister, himself. It was thrust carelessly, and even, as it seemed, contemptuously, into one of the upper divisions of the rack.

"No sooner had I glanced at this letter, than I concluded it to be that of which I was in search. To be sure, it was, to all appearance, radically different from the one of which the Prefect had read us so minute a description. Here the seal was large and black, with the D—— cipher; there it was small and red, with the ducal arms of the S—— family. Here, the address, to the Minister, was diminutive and feminine; there the superscription, to a certain royal personage, was markedly bold and decided; the size alone formed a point of correspondence. But, then, the *radicalness* of these differences, which was excessive; the dirt; the soiled and torn condition of the paper, so inconsistent with the *true* methodical habits of D——, and so suggestive of a design to delude the beholder into an idea of the worthlessness of the document; these things, together with the hyperobtrusive situation of this document, full in the view of every visitor, and thus exactly in accordance with the conclusions to which I had previously arrived; these things, I say, were strongly corroborative of suspicion, in one who came with the intention to suspect.

"I protracted my visit as long as possible, and, while

I maintained a most animated discussion with the Minister, on a topic which I knew well had never failed to interest and excite him, I kept my attention really riveted upon the letter. In this examination, I committed to memory its external appearance and arrangement in the rack; and also fell, at length, upon a discovery which set at rest whatever trivial doubt I might have entertained. In scrutinizing the edges of the paper, I observed them to be more *chafed* than seemed necessary. They presented the *broken* appearance which is manifested when a stiff paper, having been once folded and pressed with a folder, is refolded in a reversed direction, in the same creases or edges which had formed the original fold. This discovery was sufficient. It was clear to me that the letter had been turned, as a glove, inside out, re-directed, and re-sealed. I bade the Minister good morning, and took my departure at once, leaving a gold snuff-box upon the table.

"The next morning I called for the snuff-box, when we resumed, quite eagerly, the conversation of the preceding day. While thus engaged, however, a loud report, as if of a pistol, was heard immediately beneath the windows of the hotel, and was succeeded by a series of fearful screams, and the shoutings of a mob. D—— rushed to a casement, threw it open, and looked out. In the meantime, I stepped to the card-rack, took the letter, put it in my pocket, and replaced it by a fac-simile (so far as regards externals) which I had prepared at my

"I stepped to the card rack."

lodgings; imitating the D—— cipher, very readily, by means of a seal formed of bread.

"The disturbance in the street had been occasioned by the frantic behavior of a man with a musket. He had fired it among a crowd of women and children. It proved, however, to have been without ball, and the fellow was suffered to go his way as a lunatic or a drunkard. When he had gone, D—— came from the window, whither I had followed him immediately upon securing the object in view. Soon afterwards I bade him farewell. The pretended lunatic was a man in my own pay."

"But what purpose had you," I asked, "in replacing the letter by a fac-simile? Would it not have been better, at the first visit, to have seized it openly, and departed?"

"D——," replied Dupin, "is a desperate man, and a man of nerve. His hotel, too, is not without attendants devoted to his interests. Had I made the wild attempt you suggest, I might never have left the Ministerial presence alive. The good people of Paris might have heard of me no more. But I had an object apart from these considerations. You know my political prepossessions. In this matter, I act as a partisan of the lady concerned. For eighteen months the Minister has had her in his power. She has now him in hers; since, being unaware that the letter is not in his possession, he will proceed with his exactions as if it was. Thus will he inevitably commit himself, at once, to his political destruction. His downfall, too, will not be more precipitate than awkward. It is all very well to talk about the *facilis descensus Averni*; but in all kinds of climbing, as Catalani said of singing, it is far more easy to get up than to come down. In the present instance I have no sympathy—at least no pity—for him who descends. He is that *monstrum horrendum*, an unprincipled man of genius. I confess, however, that I should like very well to know the precise character of his thoughts, when, being defied by her whom the Prefect terms 'a certain personage,' he is reduced to opening the letter which I left for him in the card-rack."

"How? did you put anything particular in it?"

"Why—it did not seem altogether right to leave the interior blank—that would have been insulting. D——, at Vienna once, did me an evil turn, which I told him, quite good-humoredly, that I should remember. So, as I knew he would feel some curiosity in regard to the identity of the person who had outwitted him, I thought it a pity not to give him a clue. He is well acquainted with my MS., and I just copied into the blank sheet—

——*Un dessein si funeste,*
S'il n'est digne d'Atrée, est digne de Thyeste.

They are to be found in Crébillon's 'Atrée.' "

[*This reference of Dupin is to the Greek legend of King Atreus, who was wronged by his brother Thyestes, and waited 20 years for his terrible revenge.*]

DONALD AND LOUISE PEATTIE

The Mystery in Four-and-a-Half Street

"You can't keep me here after tomorrow," Chuck Ames told the great ugly grandfather clock in the corner of the musty curiosity shop. "I'm quitting. I'm no antique clerk!"

It was a relief to say something aloud, even if you only growled it at the old clock. Sitting there on a high stool behind the cluttered counter, with an hour or more between customers, was the deadest job on earth.

"And I thought I was pretty good to land it," Chuck reflected. "Pretty good! Well, that was over a week ago, and I was a lot younger. I know better now."

Chuck wouldn't have admitted it but he was talking to keep up his courage. He felt somehow unreasonably wary—on guard. Was there something queer about the dreary little shop and fat Utterback, its owner? Or was he just imagining it? Probably the latter. But it was uncomfortable to feel so wary.

Anyhow, he was getting out. But that was depressing too. He had been so glad to get in.

It had been on the day after Chuck had been graduated from high school that he had found Utterback's advertisement in the *News.*

WANTED: Bright, reliable, discreet boy as clerk in curiosity shop. Good wages. Apply 13 Four-and-a-Half Street.

Chuck had applied immediately, he had landed the job, and the wages *were* good. It had been on the strength of those wages that he had packed off his mother, with whom he lived alone, down to the seashore for the first rest she had had in ten years.

For three days he had hopefully tried to sell some of the junk that filled the ramshackle narrow building on Four-and-a-Half Street, which was a slantwise alley one block long, almost lost in a dingy quarter of the city. At the end of those three days he had waylaid his employer, a man with fat white flesh like lard and eyes like blue "mibs" set under colorless eyebrows.

"I'm sorry to inconvenience you, Mr. Utterback," Chuck had said, a little flushed, "but I'll be leaving you at the end of a week. I don't believe I'll ever be much good at work like this."

The fat man had given him an opaque glance, grunted

assent, tilted his derby farther over his lashless eyes, and lumbered on out.

Utterback spent little time in the shop. Occasionally he was there to meet some special customers, and these men he led up to his living quarters on the third floor— the second was filled with second-hand furniture—and there transacted business.

What that business was Chuck had had plenty of time to wonder. He had had time enough to develop a puzzled distrust of the trade that went on under the dingy sign, *Antique Shoppe*, hung over the door of Number 13. Few customers came in for any of the tawdry wares of the shop—rococo lamps, plaster statuary, oil paintings of dead mallard ducks, goldfish castles, atrocious imitations of Chinese vases, shaky tables, crack-bottomed chairs, and cheap jewelry. The show window made some pretense of living up to the sign above it, holding a few candlesticks, some snuffboxes, and a tray of old semi-precious jewels of which the chief boast was a flawed square-cut emerald.

That tray, Utterback had impressed upon Chuck, was to be his responsibility. He was to keep his eye on it when strangers were in the shop, and at night he was to put it into the desk drawer, lock that, and leave the key on the safe at the back of the shop. Sitting through the dull hours behind the cluttered counter, Chuck had rumpled his thick brown hair and wondered why

Chuck had plenty of time to wonder.

Utterback didn't keep the tray of jewels in the safe. What else was the safe for?

To Chuck, the whole air of Number 13 was furtive. The dingiest of its secrets was brought to light when a shabby woman or a ragged man came slipping into the shop with something wrapped in crumpled paper or hidden under a worn coat. When Utterback was there he turned the offered object over in his fat hands, sneeringly, and named a loan of a few cents in a contemptuous grunt. When Chuck was alone, he gave a receipt for the proffered security, and told the customer to come back later to settle with the pawnbroker.

"It's a mean business," Chuck growled, sitting there frowning on top of his high stool. "I'd rather dig ditches."

Well, tomorrow was the last day. One hour till closing time tonight. He spent that hour watching the slow-moving hand on the face of the old grandfather clock. The clock had come to seem a jailer to him, a big stout ugly jailer breathing with a ponderous ticking.

At last it boomed six slow strokes. Utterback came lumbering down the stairs, let Chuck out the front door, and locked it after him. The boy stood in the dusty heat of Four-and-a-Half Street, and heaved a sigh of relief.

The gray-haired blind man who sold pencils on the opposite corner had shut up his box and was slowly, cautiously, starting for home. At the curb he paused, listening, his stick clutched anxiously. Chuck darted forward and took the man's arm.

"Thank you, boy." The blind man's quick smile was pleasant, almost youthful, and his voice was silvery, like his hair.

"How did you know I was a boy?" asked Chuck, guiding him across the street.

"When this sense is gone—" the peddler tapped the black glasses—"this one gets sharper." He touched his ear. "A boy's lively, light step—it's as easy to read as a face. Well, here my way turns. Thank you for your thoughtfulness."

And he went on up the drab street, the tap-tap of his cane vanishing in the city noises.

Chuck got his dinner at a little restaurant and then, feeling lonely in the summer evening, dropped into a movie theater that was showing a promising Western. Carried away by the sweep of the desert and the gallop of hoofs, he was forgetting his mean job, and the problem of getting a better one, when a sudden recollection came upon him.

He hadn't put that window tray of trinkets into the desk drawer!

He ought to go back and do it, he thought reluctantly. Yet Mr. Utterback might take care of the tray, and anyway it would probably be safe enough. Chuck sat still. On the screen the sheriff's posse was galloping to the

relief of the heroine locked in the blazing telegraph
office. But at last a persistent prick of his conscience
got Chuck out of his comfortable seat, and with a sigh
he tramped back to the shop.

The summer dark was close and stuffy in Four-and-a-
Half Street. The buildings down the block were light-
less; they loomed up blackly—two warehouses, an old
office building condemned as a fire trap, the greasy
Greek fruit store, shut for the night, and Utterback's
"Antique Shoppe." At the end of the block a single
violet arc light sputtered. Distantly, Chuck could hear
the clamor of street cars and the rush of traffic, but the
slantwise strip of street seemed a sinister island of silence in the life of the city.

He could just make out the tray of jewels safe in the
shop front. Scowling at it, he told himself he had been
a fool to bother to come back. Still, here he was and if
the pawnbroker were in, he might as well confess he
had forgotten to put away the jewels. He rang the door-
bell and waited, staring in the dim shop window.

The bell sent faint echoes through the rambling old
house; beyond the dusty glass, shadows seemed to waver
in the dark shop.

"This place gets creepier than ever at night," Chuck
muttered. He had to persuade himself out of the notion
that eyes were watching him from the black doorway
of the warehouse opposite. Better go home and forget
the silly business; no one answered the bell.

But there was a stubborn streak in Chuck. And after all, putting away that tray with its probably valuable emerald was part of his job.

He'd go around to the back, he decided, and call up to Utterback's window, on the chance he was in and hadn't heard the bell.

The light in the alley was faint, a dim blue wash. The third floor was dark—was Utterback out, or asleep? Chuck cupped his hands round his mouth for a shout, and then his eyes fell to the shop's back door, and he choked back his shout to a gasp. The door was open!

He stepped closer. The staples of an obsolete outside padlock fastening remained, but the raw, splintered wood of the door frame told how the inside lock had yielded to an expert jimmy.

Only five minutes before, Chuck had seen the jewels untouched in the shop window. Then the thief, he reasoned swiftly, was now in the shop—perhaps at this moment laying hands on the square-cut emerald. He stood a moment listening and heard a faint sound like a stumble within.

There was no time to fume at himself for his carelessness. More than ever, the responsibility for that tray of trinkets lay on his head. Police in this quarter were few and far between. Without hesitation Chuck slipped noiselessly into the shop and flattened himself against the wall behind the door.

Somewhere in that thick darkness, where the big

clock tick-tocked in hollow monotone, stood the burglar, doubtless startled to cautious waiting by Chuck's peal of the bell.

Unarmed, as he was, Chuck knew he had no chance with the burglar in an open fight. That was why he had swiftly decided to wait there in the shadow by the door until the burglar should start to leave and then leap on him from behind and get a grip on his windpipe. A desperate scheme, but the best he could fix on at the moment.

He waited, trying to smother the sound of his uneven breathing, listening to the grim tick-tock of the clock, staring with baffled eyes into the murky room lit only by the faint light of the arc lamp down the street, filtering in through the dirty glass at the shop front. Then the faintest scraping sound in the alley caught his attention, and he turned, holding his breath, to see through the crack of the open door the sudden blue spurt of a match flame.

The flickering little light illuminated the fingers that held it, thin, steely fingers. The next instant, through the crack, were visible too the silvery temples and black glasses of the blind pencil vendor, bent toward the jimmied door. The match went out. But as the implication of that brief, searching little flame struck home to Chuck, his skin crawled. The next thing he realized was that the door was closing, closing, slowly—and in a second he heard the muffled rattle and click of a pad-lock slipped through the staples and snapped into lock.

Through the thudding of his heart Chuck heard down the alley the stealthy footsteps of the blind man de-parting—the blind man who lighted matches in the dark.

A board creaked. Chuck's mind snapped back to the imperative fact that he was locked in the deserted shop with an unknown housebreaker. He had no idea why the door had been furtively padlocked on them. He had no idea where the thief was, or what his own next move should be. Why didn't his fellow prisoner make a sound—a move? Sullenly the answer to that hit Chuck like a blow. Sinkingly, he realized that that brief blue flame outside the door must have betrayed his presence, have shown his staring face in silhouette against the lighted door crack.

Yet, helpless, he still waited tensely in his corner. The silence was stifling. And out of that unbroken si-lence crept slowly to Chuck Ames a significance sharper than any outcry. The clock had stopped ticking.

In a flash he guessed why. That big clock case, with its long hinged door in front, held room for a burly six-footer, if he crouched. In his mind's eye Chuck could see the key in the clock door—he sent up an agonized prayer that it was in truth in the lock—and then slowly, soundlessly, he began to steal toward the clock. Six paces from it he caught the dim light of the key in the lock—his eyes were now accustomed to the darkness— and then beneath his foot a board treacherously cried out in the stillness.

He stood there, holding his breath and as he stood he saw the clock door slowly open and two fingers slide round the edge of it!

Lunging, he flung himself on the door. There was a strangled animal cry from within the case, the fingers jerked and vanished, and Chuck banged the door tight and turned the key in the lock. He heard the pounding of a shoulder on the stout oak door of the case as he ran to the wall switch and flooded the room with light.

Blinking, he stared at the tray of trinkets untouched in the window. He turned, and saw lying beside the safe at the back of the store a dark lantern, a chisel, a crowbar, and other tools less familiar. In another moment he was at the front door. It was locked, and the key gone.

Perhaps Utterback was in, after all—perhaps he had gone to bed, taking the key. It was a desperate hope, but Chuck dashed into the little back hall, took the two flights three steps at a time, past the cluttered second floor ghostly with piles of old furniture, up to the floor of the pawnbroker's bedroom, whence issued a steady snoring. It was music to Chuck's ears. He pounded on the door.

"Mr. Utterback! Get up! Burglars!"

"Huh?" a thick sleepy voice grunted, and in a moment or two more a light flashed on in the room and the door opened on the pawnbroker's flabby figure, in a nightshirt hastily tucked into trousers.

"They were trying to break into the safe! I've locked the fellow in the clock!" panted Chuck.

Utterback's sleepiness vanished. "Into the safe!" Then his milky blue eyes narrowed to a dangerous slit. "What you doin' here at this time o' night, anyway? How'd you get in?"

Chuck started to explain but Utterback didn't wait to hear it all. He stepped back into the room for a moment, and reappeared with the deadly blue-black gleam of a revolver in his hand.

"Good!" cried Chuck. "That'll keep him in the clock till the police get here. Give me the key to the front door, sir, and I'll slip out and call Headquarters from the first phone I can get to."

"Get this," said Utterback, and there was sudden cold menace in his voice. "The police ain't in this—see? And anything you seen or will see around here tonight you're goin' to forget the minute you see it—see? Or you won't live to see daylight, kid—that's fair warning. Now get on with you."

With the cold muzzle of the gun sending chills up his spine Chuck turned and started down the black stairway, moving as in a nightmare.

He turned and started down the black stairway.

This wasn't true. It was a dream. He had often dreamed it before. Dreamed of being forced down a stairway in a strange house, a stairway that wound down into blackness. Before him lay always unknown horrors; behind him, with heavy tread, something moved relentlessly upon him, driving him on and down. At the foot of the stairs he always woke up, in a cold sweat of horror.

But now he was at the foot of the stairs, and light fell silently into the hall from the open door of the shop.

"Go on," said Utterback grimly, prodding him, and Chuck a shield for the other's cowardly bulk, stepped into the room.

It was as before—the key still stood in the clock door.

"So there you are, Spike Brent!" Utterback addressed the invisible prisoner, with a malignant humor. "I see your favorite jimmy over there by the safe. Gettin' impatient, were you? Well, you can cool off in there till I get the stuff stowed away more secure, and then I'll see what to do with you."

No sound from the clock answered him. Utterback strode to the safe and with a few swift twists of the combination had the door open and, reaching in, drew out a little black felt bag. Except for some papers, there was nothing else in the big box of a safe. Utterback turned on the boy and motioned with his revolver.

"Get in," he said.

Chuck stared at him in horror, and stood frozen.

"Oh, I'll let you out before you're smothered," the fat man said, with an unpleasant laugh that showed pink gums. "But I want you out o' the way for a while— I'll be busy. Get in," he repeated less pleasantly.

"I won't!" Chuck jerked out.

Utterback's pink face changed to a menacing purple. "You young fool!" he growled. "You'll—"

At that second came the crash of a report—a shot muffled slightly by the thick oak door of the clock case, and out of the case leaped a big burly figure that hurled itself full upon Utterback!

The burglar had shot out the lock. Chuck's mind registered that fact mechanically, as he leaped out of the onslaught and stood pressed against the wall, while the two men struggled, swaying, panting, cursing.

Utterback held the black bag high out of reach. With a sudden plunge the burglar caught the fat wrist. He bent and twisted it till the pawnbroker with a scream of pain relaxed his hold on the prize and the bag, half flung from his hand, fell with a thud six paces away. Chuck Ames dived for the light switch and plunged the room in darkness. The next moment he had his hand on the bag, had caught it up, and was running noiselessly for the stairs.

Halfway up the first nightmare steps, however, he stumbled and fell with a clatter. He was up in a minute, but running feet pounded below, and just as he made the first landing the light hanging directly over his head went on, revealing him in its sudden glare plain as a target. With one leap and a swing of the heavy little bag, Chuck crashed out the light, and leaped on up into darkness.

On the dim second floor Chuck halted, panting. Clearly, through the turmoil of his mind, stood out the recollection of a gutter pipe runing up along the back door of the shop. If he could find a window near enough to it—

This floor was thrown into one loft where the furniture loomed in piles like great distorted monsters. Taking swift bearings, Chuck slipped through this confusion toward the corner where the gutter pipe ran. Feet were pounding up the stairs. If there were only a window—

There was. But it was locked, and he couldn't budge it. The feet had halted uncertainly on the threshold. All at once, cruel and garish, the light of a bulb flashed on in the ceiling—and the next moment Chuck had crashed the black bag through the pane, smashed out the glass, and swung over the sill.

A shot seared past him as he caught the gutter pipe and swung out on it. As he hit the ground in a supple jump, another shot rang out and pain caught him agonizingly by the shoulder. Dazed with agony but triumphant, Chuck doubled up and ran down the alley —straight into the staring muzzle of a revolver.

"Hands up!" said a familiar silvery voice, and Chuck with one sick look of horror at the black glasses of the "blind" man, crumpled with a groan into his own blood on the cobbles.

He opened his eyes upon cool dazzling whiteness. A hospital, he drowsily concluded, and shut them again. He heard the rustle of a starched uniform, and heard a woman's low voice say:

"He's coming to. You may speak to him if you want to."

And then he heard that odd, light, silvery man's voice again, that last voice out of his nightmare adventure.

"Good work, boy," it said. "Very neat. How are you feeling now?"

Chuck lifted his heavy lids, and warm brown eyes twinkled into his.

"Who are you?" gasped Chuck weakly.

"Tolliver's my name. Christopher C. Tolliver, investigator. I'm sorry—I had you doped out wrong, youngster. All wrong. I thought you were a spy for that gang down on Four-and-a-Half Street."

"I had you doped out wrong, too," said Chuck, blinking.

"I don't wonder," laughed the man. "Nobody on Four-and-a-Half Street is what he seems to be. Utterback looked like a pawnbroker and was really a fence for a gang of jewel thieves. What looked like a common burglar turns out to be Spike Brent, whom we've been wanting for two years. Spike got rash because Utterback was double-crossing him, and made a play to get back the famous Bramwell jewels he stole six years ago. And

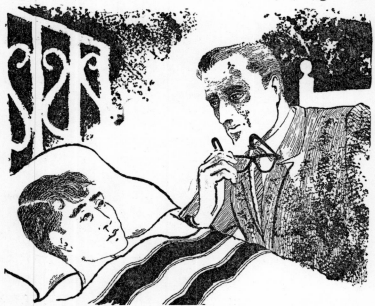

He heard the voice out of his nightmare adventure.

a kid who looked suspiciously like a cat's-paw turns out to be a darn valuable fellow with wit and nerve enough to balk two of the smartest crooks in the gallery. When you're patched up, we'll talk about a job I've got for you. Now slip off to sleep for a bit—you've lost a lot of blood."

And Chuck Ames, drowsily reflecting that the end of the Western couldn't have been half so thrilling as his evening had turned out to be, dozed off with a sleepy grin.

AUTHOR UNKNOWN

The Rescue at Sea

Mr. Robert Bruce, descended from some branch of the Scottish family of the same name, was born in humble circumstances about the close of the eighteenth century at Torguay, in the south of England, and there bred up to a seafaring life. When about thirty years of age, he was first mate on board a barque trading between Liverpool and St. John's, New Brunswick.

On one of her voyages, bound westward, being then some five or six weeks out, and having neared the eastern portion of the Banks of Newfoundland, the captain and the mate had been on deck at noon, taking an observation of the sun; after which they both descended to calculate their day's work.

The cabin, a small one, was immediately at the stern of the vessel, and the short stairway, descending to it, ran athwart-ships. Immediately opposite to this stairway, just beyond a small, square landing, was the mate's stateroom, and from that landing there were two doors, close to each other—the one opening aft, into the cabin, the other fronting the stairway into the stateroom. The desk in the stateroom was in the forward part of it, close to the door; so that anyone sitting at it, could see into the cabin.

The mate, absorbed in his calculations, which did not result as he expected, had not noticed the captain's motions. When he had completed his calculations, he cried out, without looking round, "I make our latitude and longitude so-and-so. Can that be right? How is yours, sir?"

Receiving no reply he repeated the question, glancing over his shoulder and perceiving, as he thought, the captain busy at his slate. Still no answer! Thereupon he rose and, as he fronted the cabin door, the figure he had mistaken for the captain raised his head and disclosed to the astonished mate the features of an entire stranger.

Bruce was no coward, but as he met that fixed gaze, looking directly at him in grave silence, and became assured that it was no one whom he had ever seen before, it was too much for him; and, instead of stopping to question the seeming intruder, he rushed upon deck in such evident alarm that it instantly attracted the captain's attention.

"Why, Mr. Bruce," said the latter, "what in the world is the matter with you?"

"The matter, sir? Who is that at your desk?"

"No one that I know of."

They were the features of an entire stranger.

"But there *is*, sir, there's a stranger there."

"A stranger? Why, man, you must be dreaming! You must have seen the steward there, or the second mate. Who else would venture down without orders?"

"But, sir, he was sitting in your arm-chair, fronting the door, writing on your slate. Then he looked up full in my face; and if ever I saw a man plainly and distinctly in the world I saw him."

"Him! Who?"

"Heaven knows, sir, I don't! I saw a man, and a man I have never seen in my life before."

"You must be going crazy, Mr. Bruce. A stranger, and we nearly six weeks out!"

The Captain descended the stairs, and the mate followed him. Nobody in the cabin! They examined the staterooms. Not a soul could be found.

"Well, Mr. Bruce," said the Captain, "did not I tell you that you had been dreaming?"

"It's all very well to say so, sir; but if I didn't see that man writing on the slate may I never see home and family again!"

"Ah! Writing on the slate. Then it should be there still!" And the Captain took it up. "By heaven," he exclaimed, "here's something sure enough! Is that your writing, Mr. Bruce?"

The mate took the slate, and there in plain, legible characters stood the words, "Steer to the nor'-west."

The Captain sat down at his desk, the slate before

him, in deep thought. At last, turning the slate over, and pushing it toward Bruce, he said, "Write down, Steer to the nor'-west."

The mate complied; and the Captain, comparing the two handwritings, said, "Mr. Bruce, go and tell the second mate to come down here."

He came, and at the captain's request also wrote the words. So did the steward. So in succession did every man of the crew who could write at all. But not one of the various hands resembled, in any degree, the mysterious writing.

When the crew retired, the captain sat deep in thought. "Could anyone have been stowed away?" at last he said. "The ship must be searched. Order up all hands."

Every nook and corner of the vessel was thoroughly searched; not a living soul was found.

Accordingly, the captain decided to change the vessel's course according to the instructions received. A look-out was posted, who shortly reported an iceberg, and then, shortly after, a vessel, close to it.

As they approached, the captain's glass disclosed the fact that it was a dismantled ship, apparently frozen to the ice. . . . It proved to be a vessel from Quebec, bound for Liverpool, with passengers on board. She had got entangled in the ice, and finally frozen fast; and had passed several weeks in a most critical situation. She

The captain's glass disclosed a dismantled ship.

was stove, her decks swept; in fact, a mere wreck; all her provisions and almost all her water gone. Her crew and passengers had lost all hope of being saved, and their gratitude at the unexpected rescue was proportionately great.

As one of the men who had been brought away in the third boat ascended the ship's side, the mate, catching a glimpse of his face, started back in consternation. It was the very face he had seen three or four hours before, looking up at him from the captain's desk! He communicated this fact to the captain.

After the comfort of the passengers had been seen to, the captain turned to the stranger, and said to him, "I hope, sir, you will not think I am trifling with you, but I would be much obliged to you if you would write a few words on this slate." And he handed him the slate, with that side up on which the mysterious writing was not.

"I will do anything you ask," replied the passenger, "but what shall I write?"

"A few words are all I want. Suppose you write: Steer to the nor'-west."

The passenger, evidently puzzled to make out the motive of such a request, complied, however, with a smile. The captain took up the slate and examined it closely; then stepping aside so as to conceal the slate from the passenger, he turned it over and gave it to him the other side up.

"You say that this is your handwriting?" said he.

"I need not say so," replied the other, looking at it, "for you saw me write it."

"And this?" said the captain, turning the slate over.

The man looked first at one writing, then at the other, quite confounded. At last: "What is the meaning of this?" said he. "I only wrote one of these. Who wrote the other?"

"That's more than I can tell you, sir. My mate here says you wrote it, sitting at this desk, at noon today."

The captain of the wreck and the passenger looked at each other, exchanging glances of intelligence and

"Suppose you write: Steer to the nor'-west."

surprise; then the former asked the latter: "Did you dream that you wrote on this slate?"

"No, sir, not that I remember."

"You speak of dreaming," said the captain of the barque. "What was this gentleman about at noon today?"

"Captain," rejoined the other (the captain of the

wreck), "the whole thing is most mysterious and extra-ordinary; and I had intended to speak to you about it as soon as we got a little quiet. This gentleman—point-ing to the passenger—being much exhausted, fell into a heavy sleep, or what seemed such, some time before noon. After an hour or two he awoke, and said to me: 'Captain, we shall be relieved this very day.' When I asked him what reason he had for saying so, he replied that he had dreamed that he was on board a barque, and that she was coming to our rescue. He described her appearance and rig, and, to our utter astonishment, when your vessel hove in sight, she corresponded ex-actly with his description of her. We had not put much faith in what he said; yet, still we hoped there might be something in it,—for drowning men, you know, catch at straws. As it turned out, I cannot doubt that it was all arranged by some overruling Providence."

"There is not a doubt," replied the captain of the barque, "that the writing on the slate, let it come there as it may, saved all your lives. I was steering at the time considerably south of west, and I altered my course for the nor'-west, and had a look-out aloft, to see what would come of it. But you say," he added, turning to the passenger, "that you did not dream of writing on a slate?"

"No, sir. I have no recollection whatever of doing so. I got the impression that the barque I saw in my dream was coming to rescue us; but how that impression came

I cannot tell. There is another very strange thing about it," he added. "Everything here on board seems to be quite familiar; yet I am very sure that I was never on your vessel before. It is all a puzzle to me! What did your mate see?"

Thereupon Mr. Bruce related to them all the circumstances above detailed. . . .

BARONESS ORCZY

The Fenchurch Street Mystery

The man in the corner pushed aside his glass, and leant across the table.

"Mysteries!" he commented. "There is no such thing as a mystery in connection with any crime, provided intelligence is brought to bear upon its investigation."

Very much astonished Polly Burton looked over the top of her newspaper, and fixed a pair of very severe, coldly inquiring brown eyes upon him.

She had disapproved of the man from the instant when he shuffled across the shop and sat down opposite to her, at the same marble-topped table which already held her large coffee (3d.), her roll and butter (2d.), and plate of tongue (6d.).

Now this particular corner, this very same table, that special view of the magnificent marble hall—known as the Norfolk Street branch of the Aërated Bread Company's depots—were Polly's own corner, table, and view. Here she had partaken of eleven pennyworth of luncheon and one pennyworth of daily information ever since that glorious never-to-be-forgotten day when she was enrolled on the staff of the *Evening Observer* (we'll call it that, if you please), and became a member of that illustrious and world-famed organization known as the British Press.

She was a personality, was Miss Burton of the *Evening Observer*. Her cards were printed thus:

MISS MARY J. BURTON
Evening Observer

She had interviewed Miss Ellen Terry and the Bishop of Madagascar, Mr. Seymour Hicks and the Chief Commissioner of Police. She had been present at the last Marlborough House garden party—in the cloak-room, that is to say, where she caught sight of Lady Thingummy's hat, Miss What-you-may-call's sunshade, and of various other things modistical or fashionable, all of which were duly described under the heading "Royalty and Dress" in the early afternoon edition of the *Evening Observer*.

(The article itself is signed M. J. B., and is to be found in the files of that leading halfpenny-worth.)

For these reasons—and for various others, too—Polly felt irate with the man in the corner, and told him so with her eyes, as plainly as any pair of brown eyes can speak.

She had been reading an article in the *Daily Telegraph*. The article was palpitatingly interesting. Had **Polly** been commenting audibly upon it? Certain it is

She looked at him and frowned.

that the man over there had spoken in direct answer to her thoughts.

She looked at him and frowned; the next moment she smiled. Miss Burton (of the *Evening Observer*) had a keen sense of humor, which two years' association with the British Press had not succeeded in destroying, and the appearance of the man was sufficient to tickle the most ultra-morose fancy. Polly thought to herself that she had never seen any one so pale, so thin, with such funny light-colored hair, brushed very smoothly across the top of a very obviously bald crown. He looked so timid and nervous as he fidgeted incessantly with a piece of string; his long, lean, and trembling fingers tying and untying it into knots of wonderful and complicated proportions.

Having carefully studied every detail of the quaint personality, Polly felt more amiable.

"And yet," she remarked kindly but authoritatively, "this article, in an otherwise well-informed journal, will tell you that, even within the last year, no fewer than six crimes have completely baffled the police, and the perpetrators of them are still at large."

"Pardon me," he said gently, "I never for a moment ventured to suggest that there were no mysteries to the *police*; I merely remarked that there were none where intelligence was brought to bear upon the investigation of crime."

"Not even in the Fenchurch Street *mystery*, I suppose?" she asked sarcastically.

"Least of all in the so-called Fenchurch Street *mystery*," he replied quietly.

Now the Fenchurch Street mystery, as that extraordinary crime had popularly been called, had puzzled—

as Polly well knew—the brains of every thinking man and woman for the last twelve months. It had puzzled her not inconsiderably; she had been interested, fascinated; she had studied the case, formed her own theories, thought about it all often and often, had even written one or two letters to the Press on the subject—suggesting, arguing, hinting at possibilities and probabilities, adducing proofs which other amateur detectives were equally ready to refute. The attitude of that timid man in the corner, therefore, was peculiarly exasperating, and she retorted with sarcasm destined completely to annihilate her self-complacent interlocutor.

"What a pity it is, in that case, that you do not offer your priceless services to our misguided though well-meaning police."

"Isn't it?" he replied with perfect good-humor. "Well, you know, for one thing I doubt if they would accept them; and in the second place my inclinations and my duty would—were I to become an active member of the detective force—nearly always be in direct conflict. As often as not my sympathies go to the criminal who is clever and astute enough to lead our entire police force by the nose.

"I don't know how much of the case you remember," he went on quietly. "It certainly, at first, began even to puzzle me. On the 12th of last December a woman, poorly dressed, but with an unmistakable air of having seen better days, gave information at Scotland Yard of the disappearance of her husband, William Kershaw, of no occupation, and apparently of no fixed abode. She was accompanied by a friend—a fat, oily-looking German—and between them they told a tale which set the police immediately on the move.

"It appears that on the 10th of December, at about three o'clock in the afternoon, Karl Müller, the German, called on his friend, William Kershaw, for the purpose of collecting a small debt—some ten pounds or so—which the latter owed him. On arriving at the squalid lodging in Charlotte Street, Fitzroy Square, he found William Kershaw in a wild state of excitement, and his wife in tears. Müller attempted to state the object of his visit, but Kershaw, with wild gestures, waved him aside, and—in his own words—flabbergasted him by asking him point-blank for another loan of two pounds, which sum, he declared, would be the means of a speedy fortune for himself and the friend who would help him in his need.

"After a quarter of an hour spent in obscure hints, Kershaw, finding the cautious German obdurate, decided to let him into the secret plan, which, he averred, would place thousands into their hands."

Instinctively Polly had put down her paper; the mild stranger, with his nervous air and timid, watery eyes, had a peculiar way of telling his tale, which somehow fascinated her.

"I don't know," he resumed, "if you remember the

story which the German told to the police, and which was corroborated in every detail by the wife or widow. Briefly it was this: Some thirty years previously, Kershaw, then twenty years of age, and a medical student at one of the London hospitals, had a chum named Barker, with whom he roomed together with another.

"The latter, so it appears, brought home one evening a very considerable sum of money, which he had won on the turf, and the following morning he was found murdered in his bed. Kershaw, fortunately for himself, was able to prove a conclusive *alibi*; he had spent the night on duty at the hospital; as for Barker, he had disappeared, that is to say, as far as the police were concerned, but not as far as the watchful eyes of his friend Kershaw were able to spy—at least, so that latter said. Barker very cleverly contrived to get away out of the country, and, after sundry vicissitudes, finally settled down at Vladivostok, in Easten Siberia, where, under the assumed name of Smethurst, he built up an enormous fortune by trading in furs.

"Now, mind you, every one knows Smethurst, the Siberian millionaire. Kershaw's story that he had once been called Barker, and had committed a murder thirty years ago was never proved, was it? I am merely telling you what Kershaw said to his friend the German and to his wife on that memorable afternoon of December the 10th.

"According to him Smethurst had made one gigantic

mistake in his clever career—he had on four occasions written to his late friend, William Kershaw. Two of these letters had no bearing on the case, since they were written more than twenty-five years ago, and Kershaw, moreover, had lost them—so he said—long ago. According to him, however, the first of these letters was written when Smethurst, alias Barker, had spent all the money he had obtained from the crime, and found himself destitute in New York.

"Kershaw, then in fairly prosperous circumstances, sent him a ten-pound note for the sake of old times. The second, when the tables had turned, and Kershaw had begun to go downhill, Smethurst, as he then already called himself, sent his whilom friend fifty pounds. After that, as Müller gathered, Kershaw had made sundry demands on Smethurst's ever-increasing purse, and had accompanied these demands by various threats, which, considering the distant country in which the millionaire lived, were worse than futile.

"But now the climax had come, and Kershaw, after a final moment of hesitation, handed over to his German friend the two last letters purporting to have been written by Smethurst, and which, if you remember, played such an important part in the mysterious story of this extraordinary crime. I have a copy of both these letters here," added the man in the corner, as he took out a piece of paper from a very worn-out pocketbook, and, unfolding it very deliberately, he began to read—

" 'SIR—*Your preposterous demands for money are wholly unwarrantable. I have already helped you quite as much as you deserve. However, for the sake of old times, and because you once helped me when I was in a terrible difficulty, I am willing to once more let you impose upon my good nature. A friend of mine here, a Russian merchant, to whom I have sold my business, starts in a few days for an extended tour to many European and Asiatic ports in his yacht, and has invited me to accompany him as far as England. Being tired of foreign parts, and desirous of seeing the old country once again after thirty years' absence, I have decided to accept his invitation. I don't know when we may actually be in Europe, but I promise you that as soon as we touch a suitable port I will write to you again, making an appointment for you to see me in London. But remember that if your demands are too preposterous I will not for a moment listen to them, and that I am the last man in the world to submit to persistent and unwarrantable blackmail.*

" '*I am, sir,*
" '*Yours truly,*
" '*FRANCIS SMETHURST.*'

"The second letter was dated from Southampton," continued the man in the corner calmly, "and, curiously enough, was the only letter which Kershaw professed to have received from Smethurst of which he had kept the envelope, and which was dated. It was quite brief," he added, referring once more to his piece of paper.

" '*DEAR SIR—Referring to my letter of a few weeks ago, I wish to inform you that the* Tsarskoe Selo *will touch at*

*Tilbury on Tuesday next, the 10th. I shall land there, and
immediately go up to London by the first train I can get.
If you like, you may meet me at Fenchurch Street Station,
in the first-class waiting-room, in the late afternoon. Since
I surmise that after thirty years' absence my face may not
be familiar to you, I may as well tell you that you will recognize me by a heavy Astrakhan fur coat, which I shall wear,
together with a cap of the same. You may then introduce
yourself to me, and I will personally listen to what you may
have to say.*

         " 'Yours faithfully,
                " 'FRANCIS SMETHURST.'

"It was this last letter which had caused William Kershaw's excitement and his wife's tears. In the German's
own words, he was walking up and down the room like
a wild beast, gesticulating madly, and muttering sundry
exclamations. Mrs. Kershaw, however, was full of appre-
hension. She mistrusted the man from foreign parts—
who, according to her husband's story, had already one
crime upon his conscience—who might, she feared, risk
another, in order to be rid of a dangerous enemy.
Woman-like, she thought the scheme a dishonorable
one, for the law, she knew, is severe on the blackmailer.

"The assignation might be a cunning trap, in any
case it was a curious one; why, she argued, did not
Smethurst elect to see Kershaw at his hotel the following day? A thousand whys and wherefores made her anxious, but the fat German had been won over by Kershaw's visions of untold gold, held tantalizingly before

his eyes. He had lent the necessary two pounds, with which his friend intended to tidy himself up a bit before he went to meet his friend the millionaire. Half an hour afterward Kershaw had left his lodgings, and that was the last the unfortunate woman saw of her husband, or Müller, the German, of his friend.

"Anxiously his wife waited that night, but he did not return; the next day she seems to have spent in making purposeless and futile inquiries about the neighborhood of Fenchurch Street; and on the 12th she went to Scotland Yard, gave what particulars she knew, and placed in the hands of the police the two letters written by Smethurst."

The man in the corner had finished his glass of milk. His watery blue eyes looked across at Miss Polly Burton's eager little face, from which all traces of severity had now been chased away by an obvious and intense excitement.

"It was only on the 31st," he resumed after a while, "that a body, decomposed past all recognition, was found by two lightermen in the bottom of a disused barge. She had been moored at one time at the foot of one of those dark flights of steps which lead down between tall warehouses to the river in the East End of London. I have a photograph of the place here," he added, selecting one out of his pocket, and placing it before Polly.

"The actual barge, you see, had already been removed when I took this snapshot, but you will realize
what a perfect place this alley is for the purpose of one
man cutting another's throat in comfort, and without
fear of detection. The body, as I said, was decomposed
beyond all recognition; it had probably been there
eleven days, but sundry articles, such as a silver ring
and a tie pin, were recognizable, and were identified by
Mrs. Kershaw as belonging to her husband.

"She, of course, was loud in denouncing Smethurst,
and the police had no doubt a very strong case against
him, for two days after the discovery of the body in the
barge, the Siberian millionaire, as he was already popularly called by enterprising interviewers, was arrested
in his luxurious suite of rooms at the Hotel Cecil.

"To confess the truth, at this point I was not a little
puzzled. Mrs. Kershaw's story and Smethurst's letters
had both found their way into the papers, and following my usual method—mind you, I am only an amateur,
I try to reason out a case for the love of the thing—I
sought about for a motive for the crime, which the police declared Smethurst had committed. Effectually to
get rid of a dangerous blackmailer was the generally accepted theory. Well! did it ever strike you how paltry
that motive really was?"

Miss Polly had to confess, however, that it had never
struck her in that light.

"Surely a man who had succeeded in building up an

immense fortune by his own individual efforts was not the sort of fool to believe that he had anything to fear from a man like Kershaw. He must have *known* that Kershaw held no damning proofs against him—not enough to hang him, anyway. Have you ever seen Smethurst?" he added, as he once more fumbled in his pocketbook.

Polly replied that she had seen Smethurst's picture in the illustrated papers at the time. Then he added, placing a small photograph before her:

"What strikes you most about the face?"

"Well, I think its strange, astonished expression due to the total absence of eyebrows, and the funny foreign cut of the hair."

"So close that it almost looks as if it had been shaved. Exactly. That is what struck me most when I elbowed my way into the court that morning and first caught sight of the millionaire in the dock. He was a tall, soldierly-looking man, upright in stature, his face very bronzed and tanned. He wore neither mustache nor beard, his hair was cropped quite close to his head, like a Frenchman's; but, of course, what was so very remarkable about him was that total absence of eyebrows and even eyelashes, which gave the face such a peculiar appearance—as you say, a perpetually astonished look.

"He seemed, however, wonderfully calm; he had been accommodated with a chair in the dock—being a millionaire—and chatted pleasantly with his lawyer, Sir

Arthur Inglewood, in the intervals between the calling of the several witnesses for the prosecution; whilst during the examination of these witnesses he sat quite placidly, with his head shaded by his hand.

"Müller and Mrs. Kershaw repeated the story which they had already told to the police. I think you said that you were not able, owing to pressure of work, to go to the court that day, and hear the case, so perhaps you have no recollection of Mrs. Kershaw. No? Ah, well! Here is a snapshot I managed to get of her once. That is she. Exactly as she stood in the box—over-dressed—in elaborate crêpe, with a bonnet which once had contained pink roses, and to which a remnant of pink petals still clung obtrusively amidst the deep black.

"She would not look at the prisoner, and turned her head resolutely toward the magistrate. I fancy she had been fond of that vagabond husband of hers: an enormous wedding-ring encircled her finger, and that, too, was swathed in black. She firmly believed that Kershaw's murderer sat there in the dock, and she literally flaunted her grief before him.

"I was indescribably sorry for her. As for Müller, he was just fat, oily, pompous, conscious of his own importance as a witness; his fat fingers, covered with brass rings, gripped the two incriminating letters, which he had identified. They were his passports, as it were, to a delightful land of importance and notoriety. Sir Arthur Inglewood, I think, disappointed him by stating that he had no questions to ask of him. Müller had been brimful of answers, ready with the most perfect indictment, the most elaborate accusations against the bloated millionaire who had destroyed his dear friend Kershaw, and murdered him in Heaven knows what an out-of-the-way corner of the East End.

"After this, however, the excitement grew apace. Müller had been dismissed, and had retired from the court altogether, leading away Mrs. Kershaw, who had completely broken down.

"Constable D 21 was giving evidence as to the arrest in the meanwhile. The prisoner, he said, had seemed completely taken by surprise, not understanding the cause or history of the accusation against him; however, when put in full possession of the facts, and realizing, no doubt, the absolute futility of any resistance, he had quietly enough followed the constable into the cab. No one at the fashionable and crowded Hotel Cecil had even suspected that anything unusual had occurred.

"Then a gigantic sigh of expectancy came from every one of the spectators. The 'fun' was about to begin. James Buckland, a porter at Fenchurch Street railway station, had just sworn to tell all the truth, etc. After all, it did not amount to much. He said that at six o'clock in the afternoon of December the 10th, in the midst of one of the densest fogs he ever remembers, the 5:05 from Tilbury steamed into the station, being just about an hour late. He was on the arrival platform, and was hailed by a passenger in a first-class carriage. He could see very little of him beyond an enormous black fur coat and a traveling cap of fur also.

"The passenger had a quantity of luggage, all marked F. S., and he directed James Buckland to place it all upon a four-wheeled cab, with the exception of a small handbag, which he carried himself. Having seen that all his luggage was safely bestowed, the stranger in the fur coat paid the porter, and, telling the cabman to wait until he returned, he walked away in the direction of the waiting-rooms, still carrying his small handbag.

" 'I stayed for a bit,' added James Buckland, 'talking to the driver about the fog and that; then I went about my business, seein' that the local from Southend 'ad been signaled.'

"The prosecution insisted most strongly upon the hour when the stranger in the fur coat, having seen to his luggage, walked away toward the waiting-rooms. The porter was emphatic. 'It was not a minute later than 6: 15,' he averred.

"Sir Arthur Inglewood still had no questions to ask, and the driver of the cab was called.

"He corroborated the evidence of James Buckland as to the hour when the gentleman in the fur coat had engaged him, and having filled his cab in and out with luggage, had told him to wait. And cabby did wait. He waited in the dense fog—until he was tired, until he seriously thought of depositing all the luggage in the lost property office, and of looking out for another fare —waited until at last, at a quarter before nine, whom should he see walking hurriedly toward his cab but the gentleman in the fur coat and cap, who got in quickly and told the driver to take him at once to the Hotel Cecil. This, cabby declared, had occurred at a quarter before nine. Still Sir Arthur Inglewood made no comment, and Mr. Francis Smethurst, in the crowded, stuffy court, had calmly dropped to sleep.

"The next witness, Constable Thomas Taylor, had noticed a shabbily-dressed individual, with shaggy hair and beard, loafing about the station and waiting-rooms in the afternoon of December the 10th. He seemed to be watching the arrival platform of the Tilbury and Southend trains.

"Two separate and independent witnesses, cleverly unearthed by the police, had seen this same shabbily-dressed individual stroll into the first-class waiting-room at about 6:15 on Tuesday, December 10th, and go straight up to a gentleman in a heavy fur coat and cap, who had also just come into the room. The two talked together for a while; no one heard what they said, but presently they walked off together. No one seemed to know in what direction.

"Francis Smethurst was rousing himself from his apathy; he whispered to his lawyer, who nodded with a bland smile of encouragement. The employees of the Hotel Cecil gave evidence as to the arrival of Mr.

Smethurst at about 9:30 P.M. on Tuesday, December the 10th, in a cab, with a quantity of luggage; and this closed the case for the prosecution.

"Everybody in that court already *saw* Smethurst mounting the gallows. It was uninterested curiosity which caused the elegant audience to wait and hear what Sir Arthur Inglewood had to say. He, of course, is the most fashionable man in the law at the present moment. His lolling attitudes, his drawling speech, are quite the rage, and imitated by the gilded youth of society.

"Even at this moment, when the Siberian millionaire's neck literally and metaphorically hung in the balance, an expectant titter went around the fair spectators as Sir Arthur stretched out his long loose limbs and lounged across the table. He waited to make his effect —Sir Arthur is a born actor—and there is no doubt that he made it, when in his slowest, most drawly tones he said quietly:

" 'With regard to this alleged murder of one William Kershaw, on Tuesday, December the 10th, between 6:15 and 8:45 P.M., your Honor, I now propose to call two witnesses, who saw this same William Kershaw alive on Monday afternoon, December the 16th, that is to say, six days after the supposed murder.'

"It was as if a bombshell had exploded in the court. Even his Honor was aghast, and I am sure the lady next to me only recovered from the shock of surprise in or-

der to wonder whether she need put off her dinner
party after all.

"As for me," added the man in the corner, with that
strange mixture of nervousness and self-complacency
which had set Miss Polly Burton wondering, "well, you
see, I had made up my mind long ago where the hitch
lay in this particular case, and I was not so surprised as
some of the others.

"Perhaps you remember the wonderful development
of the case, which so completely mystified the police—
and in fact everybody except myself. Torriani and a
waiter at his hotel in the Commercial Road both de-
posed that at about 3:30 P.M. on December the 10th a
shabbily-dressed individual lolled into the coffee-room
and ordered some tea. He was pleasant enough and
talkative, told the waiter that his name was William
Kershaw, that very soon all London would be talking
about him, as he was about, through an unexpected
stroke of good fortune, to become a very rich man, and
so on, and so on, nonsense without end.

"When he had finished his tea he lolled out again,
but no sooner had he disappeared down a turning of
the road than the waiter discovered an old umbrella,
left behind accidentally by the shabby, talkative individual. As is the custom in his highly respectable restaurant, Signor Torriani put the umbrella carefully
away in his office, on the chance of his customer calling
to claim it when he discovered his loss. And sure enough

nearly a week later, on Monday the 16th, at about 1:00 P.M., the same shabbily-dressed individual called and asked for his umbrella. He had some lunch, and chatted once again to the waiter. Signor Torriani and the waiter gave a description of William Kershaw, which coincided exactly with that given by Mrs. Kershaw of her husband.

"Oddly enough he seemed to be a very absent-minded sort of person, for on this second occasion, no sooner had he left than the waiter found a pocketbook in the coffee-room, underneath the table. It contained sundry letters and bills, all adressed to William Kershaw. This pocketbook was produced, and Karl Müller, who had returned to the court, easily identified it as having belonged to his dear and lamented friend 'Villiam.'

"This was the first blow to the case against the accused. It was a pretty stiff one, you will admit. Already it had begun to collapse like a house of cards. Still, there was the assignation, and the undisputed meeting between Smethurst and Kershaw, and those two and a half hours of a foggy evening satisfactorily to account for."

The man in the corner made a long pause, keeping the girl on tenterhooks. He had fidgeted with his bit of string till there was not an inch of it free from the most complicated and elaborate knots.

"I assure you," he resumed at last, "that at that very moment the whole mystery was, to me, as clear as daylight. I only marveled how his Honor could waste his

time and mine by putting what he thought were searching questions to the accused relating to his past. Francis
Smethurst, who had quite shaken off his somnolence,
spoke with a curious nasal twang, and with an almost
imperceptible soupçon of foreign accent. He calmly
denied Kershaw's version of his past; declared that he
had never been called Barker, and had certainly never
been mixed up in any murder case thirty years ago.

" 'But you knew this man Kershaw,' persisted his
Honor, 'since you wrote to him?'

" 'Pardon me, your Honor,' said the accused quietly,
'I have never, to my knowledge, seen this man Kershaw,
and I can swear that I never wrote to him.'

" 'Never wrote to him?' retorted his Honor warningly.
'That is a strange assertion to make when I have two of
your letters to him in my hands at the present moment.'

" 'I never wrote those letters, your Honor,' persisted
the accused quietly, 'they are not in my handwriting.'

" 'Which we can easily prove,' came in Sir Arthur
Inglewood's drawly tones as he handed up a packet to
his Honor, 'here are a number of letters written by my
client since he has landed in this country, and some of
which were written under my very eyes.'

"As Sir Arthur Inglewood had said, this could be
easily proved, and the prisoner, at his Honor's request,
scribbled a few lines, together with his signature, several times upon a sheet of note-paper. It was easy to
read upon the magistrate's astounded countenance, that

there was not the slightest similarity in the two hand-writings.

"A fresh mystery had cropped up. Who, then, had made the assignation with William Kershaw at Fenchurch Street railway station? The prisoner gave a satisfactory account of the employment of his time since his landing in England.

" 'I came over on the *Tsarkoe Selo*,' he said, 'a yacht belonging to a friend of mine. When we arrived at the mouth of the Thames there was such a dense fog that it was twenty-four hours before it was thought safe for me to land. My friend, who is a Russian, would not land at all; he was regularly frightened at this land of fogs. He was going on to Madeira immediately.'

" 'I actually landed on Tuesday, the 10th, and took a train at once for town. I did see to my luggage and a cab, as the porter and driver told your Honor; then I tried to find my way to a refreshment-room, where I could get a glass of wine. I drifted into the waiting-room, and there I was accosted by a shabbily-dressed individual, who began telling me a piteous tale. Who he was I do not know. He *said* he was an old soldier who had served his country faithfully, and then been left to starve. He begged of me to accompany him to his lodgings, where I could see his wife and starving children, and verify the truth and piteousness of his tale.'

" 'Well, your Honor,' added the prisoner with noble frankness, 'it was my first day in the old country. I had come back after thirty years with my pockets full of gold, and this was the first sad tale I had heard; but I am a business man, and did not want to be exactly "done" in the eye. I followed my man through the fog,

I was accosted by a shabby individual.

out into the streets. He walked silently by my side for a time. I had not a notion where I was.'

" 'Suddenly I turned to him with some question, and realized in a moment that my gentleman had given me the slip. Finding, probably, that I would not part with my money till I *had* seen the starving wife and children,

he left me to my fate, and went in search of more willing bait.'

" 'The place where I found myself was dismal and
deserted. I could see no trace of cab or omnibus. I retraced my steps and tried to find my way back to the
station, only to find myself in worse and more deserted
neighborhoods. I became hopelessly lost and fogged.
I don't wonder that two and a half hours elapsed while
I thus wandered on in the dark and deserted streets; my
sole astonishment is that I ever found the station at all
that night, or rather close to it a policeman, who showed
me the way.'

" 'But how do you account for Kershaw knowing all
your movements?' still persisted his Honor, 'and his
knowing the exact date of your arrival in England? How
do you account for these two letters, in fact?'

" 'I cannot account for it or them, your Honor,' replied the prisoner quietly. 'I have proved to you, have
I not, that I never wrote those letters, and that the man
—er—Kershaw is his name?—was not murdered by
me?'

" 'Can you tell me of any one here or abroad who
might have heard of your movements and date of your
arrival?'

" 'My late employees at Vladivostok, of course, knew
of my departure, but none of them could have written
these letters, since none of them knew a word of English.'

" 'Then you can throw no light upon these mysterious letters? You cannot help the police in any way toward the clearing up of this strange affair?'

" 'The affair is as mysterious to me as to your Honor, and to the police of this country.'

"Francis Smethurst was discharged, of course; there was no semblance of evidence against him sufficient to commit him for trial. The two overwhelming points of his defense which had completely routed the prosecution were, firstly, the proof that he had never written the letters making the assignation, and secondly, the fact that the man supposed to have been murdered on the 10th was seen to be alive and well on the 16th. But then, who in the world was the mysterious individual who had apprised Kershaw of the movements of Smethurst, the millionaire?"

The man in the corner cocked his funny thin head on one side and looked at Polly; then he took up his beloved bit of string and deliberately untied every knot he had made in it. When it was quite smooth he laid it out upon the table.

"I will take you, if you like, point by point along the line of reasoning which I followed myself, and which will inevitably lead you, as it led me, to the only possible solution of the mystery.

"First take this point," he said with nervous restlessness, once more taking up his bit of string, and forming with each point raised a series of knots which would have shamed a navigating instructor, "Obviously it was *impossible* for Kershaw not to have been acquainted with Smethurst, since he was fully apprised of the latter's arrival in England by two letters. Now it was clear to me from the first that *no one* could have written those two letters except Smethurst. You will argue that those letters were proved not to have been written by the man in the dock. Exactly. Remember, Kershaw was a careless man—he had lost both envelopes. To him they were insignificant. Now it was never *disproved* that those letters were written by Smethurst."

"But—" suggested Polly.

"Wait a minute," he interrupted, while knot number two appeared upon the scene; "it was proved that six days after the murder William Kershaw was alive, and visited the Torriani Hotel, where already he was known, and where he conveniently left a pocketbook behind, so that there should be no mistake as to his identity; but it was never questioned where Mr. Francis Smethurst, the millionaire, happened to spend that very same afternoon."

"Surely, you don't mean—?" gasped the girl.

"One moment, please," he added triumphantly. "How did it come about that the landlord of the Torriani Hotel was brought into court at all? How did Sir Arthur Inglewood, or rather his client, know that William Kershaw had on those two memorable occasions visited the hotel, and that its landlord could bring such convincing evidence forward that would forever exonerate the millionaire from the imputation of murder?"

"Surely," Polly argued, "the usual means, the police——"

"The police had kept the whole affair very dark until the arrest at the Hotel Cecil. They did not put into the papers the usual: 'If any one happens to know of the whereabouts, etc., etc.' Had the landlord of that hotel heard of the disappearance of Kershaw through the usual channels, he would have put himself in communication with the police. Sir Arthur Inglewood produced him. How did Sir Arthur Inglewood come on his track?"

"Surely, you don't mean——?"

"Point number four," he resumed imperturbably, "Mrs. Kershaw was never requested to produce a specimen of her husband's handwriting. Why? Because the police, clever as you say they are, never started on the right tack. They believed William Kershaw to have been murdered; they looked for William Kershaw.

"On December the 31st, what was presumed to be the body of William Kershaw was found by two lightermen: I have shown you a photograph of the place where it was found. Dark and deserted it is in all conscience, is it not? Just the place where a bully and a coward would decoy an unsuspecting stranger, murder him first, then rob him of his valuables, his papers, his very identity, and leave him there to rot. The body was found in a disused barge which had been moored for some time against the wall, at the foot of these steps. It was in the last stages of decomposition, and, of course, could not be identified; but the police would have it that it was the body of William Kershaw.

"It never entered their heads that it was the body of *Francis Smethurst, and that William Kershaw was his murderer.*

"Ah! it was cleverly, artistically conceived! Kershaw is a genius. Think of it all! His disguise! Kershaw had a shaggy beard, hair, and mustache. He shaved up to his very eyebrows! No wonder that even his wife did not recognize him across the court; and remember she never saw much of his face while he stood in the dock. Kershaw was shabby, slouchy, he stooped. Smethurst, the millionaire, might have served in the Prussian army.

"Then that lovely trait about going to revisit the Torriani Hotel. Just a few days' grace, in order to purchase mustache and beard and wig, exactly similar to what he had himself shaved off. Making up to look exactly like himself! Splendid! Then leaving the pocketbook behind! He! he! he! Kershaw was not murdered! Of course not. He called at the Torriani Hotel six days after the murder, whilst Mr. Smethurst, the millionaire, hobnobbed in the park with duchesses! Hang such a man! Fie!"

He fumbled for his hat. With nervous, trembling fingers he held it deferentially in his hand whilst he rose from the table. Polly watched him as he strode up to the desk, and paid two-pence for his glass of milk and his bun. Soon he disappeared through the shop, whilst she still found herself hopelessly bewildered, with a number of snapshots before her, still staring at a long piece of string, smothered from end to end in a series of knots, as bewildering, as irritating, as puzzling as the man who had lately sat in the corner.

SAX ROHMER

The Owl Hoots Twice

It was dark when I got back to the barn. There was no one in Quarry Lane as I climbed over the stile, and the night was still and humid. Except for the people who had a week-end cottage at the top, practically nobody came along at this season.

Using the light sparingly, I made a careful search of the barn's ground floor before I ventured in. It was empty.

The bread and cheese and pickled onions I had eaten at the Forester Arms had satisfied my appetite. The ale was pretty weak—but we had got used to weak ale in England since the war. I felt sleepy. Perhaps that quart had been a mistake. But, God knows, I had needed it.

Back up in the loft I felt safe again. There were plenty of spy holes and I didn't think it likely I should be taken by surprise. I sleep lightly, and wake like a weasel at the faintest stirring.

As I lay down on my tramp's bed I thought about Mary Maguire, wondering if she suspected me.

I closed my eyes and studied the mental picture. Old Bill Maguire, landlord of the Forester, came into it, but right in the foreground stood his daughter. Mary Maguire, with her high cheekbones and wide-spaced blue eyes, hardly conformed to the standard concept of a pretty girl—but she had a remarkable figure, and the eager friendliness of her smile made her seem beautiful. I wondered about her.

The Celts are unpredictable, in my experience—and I knew that Superintendent Stopes of the local police used the Forester. I had left by one door that evening as he had come in at another. And those wide-spaced eyes of Mary's could see a long way.

I wondered.

Just as I was dozing off an unearthly yell jerked me from half dreams, and I sat up, tensely alert. The next moment I knew it was the big white owl whose quarters I had invaded, setting out on a night's hunting. It had dropped the body of a young rat on my head only a few nights before and so I had a friendly feeling for the bird.

Rain had begun to patter on those parts of the roof that remained intact.

I was settling down again, hoping the downpour wouldn't reach the spot I had chosen when I saw a faint light shining through a cranny in the wall.

Almost before I knew it I was flat on the boards, peering down.

She regarded me in her grave way.

Someone holding a flashlight was coming toward the barn.

There was no sound but that of the rain on the roof and a faint sighing from the fir trees which grew close up to the barn. Fir trees always sigh when it rains. Whoever held the light had come into the barn and was standing stock-still.

Then, came a call: "Jim!"

It was Mary's voice, and Jim was the name by which she knew me. I had been in the Forester a number of times when the bar was empty, and she and I had got talking; she had the trick of making friends quickly.

I lay still. "Jim!" she called again.

I balanced the chances. She must have followed me. The bar had been closing when I left. Whatever her motive, she had cool nerves. I had to face it out.

"Hullo, there! Who is it?" I shouted.

"Mary Maguire. Did I wake you up?"

"You did. But it doesn't matter. I'll come down."

I climbed down the ladder. There was a plank there, set on trestles, which at some time had been used as a saw bench. She had put the lamp on the plank and was sitting beside it. She wore a raincoat and had a striped handkerchief tied over her hair.

I sat down beside her—and her eyes regarded me gravely. There was a depth of discernment in the gravity of her eyes that I found disturbing. There in the dimness I wondered why she ventured after me. What did she suspect?

I pulled out a pack of cigarettes and offered her one. She shook her head, and from under the wet coat produced a full pack. "Keep yours. They're hard to come by—and expensive."

She put a cigarette between her lips as I snapped my lighter.

"Why did you follow me, Mary?"

She blew a smoke ring. "I wanted to find out where you lived."

"Why?"

"Well"—she hesitated, her eyes searching mine—"it's a hard world the peace has brought us, and I thought I might be able to help you. Did you find anything today?"

I shook my head. "Not a thing."

"It's taking chances to employ a man except through the Labor Exchange."

"I know it is."

She regarded me in her grave way before speaking again: "Are you a deserter, Jim?" she asked softly.

Her eyes were almost eager as she waited; and I think if I could have given her an honest answer I would have been, for a moment, the happiest man in England. "Yes," I lied, and looked away.

"Oh!" It was a sigh of relief. "I thought that was what you were hiding. Whatever made you do it? Is there someone—you just had to get to?"

"No. No one. It wasn't that."

"Well, it's none of my business, and you don't have to tell me if you don't want to. But you're a stranger in these parts, and you couldn't be in a worse place just now."

"How's that?"

Her eyes searched mine again, almost fearfully. "The murder."

"What murder?"

"Surely you heard them talking about it in the bar? They talk of little else."

I conjured up what was meant to be a puzzled expression, then nodded slowly. "I remember—I did. But why should it bother *me*?"

She was watching me, intently. "The superintendent asked me, tonight, if I knew you, and where you're from."

I whistled and silently cursed my carelessness. I could have got meals somewhere else. But I had been drawn to the Forester—and at this moment I knew it was Mary who had drawn me. Once I had found out that Stopes frequented the house common sense should have kept me away.

"You told him you didn't know?"

"Of course. I didn't—then."

"Is—the superintendent—a particular friend of yours?"

She stared past me, dreamily shaking her head.

"Perhaps he'd like to be."

"Perhaps. But if you want to get arrested, stay here. And it won't be just a court-martial you'll be facing."

"What do you mean?"

Her eyes were fixed on me again. "They think the

man who killed old Pettigrew is still in the neighborhood."

"He's a fool if he is." I paused, doubtful if it would be wise to say more; then: "Who was old Pettigrew, anyway? I haven't been keeping up."

Mary watched me for what seemed a very long time before she started to tell me about the murder of Cyrus Pettigrew. Some of her statements were wide of the mark and I had to guard my tongue. She never once looked at me while she related it.

Cyrus Pettigrew, she said, had lived the life of a hermit in a broken-down bungalow less than a hundred yards from the barn where we sat. He had no relatives and no friends and he had the reputation of being a miser. And in this case it was well deserved.

About a month before, his bungalow had been burgled during one of his rare absences. With great reluctance he had reported the matter to the police, assuring them he had no valuables in the place which could account for the burglary. And the ramshackle interior of the bungalow seemed to support his statement.

Three weeks later he was found dead in the lane beside his old push bike, and Superintendent Stopes had a job on his hands.

It was clear that old Pettigrew—he was close on seventy—had been knocked off his bicycle, for although the attack took place after dark, Pettigrew knew every foot of Quarry Lane and there was no obstruction which might have upset him. Furthermore, there had been some attempt to stanch the bleeding from a wound on his skull, as medical evidence proved.

Investigations threw more light on the mystery—but none on the identity of the murderer.

Cyrus Pettigrew distrusted banks and had a considerable fortune in notes hidden in the bungalow. Latterly, he had grown to distrust the Socialist government as well and had begun to convert his hoard into diamonds, to purchase which he paid periodical visits to a dealer in Hatton Garden.

He had returned from such a visit on the evening of his death, coming down from London by the 6:45 train —third class—and reaching Lowerwood at 7:42. His push bike was parked at the little station, and the last man—excepting, presumably, his murderer—to see him alive was the Lowerwood stationmaster.

Further investigation disclosed that he had left the Hatton Garden dealer with four thousand pounds' worth of diamonds in his possession. Many other packets, to the value of twenty-five to thirty thousand, were found buried under the bedroom floor, together with a hoard of notes not yet converted.

When his body was found—by a veterinary surgeon from Underhill who had lost his way in the dark—the diamonds were gone. Cyrus Pettigrew at this time could not have been dead more than ten minutes, the police surgeon said.

"He lay in the lane right outside this barn," Mary said, watching me fixedly.

She offered me another cigarette, but I shook my head.

I looked around me into the shadowy corners of the barn. Mary blew smoke which hung in the still air like a veil between us.

"And you knew nothing about it?" she asked.

It was hard, with her eyes on me, but I lied again. "No."

The rain was increasing, becoming a tattoo on the roof above. The sighing of the firs had risen to a whisper, so that I caught myself trying to hear what they were saying.

Mary stood up.

"Get away early in the morning." She pulled the raincoat over her shoulders. "Take my advice."

She moved to go.

"Mary—"

She half turned.

"Promise you won't say a word—about me being here."

Then she turned right around. She was holding the lamp to shine down onto the littered floor and I could barely see her eyes. But I thought there was a new expression there.

She was silent while I could have counted ten.

"All right," she said.

A shadowy shape swept past, silently, like a mocking phantom. The white owl's hoot echoed mournfully around the barn.

I followed Mary to where a sheet of rain curtained the doorway. And I began to wonder again.

"It's a vile night," I said.

She spoke with her back to me. "Did you ever hear a barn owl hoot twice? I mean just twice, no more."

I was puzzled. "I don't know if I ever did."

"They'd tell you, where I come from: If ever you do, look out. It means black luck—for somebody."

The light shone down onto the muddy path as she made her way out.

"Good night, Mary—and thank you."

But I heard no reply, although I stood there for a long time, listening to the firs whispering.

I passed an uneasy night. The rain stopped just as gray light began to creep in at gaps in the roof and wall. The home-coming bats had wakened me.

There are quarrelsome things in a man's make-up, I suppose, and few of us will take the trouble to analyze our impulses. All I know is I decided to shave off my two days' growth of beard that morning and leave the refuge of the barn. The odds against me, during the day, were high—whether I was in the barn or out of it.

Anyway, I made an attempt to spruce myself up a bit. I noted, from a spy hole I had discovered, certain activity in Pettigrew's bungalow along the lane. I believe a constable was still kept on duty there. But no one came into the barn.

Leaving the barn by way of some loose boards on the side away from the bungalow, I headed for the stile; it was around ten o'clock. I knew I was mad—but I was going to the Forester again. It was a dull, damp morning, and the mud came over my shoes as I crossed the orchard to the farther stile.

Once in the cubbyhole—a tiny bar with only one high-backed wooden bench, wedged in beside the more exclusive saloon—I felt temporarily secure. It smelled of beer and stale tobacco. Service was through a hatch. The hatch open, all that went on in the saloon could be heard easily enough.

When I rapped, Mary opened the hatch.

"Good morning," I said.

She stared at me very hard. There was no smile, no welcome in her eyes.

"So you didn't take my advice," was all she replied.

She set a tankard in front of me, swept the coins off into a till and turned aside impassively as someone came into the next room.

"Good morning, sir," I heard. "We don't often see you so early."

"No," said a man's deep voice, "I picked up a friend at the station. We're driving home—and it's a damp morning."

I knew the voice. Edward Larkin was an Underhill town councilor. When Mary had served their whiskies, I hoped she'd come back and talk to me. But she didn't.

"This is a tricky job, Larkin." I didn't recognize the other voice. "In fact, I hardly know where to begin. As a brother accountant, what's your own opinion?"

Someone struck a match.

"Well, Martin, frankly we fear he's been dipping pretty freely into funds raised for charity. He drinks hard, and he's separated from his wife. Apart from which"—the councilor dropped his voice—"he has his eye on—" Larkin paused.

"H'm. Good-looking girl," said the other speculatively.

"He never misses one. Of course, he's a good-looking fellow, himself, and smart, too. But—"

"Suppose—I only say suppose—I find a serious deficit? Shall you give him time to make it good?"

"It wouldn't rest with me. But he'd certainly have to resign. In many ways, the higher-ups aren't satisfied with the way things are run in this neighborhood. Take the murder along in Quarry Lane, for instance. Whoever did it must have known the old man's habits."

"Have the police no clues?"

I suppose Mr. Larkin shook his head, for the man called Martin went on: "If the locals are stuck, I should have thought it was a matter for Scotland Yard."

"So should I."

There was a pause.

"To come back to my job, Larkin—am I to regard it as a confidential audit?"

"As much as possible, Martin. No scandal, if it can be avoided."

There came a sudden silence, and I heard someone else walk into the saloon. Mary reappeared. I could just see her, through the hatch, where she stood. She smiled at the new arrival, and I thought a faint blush came to her cheeks. When he spoke, I knew.

"Top o' the mornin', Mary!" came a genial voice, but the Irish brogue was a poor imitation. "Why, Mr. Larkin!" the new voice exclaimed. "This is a pleasant surprise, sir."

"Good morning, Super," Mr. Larkin replied. "Meet a friend of mine, Mr. Martin Aloys. Martin—Police Superintendent Stopes."

I heard murmured greetings.

"I'm on my way to Quarry Lane, Mr. Larkin, and I just looked in to say how d'you do to Mary. I'm not satisfied with the way the inquiry is going. You will join me in a drink, gentlemen?"

Mary, with her back to me, stood at the till writing

something. Now, she came across, whisked my tankard away and dropped a scrap of paper on the ledge.

She was leaning over the adjoining bar, smiling at Stopes and waiting for his order, when I picked the paper up.

It said: *Get out. Quick.*

The words gave me a queer thrill. I went. And I went in a hurry. One false move now and I was lost.

From what I knew of his habits, what with Mary being there, I didn't expect the superintendent to leave the Forester in time to reach the lane ahead of me, although I had seen his car outside the inn.

I was right. I got back into the barn without sighting a soul, after I left the highroad and climbed the orchard stile. I wasted no time, though, getting inside. But I didn't forget to look carefully before I went in. Nothing was disturbed.

Up in the loft, I gave a deep sigh of relief. Every time I left it, even for an hour, I took tremendous chances— but I had to eat.

To get a view of the bungalow, through my spy hole, it was necessary to stand on a rafter and peer through a gap in the roof. It was tiring, for I could only support myself by holding on with both hands. But I stood there until I saw the superintendent drive up to the bungalow.

As a rule, a police sergeant drove his car. But Stopes was alone this morning.

I watched him go in. Then I lay down, with my eyes glued to the crack in the floor, waiting. If he came to the barn, he must hear no movement above. I got into as comfortable a position as I could.

There I waited. A sudden rustling broke the silence —and a huge rat crossed the floor below, halting for a moment by the bench where I had sat with Mary.

The minutes passed and nothing happened. I don't know how long I had lain there when I heard the sound of an engine starting.

I got back on the rafter in what would have been good going for a squirrel.

The superintendent was driving away.

I don't think any day before had ever seemed so long as that day. I had nothing to eat, and no chance to get anything.

And thoughts of Mary haunted me until they became an obsession.

Shouldn't I have taken her into my confidence when she invited me? The facts, as I could have put them, would have changed the complexion of the matter. Why hadn't I trusted my instincts, which had prompted me to make a clean breast of it? I had been a blind fool.

As a result she thought the worst of me, and I couldn't blame her.

About noon it grew very dark and rain began to fall again. It went on steadily all through the afternoon and only once was the lane disturbed by a footstep. A wild hope—that Mary was coming to look for me—died almost as soon as it was born.

In the first place, the footsteps were coming from the wrong direction. In the second place, they were slow and shambling.

A ragged object, a real tramp of the old school with a shapeless bundle swung on his back, pulled up just outside the door of the barn and stood there looking in, moisture trickling from the brim of a crazy felt hat.

I knew he was considering the idea of spending the night there, and I knew that at whatever cost he must be kept out. I had too much at stake to be squeamish. But as if the dark, cavernous interior of the place had cast a chill on his spirits, he turned and shambled off down the lane.

From then to dusk no one came near the barn.

Rain ceased about nightfall. I was terribly hungry and hopelessly depressed. Lack of food was bringing on a sort of drowsiness, and I began to wonder if I should be able to keep awake. I clenched my teeth. Tonight, I *must* keep awake.

It was, roughly, at eight o'clock that I was disturbed again. As I heard those quiet, purposeful steps drawing quickly nearer, I jumped to my lookout in the floor of the loft and settled down to watch.

At the door of the barn the footsteps stopped. I knew that the man (the steps were those of a man) was

He knelt at the base of the tree.

standing there listening. I relaxed every muscle, breathing slowly.

He moved a little left of the entrance, shining the ray of a flashlight ahead of him. I saw him kneel down at the base of a fir tree which stood like a sentinel before the door—and I knew what he was looking for.

Less than a minute he stayed there, then got up and came into the barn.

He swept his light around the barn's interior. When he directed it upward, I closed my eyes—stopped breathing. When I opened them again the beam of light was once more directed downward. The man was bending down in the far, right-hand corner, scooping out ancient rubbish piled against the brickwork foundation.

I inhaled one deep breath. He was going to open the secret cache!

I saw him remove two or three bricks from their places and put his hand into the gap. He pulled something out and slipped it in his pocket. He pulled out something else and dropped it on the pile of rubbish beside him. Then, into the hole he thrust a coil of thin wire.

He paused. He seemed to be listening again.

I knew that the wire, which had been stretched across the lane just before old Pettigrew came along, was only intended to pitch him off his bicycle. It did. And the fall killed him. There was medical evidence to show that an attempt had been made to stanch the wound on his head.

Interrupted by the unforeseen arrival of a car, the man responsible for the killing had only time to grab the wire away from the road and run into the near-by barn. But the thin strand had broken as Pettigrew crashed. Part of it remained fastened to a tree—a clue never discovered by the local police.

Now, I had seen the fragment of wire being untied from the base of the fir tree, the stained handkerchief and the packet of diamonds Pettigrew had carried being taken out of their hiding place.

The game was nearly up. I watched more tensely than ever.

Satisfied that nothing stirred, the man in the barn below put the loose bricks back and replaced the rubbish. He wrapped the handkerchief in a piece of newspaper which he had with him and put the bundle in his pocket.

I could have told him it was useless as evidence— stained with the blood of a dead rat. The handkerchief that had been actually used to stanch Pettigrew's blood lay safe in my knapsack. Stamped on it were incriminating laundry marks.

Just as he had finished what he had to do, the man below me sprang suddenly upright and snapped out his light.

The white owl, circling outside, and disturbed by an unfamiliar light, had hooted—twice.

At the door of the Forester I checked for a moment, to get my breath. I had had nothing to eat all day, and it had been a test of endurance to sprint across the muddy orchard and so to the highroad. But I had all my possessions with me, and my knapsack on my back.

I inhaled deeply, clenched my teeth, and opened the door.

There were only three customers in the saloon. One, a local farmer, I knew by sight; another, standing bolt upright in a corner I recognized as a sergeant of the Underhill police who lived hard by; and the third was Superintendent Stopes. His car stood outside. Both the police officers wore plain clothes.

There was no one behind the bar.

I rapped on the counter.

"A double Scotch and soda, please."

Maguire, who had been reading an evening paper in his armchair over by the window, gave me an unwelcoming glance but stood up to serve me. He still had his back to the bar when the superintendent spoke. "I think I have seen you before," he said.

I turned and looked at him. He was a good figure of a man in his well-cut tweed suit, and except that he was rather puffy under his brown eyes, his features were good, too, a touch of gray in the crisp dark hair adding distinction to his looks.

"It's possible."

"It's certain—and I shall be glad if you will show me your identity card, and any other papers you may have."

In a mirror across the saloon I could see Maguire, the bottle of whisky in his hand, staring open-mouthed. The police sergeant put his tankard on a table and took a step forward.

"Before I do that, Superintendent, I should like a word with you."

And as I spoke, Mary came in. I saw her through the mirror and glanced back.

When our glances met, she flushed hotly, then grew white as marble. Her eyes seemed to be alight as she looked from me to the superintendent. I turned away. If my heart had jumped when I got her note that morning, it sang now.

"Make it snappy. I'm waiting," Superintendent Stopes said.

"I should prefer it to be private—if you and the sergeant, there, would step outside for a minute."

Two blue eyes were fixed on me through the mirror. The superintendent and the sergeant exchanged looks.

"It concerns the death of Cyrus Pettigrew," I added.

Superintendent Stopes' expression changed as if a wet sponge had been swept over a painted face. He stared at me; I knew what he was going to say.

"Stand by here, Sergeant. I'll talk to this man, alone."

"I prefer the sergeant to be present."

The farmer looked riveted to his chair. Maguire still had the bottle gripped in his hand as though he'd been hypnotized.

There was nothing else for it. The three of us went outside. It seemed very dark, after the lighted saloon.

"The man who killed Pettigrew," I said, "was in financial difficulty. That was the motive. He must have tried, many times, to get alone to the spot, recover the diamonds and remove the evidence. But, for one in his position, it wasn't easy. He managed it tonight, though."

In a dead silence I swung my knapsack from my shoulder.

"The wire used in the crime is still in the old barn where the criminal hid it—and where I found it more than a week ago. There may be fingerprints. The packet of diamonds is in his pocket."

I opened the knapsack.

"You asked me for my identity card. Here it is. Sergeant, will you take it?"

I gave the card to the police sergeant and snapped on my flashlight to let him read it. What he read was:

Detective Inspector Jas. Yeoward
Criminal Investigation Department
New Scotland Yard. S.W.I.

"It's a painful duty, Superintendent Stopes, to arrest a senior officer. But I have to charge you with the mur-

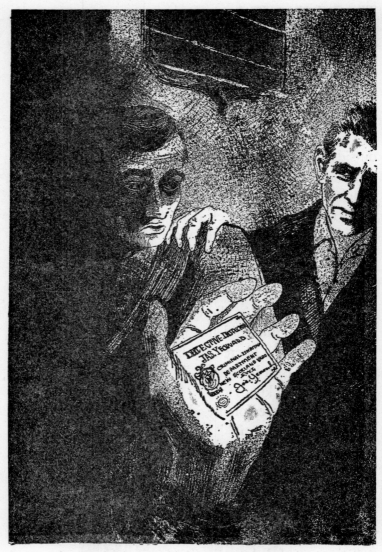

I snapped on my flashlight to let him read it.

der of Cyrus Pettigrew on the night of the nineteenth
of October. I warn you that anything you may say.
. . ."

When I got back to the Forester from Underhill police station (I was in a hurry and I came in a patrol car)
the bar was just closing.

But Mary was waiting.

She whispered: "Jim, how could you do it to me?
Didn't you trust me? Oh, I'll never forgive you—"

It's lucky that women don't always mean what they
say.

WILLIAM AUSTIN

Peter Rugg

(FROM JONATHAN DUNWELL OF NEW YORK TO
MR. HERMAN KRAUFF.)

SIR—Agreeably to my promise, I now relate to
you all the particulars of the lost man and child which
I have been able to collect. It is entirely owing to the
human interest you seemed to take in the report that I
have pursued the inquiry to the following result.

You may remember that business called me to Boston
in the summer of 1820. I sailed in the packet to Providence; and when I arrived there, I learned that every
seat in the stage was engaged. I was thus obliged either
to wait a few hours, or accept a seat with the driver,
who civilly offered me that accommodation. Accordingly I took my seat by his side, and soon found him
intelligent and communicative. When we had travelled
about ten miles, the horses suddenly threw their ears
on their necks as flat as a hare's. Said the driver, "Have
you a surtout with you?"

"No," said I; "why do you ask?"

"You will want one soon," said he. "Do you observe the ears of all the horses?"

"Yes; and was just about to ask the reason."

"They see the storm-breeder, and we shall see him soon."

At this moment there was not a cloud visible in the firmament, soon after a small speck appeared in the road.

"There," said my companion, "comes the storm-breeder; he always leaves a Scotch mist behind him. By many a wet jacket do I remember him. I suppose the poor fellow suffers much himself—much more than is known to the world."

Presently a man with a child beside him, with a large black horse and a weather-beaten chair, once built for a chaise-body, passed in great haste, apparently at the rate of twelve miles an hour. He seemed to grasp the reins of his horse with firmness, and appeared to anticipate his speed. He seemed dejected, and looked anxiously at the passengers, particularly at the stage-driver and myself. In a moment after he passed us, the horses' ears were up, and bent themselves forward so that they nearly met.

"Who is that man?" said I; "he seems in great trouble."

"Nobody knows who he is; but his person and the child are familiar to me. I have met him more than a

A man with a child beside him passed in great haste.

hundred times, and have been so often asked the way to Boston by that man, even when he was travelling directly from that town, that of late I have refused any communication with him; and that is the reason he gave me such a fixed look."

"But does he never stop anywhere?"

"I have never known him to stop anywhere longer than to inquire the way to Boston. And let him be where he may, he will tell you he cannot stay a moment, for he must reach Boston that night."

We were now ascending a high hill in Walpole; and as we had a fair view of the heavens, I was rather disposed to jeer the driver for thinking of his surtout, as not a cloud as big as a marble could be discerned.

"Do you look," said he, "in the direction whence the man came; that is the place to look. The storm never meets him, it follows him."

We presently approached another hill; and when at the height the driver pointed out in an eastern direction a little black speck about as big as a hat,—"There," said he, "is the seed storm; we may possibly reach Polley's before it reaches us, but the wanderer and his child will go to Providence through rain, thunder, and lightning."

And now the horses, as though taught by instinct, hastened with increased speed. The little black cloud came on rolling over the turnpike, and doubled and trebled itself in all directions. The appearance of this cloud attracted the notice of all the passengers; for after it had spread itself to a great bulk, it suddenly became more limited in circumference, grew more compact, dark and consolidated. And now the successive flashes of chain lightning caused the whole cloud to appear like a sort of irregular network, and displayed a thousand fantastic images. The driver bespoke my attention to a remarkable configuration in the cloud; he said every flash of lightning near its centre discovered to him distinctly the form of a man sitting in an open carriage drawn by a black horse. But in truth I saw no such thing. The man's fancy was doubtless at fault. It is a common thing for the imagination to paint for the senses, both in the visible and invisible world.

In the mean time the distant thunder gave notice of a shower at hand; and just as we reached Polley's tavern the rain poured down in torrents. It was soon over, the cloud passing in the direction of the turnpike toward Providence. In a few moments after, a respectable-looking man in a chaise stopped at the door. The man and child in the chair having excited some little sympathy among the passengers, the gentleman was asked if he had observed them. He said he had met them; that the man seemed bewildered, and inquired the way to Boston; that he was driving at great speed, as though he expected to outstrip the tempest; that the moment he had passed them, a thunder clap broke directly over the man's head, and seemed to envelop both man and

child, horse and carriage. "I stopped," said the gentleman, "supposing the lightning had struck him; but the
horse only seemed to loom up and increase his speed;
and as well as I could judge, he travelled just as fast as
the thundercloud."

While this man was speaking, a pedlar with a cart of
tin merchandise came up all dripping; and on being
questioned, he said he had met that man and carriage,
within a fortnight, in four different states; that each
time he had inquired the way to Boston, and that a
thunder shower, like the present, had each time deluged
his wagon and his wares, setting his tin pots, etc., afloat,
so that he had determined to get marine insurance done
for the future. But that which excited his surprise most
was the strange conduct of his horse; for that long before he could distinguish the man in the chair, his own
horse stood still in the road, and flung back his ears. "In
short," said the pedlar, "I wish never to see that man
and horse again; they do not look to me as though they
belonged to this world."

This was all I could learn at that time; and the occurrence soon after would have become with me "like one
of those things that had never happened," had I not, as
I stood recently on the doorstep of Bennett's Hotel in
Hartford, heard a man say, "There goes Peter Rugg and
his child! He looks wet and weary, and farther from Boston than ever." I was satisfied it was the same man I
had seen more than three years before; for whoever has

once seen Peter Rugg can never after be deceived as to his identity.

"Peter Rugg!" said I; "and who is Peter Rugg?"

"That," said the stranger, "is more than anyone can tell exactly. He is a famous traveller, held in light esteem by all inn-holders, for he never stops to eat, drink, or sleep. I wonder why the Government does not employ him to carry the mail."

"Ay," said a bystander, "that is a thought bright only on one side. How long would it take in that case to send a letter to Boston?—for Peter has already, to my knowledge, been more than twenty years travelling to that place."

"But," said I, "does the man never stop anywhere? Does he never converse with anyone? I saw the same man more than three years since near Providence, and I heard a strange story about him. Pray, sir, give me some account of this man."

"Sir," said the stranger, "those who know the most respecting that man say the least. I have heard it asserted that Heaven sometimes sets a mark on a man either for judgment or a trial. Under which Peter Rugg now labors, I cannot say; therefore I am rather inclined to pity than to judge."

"You speak like a humane man," said I; "and if you have known him so long, I pray you will give me some account of him. Has his appearance much altered in that time?"

"Why, yes; he looks as though he never ate, drank, or slept; and his child looks older than himself; and he looks like time broken off from eternity, and anxious to gain a resting-place."

"And how does his horse look?" said I.

"As for his horse, he looks fatter and gayer, and shows more animation and courage, than he did twenty years ago. The last time Rugg spoke to me he inquired how far it was to Boston. I told him just one hundred miles.

" 'Why,' said he, 'how can you deceive me so? It is cruel to mislead a traveller. I have lost my way; pray direct me the nearest way to Boston.'

"I repeated, it was one hundred miles.

" 'How can you say so?' said he; 'I was told last evening it was but fifty, and I have travelled all night.'

" 'But,' said I, 'you are now travelling from Boston. You must turn back.'

" 'Alas!' said he, 'it is all turn back! Boston shifts with the wind and plays all around the compass. One man tells me it is to the east, another to the west; and the guide-posts, too, they all point the wrong way.'

" 'But will you not stop and rest?' said I; 'you seem wet and weary.'

" 'Yes,' said he; 'it has been foul weather since I left home.'

" 'Stop, then, and refresh yourself.'

" 'I must not stop; I must reach home tonight, if pos-

sible; though I think you must be mistaken in the distance to Boston.'

"He then gave the reins to his horse, which he re-
strained with difficulty, and disappeared in a moment.
A few days afterward I met the man a little this side of
Claremont, winding around the hills in Unity, at the
rate, I believe, of twelve miles an hour."

"Is Peter Rugg his real name, or has he accidentally
gained that name?"

"I know not, but presume he will not deny his name;
you can ask him—for see, he has turned his horse, and
is passing this way."

In a moment a dark-colored, high-spirited horse approached, and would have passed without stopping; but
I had resolved to speak to Peter Rugg, or whoever the
man might be. Accordingly I stepped into the street,
and as the horse approached, I made a feint of stopping
him. The man immediately reined in his horse. "Sir,"
said I, "may I be so bold as to inquire if you are not Mr.
Rugg?—for I think I have seen you before."

"My name is Peter Rugg," said he: "I have unfortunately lost my way. I am wet and weary, and will take it
kindly of you to direct me to Boston."

"You live in Boston, do you?—and in what street?"

"In Middle Street."

"When did you leave Boston?"

"I cannot tell precisely; it seems a considerable time."

"But how did you and your child become so wet? It has not rained here today."

"It has just rained a heavy shower up the river. But I shall not reach Boston tonight if I tarry. Would you advise me to take the old road or the turnpike?"

"Why, the old road is one hundred and seventeen miles, and the turnpike is ninety-seven."

"How can you say so? You impose on me! It is wrong to trifle with a traveller. You know it is but forty miles from Newburyport to Boston."

"But this is not Newburyport; this is Hartford."

"Do not deceive me, sir. Is not this town Newburyport, and the river that I have been following the Merrimac?"

"No, sir; this is Hartford, and the river the Connecticut."

He wrung his hands and looked incredulous.

"Have the rivers, too, changed their courses, as the cities have changed places? But see! the clouds are gathering in the south, and we shall have a rainy night. Ah, that fatal oath!"

He would tarry no longer. His impatient horse leaped off, his hind flanks rising like wings; he seemed to devour all before him and to scorn all behind.

I had now, as I thought, discovered a clew to the history of Peter Rugg, and I determined, the next time my business called me to Boston, to make a further inquiry.

Soon after, I was enabled to collect the following particulars from Mrs. Croft, an aged lady in Middle Street, who has resided in Boston during the last twenty years. Her narration is this:

The last summer, a person, just at twilight, stopped at the door of the late Mrs. Rugg. Mrs. Croft, on coming to the door, perceived a stranger, with a child by his side, in an old weather-beaten carriage, with a black horse. The stranger asked for Mrs. Rugg, and was informed that Mrs. Rugg had died in a good old age more than twenty years before that time.

The stranger replied, "How can you deceive me so? Do ask Mrs. Rugg to step to the door."

"Sir, I assure you Mrs. Rugg has not lived here these nineteen years; no one lives here but myself, and my name is Betsey Croft."

The stranger paused, and looked up and down the street, and said: "Though the painting is rather faded, this looks like my house."

"Yes," said the child; "that is the stone before the door that I used to sit on to eat my bread and milk."

"But," said the stranger, "it seems to be on the wrong side of the street. Indeed everything here seems to be misplaced. The streets are all changed, the people are all changed, the town seems changed; and what is strangest of all, Catherine Rugg has deserted her husband and child. Pray," continued the stranger, "has John Foy came home from sea? He went a long voyage;

he is my kinsman. If I could see him, he could give me some account of Mrs. Rugg."

"Sir," said Mrs. Croft, "I never heard of John Foy. Where did he live?"

"Just above here, in Orange Tree Lane."

"There is no such place in this neighborhood."

"What do you tell me? Are the streets gone? Orange Tree Lane is at the head of Hanover Street, near Pemberton's Hill."

"There is no such lane now."

"Madam! you cannot be serious. But you doubtless know my brother, William Rugg. He lives in Royal Exchange Lane, near King Street."

"I know of no such lane, and I am sure there is no such street as King Street in this town."

"No such street as King Street! Why, woman, you mock me! You may as well tell me there is no King George! However, madam, you see I am wet and weary; I must find a resting-place. I will go to Hart's tavern, near the market."

"Which market, sir?—for you seem perplexed; we have several markets."

"You know there is but one market,—near the Town dock."

"Oh, the old market; but no such person has kept there these twenty years."

Here the stranger seemed disconcerted, and uttered to himself quite audibly: "Strange mistake! How much this looks like Boston! It certainly has a great resemblance to it; but I perceive my mistake now. Some other Mrs. Rugg, some other Middle Street."

"Then," said he, "madam, can you direct me to Boston?"

"Why, this is Boston, the city of Boston. I know of no other Boston."

"City of Boston it may be; but it is not the Boston where I live. I recollect now, I came over a bridge instead of a ferry. Pray what bridge is that I just came over?"

"It is Charles River Bridge."

"I perceive my mistake; there is a ferry between Boston and Charlestown; there is no bridge. Ah, I perceive my mistake. If I were in Boston my horse would carry me directly to my own door. But my horse shows by his impatience that he is in a strange place. Absurd, that I should have mistaken this place for the old town of Boston! It is a much finer city than the town of Boston. It has been built long since Boston. I fancy it must lie at a distance from this city, as the good woman seems ignorant of it."

At these words his horse began to chafe and strike the pavement with his fore-feet. The stranger seemed a little bewildered, and said, "No home tonight"; and giving the reins to his horse, passed up the street.

"I saw him no more."

It was evident that the generation to which Peter Rugg belonged had passed away.

This was all the account of Peter Rugg I could obtain from Mrs. Croft; but she directed me to an elderly man, Mr. James Felt, who lived near her, and who had kept a record of the principal occurrences for the last fifty years. At my request she sent for him; and after I had related to him the object of my inquiry, Mr. Felt told me he had known Rugg in his youth; that his disappearance had caused some surprise; but as it sometimes happens that men run away, sometimes to be rid of others, and sometimes to be rid of themselves; and Rugg took his child with him, and his own horse and chair; and as it did not appear that any creditors made a stir, —the occurrence soon mingled itself in the stream of oblivion, and Rugg and his child, horse and chair, were soon forgotten.

"It is true," said Mr. Felt, "sundry stories grew out of Rugg's affair,—whether true or false I cannot tell; but stranger things have happened in my day, without even a newspaper notice."

"Sir," said I, "Peter Rugg is now living; I have lately seen Peter Rugg and his child, horse and chair. Therefore I pray you to relate to me all you know or have ever heard of him."

"Why, my friend," said James Felt, "that Peter Rugg is now a living man, I will not deny; but that you have

seen Peter Rugg and his child is impossible, if you mean
a small child; for Jenny Rugg, if living, must be at least
—let me see—Boston Massacre, 1770—Jenny Rugg
was about ten years of age. Why, sir, Jenny Rugg, if
living must be more than sixty years old. That Peter
Rugg is living, is highly probable, as he was only ten
years older than myself, and I was only eighty last
March; and I am as likely to live twenty years longer as
any man."

Here I perceived that Mr. Felt was in his dotage; and
I despaired of gaining any intelligence from him on
which I could depend.

I took my leave of Mrs. Croft, and proceeded to my
lodgings at the Marlborough Hotel.

If Peter Rugg, thought I, has been travelling since
the Boston Massacre, there is no reason why he should
not travel to the end of time. If the present generation
know little of him, the next will know less; and Peter
and his child will have no hold on this world.

In the course of the evening I related my adventure
in Middle Street.

"Ha!" said one of the company, smiling, "do you
really think you have seen Peter Rugg? I have heard my
grandfather speak of him as though he seriously believed
his own story."

"Sir," said I, "pray let us compare your grandfather's
story of Mr. Rugg with my own."

"Stranger things have happened in my day. . . ."

"Peter Rugg, sir, if my grandfather was worthy of credit, once lived in Middle Street, in this city. He was a man in comfortable circumstances, had a wife and one daughter, and was generally esteemed for his sober life and manners. But, unhappily, his temper at times was altogether ungovernable; and then his language was terrible. In these fits of passion, if a door stood in his way, he would never do less than kick a panel through. He would sometimes throw his heels over his head and come down on his feet, uttering oaths in a circle; and thus in a rage he was the first who performed a somerset, and did what others have since learned to do for merriment and money. Once Rugg was seen to bite a tenpenny nail in halves. In those days everybody, both men and boys, wore wigs; and Peter, at these moments of violent passion, would become so profane that his wig would rise up from his head. Some said it was on account of his terrible language; others accounted for it in a more philosophical way, and said it was caused by the expansion of his scalp,—as violent passion, we know, will swell the veins and expand the head. While these fits were on him Rugg had no respect for heaven or earth. Except this infirmity, all agreed that Rugg was a good sort of man; for when his fits were over, nobody was so ready to commend a placid temper as Peter.

"It was late in autumn, one morning, that Rugg, in his own chair, with a fine large bay horse, took his daughter and proceeded to Concord. On his return a violent storm overtook him. At dark he stopped at Menotomy, now West Cambridge, at the door of a Mr. Cutter, a friend of his, who urged him to tarry the night. On Rugg's declining to stop, Mr. Cutter urged him vehemently. 'Why, Mr. Rugg,' said Cutter, 'the storm is overwhelming you: the night is exceeding dark: your little daughter will perish: you are in an open chair, and the tempest is increasing.' '*Let the storm increase,*' said Rugg, with a fearful oath, '*I will see home tonight, in spite of the last tempest, or may I never see home!*' At these words he gave his whip to his high-spirited horse, and disappeared in a moment. But Peter Rugg did not reach home that night or the next; nor, when he became a missing man, could he ever be traced beyond Mr. Cutter's in Menotomy.

"For a long while after, on every dark and stormy night, the wife of Peter Rugg would fancy she heard the crack of a whip, and the fleet tread of a horse, and the rattling of a carriage passing her door. The neighbors, too, heard the same noises; and some said they knew it was Rugg's horse, the tread on the pavement was perfectly familiar to them. This occurred so repeatedly, that at length the neighbors watched with lanterns, and saw the real Peter Rugg, with his own horse and chair, and child sitting beside him, pass directly before his own door, his head turned toward his house, and himself making every effort to stop his horse, but in vain.

"The next day the friends of Mrs. Rugg exerted themselves to find her husband and child. They inquired at every public-house and stable in town; but it did not appear that Rugg made any stay in Boston. No one, after Rugg had passed his own door, could give any account of him; though it was asserted by some that the clatter of Rugg's horse and carriage shook the houses on both sides of the streets. And this is credible, if indeed Rugg's horse and carriage did pass on that night. For at this day, in many of the streets, a loaded truck or team in passing will shake the houses like an earthquake. However, Rugg's neighbors never afterward watched; some of them treated it all as a delusion, and thought no more of it. Others, of a different opinion, shook their heads and said nothing.

"Thus Rugg and his child, horse and chair, were soon forgotten, and probably many in the neighborhood never heard a word on the subject.

"There was, indeed, a rumor that Rugg afterwards was seen in Connecticut, between Suffield and Hartford, passing through the country with headlong speed. This gave occasion to Rugg's friends to make further inquiry. But the more they inquired, the more they were baffled. If they heard of Rugg one day in Connecticut, the next they heard of him winding round the hills of

He held a large three-legged stool.

New Hampshire; and soon after, a man in a chair with a small child, exactly answering the description of Peter Rugg, would be seen in Rhode Island inquiring the road to Boston.

"But that which chiefly gave a color of mystery to the story of Peter Rugg was the affair at Charlestown Bridge. The toll-gatherer asserted that sometimes on the darkest and most stormy nights, when no object could be discerned, about the time Rugg was missing, a horse and wheel carriage, with a noise equal to a troop, would at midnight, in utter contempt of the rates of toll, pass over the bridge. This occurred so frequently, that the toll-gatherer resolved to attempt a discovery. Soon after, at the usual time, apparently the same horse and carriage approached the bridge from Charlestown Square. The toll-gatherer, prepared, took his stand as near the middle of the bridge as he dared, with a large three-legged stool in his hand. As the appearance passed, he threw the stool at the horse, but heard nothing, except the noise of the stool skipping across the bridge. The toll-gatherer, on the next day, asserted that the stool went directly through the body of the horse; and he persisted in that belief ever after. Whether Rugg, or whoever the person was, ever passed the bridge again, the toll-gatherer would never tell; and when questioned, seemed anxious to waive the subject. And thus,

Peter Rugg and his child, horse and carriage, remain a mystery to this day."

This, sir, is all that I could learn of Peter Rugg in Boston.

A. A. MILNE

Nearly Perfect

"Kindness doesn't always pay," said Coleby, "and I can tell you a very sad story that proves it."

"Kindness is its own reward," I said. I knew that somebody else would say it if I didn't.

"The reward in this case was the hangman's rope. Which is what I was saying."

"Is it a murder story?"

"Very much so."

"Good."

"What was the name of the kind gentleman?" asked Sylvia.

"Julian Crayne."

"And he was hanged?"

"Very unfairly, or so he thought. And if you will listen to the story instead of asking silly questions, you can say whether you agree with him."

"How old was he?"

"About thirty."

"Good-looking?"

"Not after he was hanged. Do you want to hear this story, or don't you?"

"Yes!" said everybody.

So Coleby told us the story.

Julian Crayne (he said) was an unpleasantly smooth young man who lived in the country with his Uncle Marius. He should have been working, but he disliked work. He disliked the country, too, but a suggestion that Julian should help the export drive in London—with the aid of a handsome allowance from Marius—met with an unenthusiastic response even when Julian threw in an offer to come down regularly for weekends and bring some of his friends with him. Marius didn't particularly like his nephew, but he liked having him about. Rich, elderly bachelors often become bores, and bores prefer to have somebody at hand who cannot escape. Marius did not intend to let Julian escape. To have nobody to talk to through the week, and then to have a houseful of rowdy young people at the weekend, none of whom wanted to listen to him, was not his idea of pleasure. He had the power over his nephew that money gives, and he preferred to use it.

"It will all come to you when I die, my boy," he said, "and until then you won't grudge a sick old man the pleasure of your company."

"Of course not," said Julian. "It was only that I was afraid you were getting tired of me."

If Marius had really been a sick old man, any loving nephew such as Julian might have been content to wait. But Marius was a sound sixty-five, and in that very morning's newspaper there had been talk of somebody at Runcorn who had just celebrated his hundred-and-fifth birthday. Julian didn't know where Runcorn was, but he could add forty years to his own age, and ask himself what the devil would be the use of this money at seventy; whereas now, with £150,000 in the bank, and all life to come— Well, you can see for yourself how the thing would look to him.

I don't know if any of you have ever wondered about how to murder an uncle—an uncle whose heir and only relation you are. As we all know, the motives for murder are many. Revenge, passion, gain, fear, or simply the fact that you have seen the fellow's horrible face in the paper so often that you feel it to be almost a duty to eliminate it. The only person I have ever wanted to murder is— Well, I won't mention names, because I may do it yet. But the point is that the police, in their stolid, unimaginative way, always look first for the money motive, and if the money motive is there, you are practically in the bag.

So you see the very difficult position in which Julian was placed. He lived alone with his uncle, he was his uncle's heir, and his uncle was a very rich man. However subtly he planned, the dead weight of that £150,000 was against him. Any other man might push Marius into the river, and confidently wait for a verdict of accidental death; but not Julian. Any other man might place a tablet of some untraceable poison in the soda-mint bottle, and look for a certificate of "Death from Natural Causes"; but not Julian. Any other man might tie a string across the top step of the attic stairs— But I need not go on. You see, as Julian saw, how terribly unfair it was. The thing really got into his mind. He used to lie awake night after night thinking how unfair it was, and how delightfully easy it would be if it weren't for that £150,000.

The trouble was that he had nobody in whom to confide. He wished now, and for the first time, that he were married. With a loving wife to help him, how blithely they could have pursued, hand in hand, the search for the foolproof plan. What a stimulant to his brain would have been some gentle, fair-haired creature of the intelligence of the average policeman, who would point out the flaws and voice the suspicions the plan might raise. In such a delicate matter as this, two heads were better than one, even if the other head did nothing but listen with its mouth slightly ajar. At least he would then have the plan out in the open and be able to take a more objective view of it.

Unfortunately, the only person available was his uncle.

What he had to find—alone, if so it must be—was an alternative suspect to himself; somebody, in the eyes

He used to lie awake at night thinking.

of the police, with an equally good motive. But what other motive could there be for getting rid of such an estimable man as Marius Crayne? A bore, yes; but would the average Inspector recognize boredom as a reasonable motive? Even if he did, it would merely be an additional motive for Julian. There was, of course, the possibility of "framing" somebody, a thing they were always doing in detective stories. But the only person in a position to be framed was old John Coppard, the gardener, and the number of footprints, fingerprints, blunt instruments, and blood-stained handkerchiefs with the initials J. C. on them that would be necessary to offset the absence of motive was more than Julian cared to contemplate.

I have said that Uncle Marius was a bore. Bores can be divided into two classes: those who have their own particular subject, and those who don't need a subject. Marius was in the former, and less offensive class. Shortly before his retirement (he was in the tea business), he had brought off a remarkable double. He had filled in his first football-pool form "just to see how it went," distributing the numbers and the crosses in an impartial spirit, and had posted it "just for fun." He followed this up by taking over a lottery ticket from a temporarily embarrassed but rather intimidating gentleman whom he had met on a train. The result being what it was, Marius was convinced that he had a flair —as he put it, "a nose for things." So when he found that through the long winter evenings—and, indeed, during most of the day—there was nothing to do in the country but read detective stories, it soon became obvious to him that he had a nose for crime.

Well, it was this nose poor Julian had had to face. It was bad enough, whenever a real crime was being exploited in the papers, to listen to his uncle's assurance that once again Scotland Yard was at fault, as it was obviously the mother-in-law who had put the arsenic in the gooseberry tart; it was much more boring when the murder had taken place in the current detective story, and Marius was following up a confused synopsis of the first half with his own analysis of the clues.

"Oh, I forgot to tell you, this fellow—I forget his name for a moment—Carmichael, something like that —had met the girl, Doris—I mean Phyllis—had met Phyllis accidentally in Paris some years before—well, a year or two, the exact time doesn't matter—it was just that she and this fellow, what did I call him, Arbuthnot? . . ."

And it was at just such a moment as this that Julian was suddenly inspired.

"You know, Uncle Marius," he said, *"you* ought to write a detective story."

Marius laughed self-consciously, and said he didn't know about that.

"Of course you could! You're just the man. You've got a flair for that sort of thing, and you wouldn't make the silly mistakes all these other fellows make."

"Oh, I dare say I should be all right with the deduction and induction and so on—that's what I'm really interested in—but I've never thought of myself as a writer. There's a bit of a knack to it, you know. More in your line than mine, I should have thought."

"Uncle, you've said it!" cried Julian. "We'll write it together. Two heads are better than one. We can talk it over every evening and criticize each other's suggestions. What do you say?"

Marius was delighted with the idea. So, of course, was Julian. He had found his collaborator.

Give me a drink, somebody.

Yes (went on Coleby, wiping his mouth), I know what you are expecting. Half of you are telling yourselves that, ironically enough, it was Uncle who thought of the foolproof plan for murder that Nephew put into execution; and the rest of you are thinking what much more fun it would be if Nephew thought of the plan, and, somewhat to his surprise, Uncle put it into execution. Actually, it didn't happen quite like that.

Marius, when it came to the point, had nothing much to contribute. But he knew what he liked. For him, one murder in a book was no longer enough. There must be two, the first one preferably at a country house party, with plenty of suspects. Then, at a moment when he is temporarily baffled, the Inspector receives a letter inviting him to a secret *rendezvous* at midnight, where the writer will be waiting to give him important information. He arrives to find a dying man, who is just able to gasp out "Horace" (or was it Hoxton?) before expiring in his arms. The murderer has struck again!

"You see the idea, my boy? It removes any doubt in the reader's mind that the first death was accidental, and provides the detective with a second set of clues. By collating the two sets—"

"You mean," asked Julian, "that it would be taken for granted that the murderer was the same in the two cases?"

"Well, of course, my dear boy, of course!" said Marius, surprised at the question. "What else? The poacher, or whoever it was, had witnessed the first murder but had foolishly given some hint of his knowledge to others—possibly in the bar of the local public house. Naturally the murderer has to eliminate him before the information can be passed on to the police."

"Naturally," said Julian thoughtfully. "Yes. . . . Exactly. . . . You know"—and he smiled at his uncle—"I think something might be done on those lines."

For there, he told himself happily, was a foolproof plan. First, commit a completely motiveless murder, of which he could not possibly be suspected. Then, which would be easy, encourage Uncle Marius to poke his "nose for things" into the case, convince him that he and he alone had found the solution, and persuade him to make an appointment with the local inspector. And then, just before the Inspector arrives, "strike again." It was, as he was accustomed to say when passing as a Battle of Britain pilot in Piccadilly bars, a piece of cake.

It may seem to some of you that in taking on this second murder Julian was adding both to his difficulties and his moral responsibility. But you must remember that through all these months of doubt he had been obsessed by one thing only, the intolerable burden of motive, so that suddenly to be rid of it, and to be faced with a completely motiveless killing, gave him an exhilarating sense of freedom in which nothing could go wrong. He had long been feeling that such a murder would be easy. He was now persuaded that it would be blameless.

The victim practically selected himself, and artistically, Julian liked to think, was one of whom Uncle Marius would have approved. A mile or two away at Birch Hall lived an elderly gentleman by the name of Corphew. Not only was he surrounded by greedy relations of both sexes, but in his younger days he had lived a somewhat mysterious life in the East. It did not outrage credibility to suppose that, as an innocent young man, he might have been mixed up in some Secret Society, or, as a more experienced one, might have robbed some temple of its most precious jewel. Though no dark men had been seen loitering in the neighborhood lately, it was common knowledge that Sir George had a great deal of money to leave and was continually altering or threatening to alter his will. In short, his situation fulfilled all the conditions Uncle Marius demanded of a good detective story.

At the moment Julian had no personal acquaintance with Sir George. Though, of course, they would have to be in some sort of touch with each other at the end, his first idea was to remain discreetly outside the family circle. Later reflection, however, told him that in this case he would qualify as one of those mysterious strangers who were occasionally an alternative object of suspicion for the police—quite effectively, because Julian was of a dark, even swarthy, complexion. It would be better, he felt, to be recognized as a friendly acquaintance; obviously harmless, obviously with nothing to gain, even something to lose, by Sir George's death.

In making this acquaintance with his victim, Julian was favored by fortune. Rejecting his usual method of approach to a stranger (an offer to sell him some shares in an oil well in British Columbia), he was presenting himself at the Hall as the special representative of a paper interested in Eastern affairs, when he heard a cry for help from a little coppice that bordered the drive. Sir George, it seemed, had tripped over a root and sprained his ankle. With the utmost good will, Julian carried him up to the house. When he left an hour later, it was with a promise to drop in on a bedridden Sir

Julian allowed Sir George the pleasure of beating him.

George the next day, and play a game of chess with him.

Julian was no great chess player, but he was sufficiently intimate with the pieces to allow Sir George the constant pleasure of beating him. Between games, he learned all he could of his host's habits and the family's members. There seemed to him to be several admirable candidates for chief suspect, particularly a younger brother of sinister aspect called Eustace, who had convinced himself that he was to be the principal legatee. Indeed, the possibility of framing Eustace did occur to him, but he remembered in time that a second framing for the murder of Marius would then be necessary, and might easily be impracticable. Let them sort it out. The more suspects the better.

Any morbid expectations you may now have of a detailed account of the murder of Sir George Corphew will not be satisfied. It is enough to say that it involved the conventional blunt instrument, and took place at a time when at least some of the family would not be likely to have an alibi. Julian was not at this time an experienced murderer, and he would have been the first to admit that he had been a little careless about footprints, fingerprints, and cigarette ashes. But as he would never be associated with the murder, this did not matter.

All went as he had anticipated. A London solicitor had produced a will in which all the family was heavily involved, and the Inspector had busied himself with their alibis, making it clear that he regarded each one with the liveliest suspicion. Moreover, Uncle Marius was delighted to pursue his own line of investigation, which, after hovering for a moment round the Vicar, was now rapidly leading to a denunciation of an under-gardener called Spratt.

"Don't put anything on paper," said Julian kindly. "It might be dangerous. Ring up the Inspector, and ask him to come in and see you tonight. Then you can tell him all about it."

"That's a good idea, my boy," said Marius. "That's what I'll do."

But, as it happened, the Inspector was already on his way. A local solicitor had turned up with a new will, made only a few days before. "In return for his kindness in playing chess with an old man," as he put it, Sir George had made Julian Crayne his sole legatee.

W. J. WALLACE

The Dead Run

Randall pressed himself down against the rock, breathing hard. A bullet snicked above him somewhere, and then the gun that had shot it banged far below. There was a pause, during which he listened to the sound of his breathing and the cry of a bird nearby; and then another snick came off the rock above and a bang from below. He knew that one of the men was keeping him pinned here while the rest came up to get him. The muscles of his thighs twitched with fatigue and his chest hurt where the camera pressed into him. He breathed heavily with terror.

Twenty feet farther up, the gully turned to the left; there the rocks glistened a bright red in the evening sun, but to someone down below, the place where he lay must seem deep in shadow. If he did not move now, he would probably never move again. He began to scramble toward the red spot above him. The stones his feet and hands dislodged clattered down; the clatter echoed in the dry watercourse until it sounded as if bullets were striking all around him. From below came the steady bang of the gun. Surely he would be hit. Surely he would not make it. As he crawled over the lip of the gully, the sun blinded him. He was running on nearly level ground now. He was out of the sniper's range and safe for a moment.

The sun was setting behind a range of mountains that stretched across the Highlands of Scotland. On his right he could see Ben Lawers, one of the highest of them all, towering bright green in the last sunlight. He was running north; they were driving him straight away from civilization, into the wilds. The country below Ben Lawers was in darkness, but he could see a strip of bright blue water which must be Loch Tay. He turned that way, and ran with the sun behind him. The ground sloped downward; heather caught at his legs, and croppings of rocks hurt his feet. He didn't think he could go much farther. His ankle turned and he pitched forward, landing in a washout that slanted away into darkness. He let himself roll, over and over on loose rock. Pain possessed him entirely. Finally he stopped and he lay, deep in a patch of heather, gasping and moaning softly. Let them come for him. . . .

Three hours before, Randall had stood on the terrace of a hotel beside Loch Awe, feeling pleased with himself for having arranged the job he was doing. In his suitcase upstairs was the contract with the airline back

He was running straight away from civilization.

home in the States for color pictures of Scotland, a real plum for any free-lance photographer to get. The camera was an instrument he knew how to use. It was going to be easy to communicate the appeal of this beautiful country to potential travelers.

At the end of the terrace was a group of happy-looking English tourists; they were perfectly located for a shot of the green islands and blue water beyond. Looking into the finder, he saw the composition was perfect. The camera clicked; he rolled the film, clicked the camera again, turned the film again.

Something had gone wrong with the composition. In the finder he saw that the people at the end of the terrace had gathered too close together and were looking at him. As he looked up, a bulky man in green tweeds detached himself from the group and stepped forward.

"I say, old chap, I'll have to have that film," the man said.

"Sorry," Randall said, smiling. "I should have asked your permission. I just had your group in one corner of a shot of the Loch. I'll give you the negatives and prints when I develop the roll tonight."

"I'll have the roll right now," the man said.

"No," Randall said. "This film costs too much for that. I'll use the rest and then give you the part which has you in it."

"You'll give me the whole bloody lot," the man said, reaching forward and grabbing the camera.

The camera, and fitting attached to it, had cost Randall over a thousand dollars. It was his livelihood, and he loved it in the same way a rancher loves his best horse. With an almost instinctive gesture, Randall faked a blow at the man's face. The man let go of the camera to cover himself. Randall turned and ran for the door of the hotel. As he went in, he looked back and saw the man coming after him, followed by the others from the end of the terrace.

Halfway up the stairs to his room, common sense returned to Randall and he stopped. This was silly. All he had to do was invite this fellow to be with him when he did the developing, thus proving to him that the negatives in question had been turned over and no prints made. He could put the matter before the manager of the hotel, to make sure this crowd of supersensitive maniacs didn't throw any punches. Why such a fuss over a couple of innocent pictures? He turned and started down toward the lobby.

At the last turning of the staircase, he looked down and saw the man in green standing at the hotel desk.

"Oh, you must mean Mr. Randall, the American photographer in Room 210," the telephone girl was saying.

The furious look on the man's face as he turned and started for the stairs stopped Randall where he stood.

He saw the man reach inside his jacket, and quite distinctly he heard a click that sounded like the safety catch on a pistol. Frightened, Randall turned and went up one flight, two flights, three flights, running silently on the thick carpet. He stopped and listened; there was silence. Was the man listening too, or had he gone down the corridor below to Room 210? Randall walked quickly along the corridor of the floor he was on, went around one corner, then another, and finally came to a back staircase. He lifted the camera and shoved it beneath his sweater, settling the lanyard on which it hung under the collar of his shirt. He started down the stairs. Somewhere a door slammed shut.

He gave up trying to move quietly, and plunged down. The steps ended in a tiny hall with two doors; one opened outside and the other was for the hotel kitchen. He looked into the kitchen. A lean old Scotsman, whom he recognized as the porter, looked up and stared at him vacantly.

"Would you be wanting something?" the porter asked.

Randall stood for a moment indecisively, wondering if this old man would be any help. On the far side of the kitchen, he saw a door opening slowly. He turned and ran outside. Five feet away, the car he had rented for this trip stood like a friend beckoning. He got in, started the engine and pulled away. As he slowed down at the gate of the hotel yard to make the sharp turn onto the road to the east, he looked back. The man in green tweeds was standing in the front doorway, searching through his pockets and shouting to someone behind him.

Randall laughed, thinking the man was trying to locate his car key and that this might give time to get away. The sound of his own laughter startled him. What was he doing? He was not thinking straight; it was stupid to leave the hotel. Where was he going? He wanted a policeman, and failing a policeman, he wanted to get lost. He did not want to get involved with anyone who intended to use a gun for persuasion.

He had rented a low-horsepower sedan, because it was cheap and yet had room for all his gear. He had it up to 65 by the time he hit the village of Dalmally. There was no one in the street but a boy leading a cart horse, so he did not slow down. The car would not go above 65, and when climbing it lost speed. But the run along Loch Lomond toward Glasgow would be fairly flat. On the top of a hill he looked in the mirror and saw a car far behind him. It looked like a Daimler. Daimlers will do as much speed as the road allows. Terror began to mount in him. A road sign pointed to the right for Glasgow. In desperation, he chose the road to the left which ran northeast toward Loch Tay. When he had rounded a curve, he stopped. Pulling his sweater up to get at the camera, he rolled the film through, took out the spool, put it in a metal container, sealed it and held it for a moment in his hand. He had an impulse to throw it away. You fool, he told himself, if you lose this you lose all chance to bargain. Taking an oilskin pouch from the glove compartment, he wrapped the film container in it and put it in his pocket. He heard the squeal of brakes, and then the gradually fading roar of an engine. The big car had taken the Glasgow road; he had another start.

The speedometer needle was close to 70; the downhill run to Loch Tay had started. Hills rose high on both sides. Then, as he slowed to make a turn and go under a railway bridge, Randall saw the Daimler a half mile or so back on the straightaway. The railway ran parallel to the road for a while, and then crossed over it again. Coming out into the light beyond this second underpass, a truck loomed ahead of Randall, filling half the road. To the right of the truck, filling the other half of the road, men stood with shovels, and one waved a red danger flag. Randall knew he must hit the men, the truck or take to the ditch. He turned the wheel to the left, pulled on the hand brake, and covered his head with his arms. The car dropped, bounced, hit something soft, slid, hit something hard, turned and came to rest upside down. Before he had time to think about it, he crawled out of the car, scrambled to his feet and started climbing. Behind him he heard the road workers shouting.

He was on the far side of a hill before he heard the

big car hit the truck. It was not much of a bang; they must have slowed for the underpass.

When he got to the top of the next rise, he heard the first shot. Crouching and looking back, he could see the man in green standing on the road with a gun in his hand, gesticulating while three men fanned out and began to climb.

The escape from the gully had come later. Lying now in the heather, Randall knew his only hope was to stay perfectly still. He heard shouts above him; then heavy boots came down the washout through which he had tumbled. The sun had gone and darkness was falling swiftly. The beat of his heart made a drumming in his ears.

"Chambers," a voice from the hillside called, "we'll never find the blighter this way. We've got to get back to the hotel and explain his disappearance there."

"You and Ron do that," the man in the boots said. "Mace and I will get to a telephone and start organizing a snare. Be sure you square those chums on the road. We don't want this blowing up on us now."

The speaker moved; he came so close that Randall thought he would be stepped on. He controlled an urge to jump up and run. The steps passed by.

"We haven't a prayer of finding him in this heather at night," another voice said. "We'd better put our lads on the roads and block the whole area. In the morning, we can get him, but we've got to pin him down."

Their footsteps rattled on the loose rock, and then were gone. Randall lay thinking. He saw that fear had muddled him; every step he had taken had been a wrong one. He should never have left the hotel. He knew nothing about the police system in the Highlands of Scotland, but he could not recall ever seeing a single agent of the law since he'd left Glasgow. He had to find a telephone, or get out of the region completely. These men would have an efficient organization, so he was not going to be able to go around asking directions of strangers. Raising his head, he saw lights twinkling in the east. That must be Killin, the settlement at the south end of Loch Tay. He got up. The muscles of his legs protested, and his ankle was stiff, but he found he could hobble along.

By the time he got to Killin, the village was dark. A single light showed down the street, and he limped cautiously toward it. It had to be a telephone box. Suddenly the tops of the trees ahead of him were flooded with light—a car was climbing the small hill behind him. He stepped off the land and into a ditch just in time to avoid the glare of lights as the car breasted the hill and sped into the village. It stopped beside the telephone box and a man got out. The car drove away. The man had a deer-stalker cap on; his left arm cradled a shotgun. He reached into the booth and turned off the light.

Randall felt a tired rage inside him. If he jumped the

man, he could get to the telephone and call for help. But with a bad ankle, he couldn't risk it. One more mistake was likely to finish him. He worked his way through the hedge and crept blindly away from the lane at a right angle. Barbed wire gashed his head, and he cursed softly as he lay flat to crawl under it. The ground sloped suddenly, and then he was sliding forward.

He was elbow-deep in moving water; something solid was pushing against him. It was a canoe. This was his first really positive stroke of luck, and he began to take hope.

The canoe was the kayak type, about ten feet long, with a cockpit just big enough for one person. Randall floated it, put the long paddle with blades at each end—which had been stowed inside—crosswise, to help him balance, and slid his legs into the cockpit. The craft sat very low in the water. Leaning forward to give as little silhouette as possible, he let the current take him. The stream turned, ran straight, turned again, and then seemed to stop. He must be in the Loch.

Cautiously at first, and then with as much strength as he could master, he paddled. It was hard to determine the shape of the lake, but a west wind blew from behind him, and he tried to keep the dark blob of the right bank close at hand, to make the most of this extra push. From his boyhood on the rivers of Wisconsin, Randall knew how to manage the American Indian type of canoe, where you sit or kneel fairly high off the water and propel yourself with a single-bladed paddle. The double motion required for this double-bladed one quickly tired him, but he was determined to keep going. Twice his arms gave out, and he had to rest them, while the wind eased him on. The water was choppy, and it kept splashing into the canoe. His legs were numb, and the blisters that formed on his hands broke and bled. Once he found himself leaning over the front deck asleep, and he realized that the sky was getting lighter. If he was out on this long, narrow lake when the sun came up, he would be finished.

In the increasing light, he saw what he supposed was the place where Loch Tay flowed into the River Tay and onward to the sea. There was a church on a promontory, and roofs beyond. Near him, to the left, there was a tiny island with a heavy growth of trees and a ruined building on it. He made for this. Poling the canoe under a tree that hung over the water, he tried to get out. His cramped legs failed him. He grabbed a branch of the tree and pulled himself up; then he crawled onto the bank and slept.

When Randall woke, the sun was low in the sky. His canoe was still anchored where he had left it. He sat up, looking out at the lake, wondering what he should do next; he hoped he had some cunning left. His pursuers had probably expected him to go south, toward Glasgow, but by now they had probably got tired of beating the hills at the other end of the Loch and begun to think about the water. From where he was, the River Tay ran northeast for about fifteen miles, and then cut south toward Perth. As soon as it grew dark, he would try that course.

As the current took him under the middle span of the bridge and into the river, he saw reflected lights on the water ahead of him. He steered to the shore, pulled the canoe up, and crept along the bank. The lights came from a hotel; the kitchen door was open. A woman was standing with her back to him, humming as she stirred something in a pot on the stove; on the table behind her lay a huge ham. A bell rang, and the woman muttered and left the room. He dodged in, grabbed the ham, and ran for his canoe. As the canoe moved out of the lighted patch of water he heard a woman's voice shouting angrily. His mouth was too full for him to laugh.

A sound in the river ahead of him made Randall drop the ham between his knees and pick up the paddle. He could see white water churning before him. The speed of the river increased.

Randall struggled to guide the canoe where the surface was darkest. The branches of a tree rushed at him, slashed his face. The spidery outline of a footbridge passed above him. The speed of the current lessened.

He hit two more bad stretches like that before midnight. Then he heard a rumble ahead which horrified him. While there was still time, he struggled to the side, beached his canoe and scrambled along the bank,

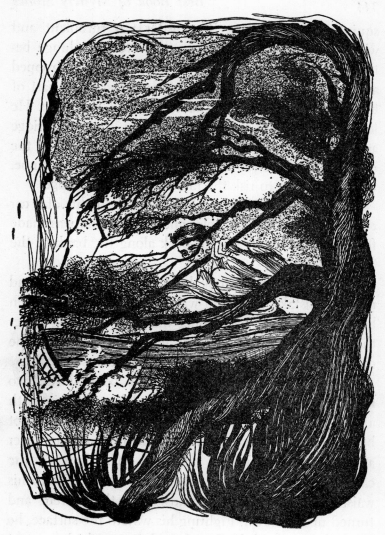

He tried to get out of the canoe.

squinting at the river. The water ran turbulent and white for a long stretch, then narrowed to plunge between two immense rocks, swerved twice, then dropped and ran free. A sign by a bridge over the worst part of this told him he was at the village of Grandtully. He looked wistfully at a road curving away from the bridge and through a cluster of dark houses. He looked at the rapids. They were too long for him to portage the canoe. He would have to risk the rapids or risk the village.

As had happened the night before, the lights of a car cut off hope of human help, and his decision was made for him. Quickly he started back along the bank to the canoe.

When the current took him, Randall knew he had made a mistake. The pull was harder than it had been before. The effort of keeping the canoe moving faster than the water made his chest and spine ache; yet if he did not do so, he could not control his course at all.

Suddenly the white shallows were behind; the two rocks loomed ahead. Randall dug his paddle in with all his weight, turned, nearly rolled, then steadied, shot between the rocks, plunged into roaring, churning water and dropped downward helplessly. The bow of the canoe tilted, swept under. He felt the water rise to his waist. The craft swung broadside to the current and turned upside down. Fighting his way to the surface, he reached down with his legs for a bottom which was not there and realized that he was through the rapids and in deep water. The canoe bumped into him, submerged and moving sluggishly. He hugged the tapering bow to him and waited. The bank of the stream moved slowly by; then his feet touched the bottom. He had made it.

After a rest, he managed to right the canoe and tip enough water out of it to be able to raise one end, drain it and refloat it. He reached far up under the front deck and found the ham still wedged in the bow.

The river grew wider and deeper, and did not carry him so rapidly now. When it joined another stream in a wide curve, he knew he was traveling south at last. He got out the ham and ate some of it. The still of the night was broken by the sound of a train somewhere ahead. The sound dwindled, leaving behind it another sound, a steady popping sound. There was a motorboat coming upstream.

Randall took up his paddle and worked over to the side. There was a place in the rocks along the bank that was big enough to conceal the canoe, but not him. He got out and waded ashore, then he climbed up into the rocks and hid. The sound of the motorboat was growing louder. He pulled farther back, and thought he heard a nearer, softer sound. Slowly he turned his head. Beside him crouched a lanky man, with a long white face and staring eyes.

Screaming like a trapped animal, Randall leaped at

the man and grabbed his throat. "You're one of them!"
he gasped. "You won't get a chance to signal them.
I'll kill you!"

The man kicked him in the belly and rolled free. "Are
you daft?" he whispered. "I'm a poacher like yourself,
man. And if you don't keep mum, you'll hae them down
on us."

Randall lay where he had fallen. The man squatted
behind the brush, peering at the river. The sound of
the motorboat grew. The shrubbery along the bank
sprang into light, and then darkened.

"I doubt he'll have got this far," a voice said. "We'll
go up stream for a mile or so, and then use the oars."

The boat went on, the sound growing duller.

"Jings, that was a close one," the lanky man whispered. He reached out, picked up a sack which lay at his
feet, and stood up. "I'm off," he said. "I'll be lifting no
more salmon from this stream the night, with yon bogies
prowling about like they are. And if you're no daft,
you'll pack it in too."

He was gone. Randall crawled to the edge of the
stream, put his head down and drank. He slid his arm
into the canoe and dragged out the ham. He crept back
to his bush and ate. Then he slept.

The heat of the midday sun woke him. From where
he lay, he could see fields, a line of telephone wires and a
farmhouse. He wanted to go there, but he was afraid.
Someone was learning to play the bagpipes; the same

phrase squealed out over and over again. A cloud of gnats attacked Randall, and he buried his face in his arms. He would run until he was caught. That was the way to do. He slept again.

When darkness came, he started downstream, keeping as close to the bank as possible. His hands were toughening, and he moved the canoe with greater efficiency, concentrating entirely on the paddling. Dawn found him still on the river. Ahead, there was a rumble; high banks rose on either side. There was no way out of this one. He slumped over the paddle. The canoe rose, poised, dropped, dived, rolled and pulled free of him. He lost the paddle. He was gone.

A bright light was shining in Randall's eyes. Someone had a tight hold on his shoulders. A sharp object was cutting his lips. "Aye, that's the lad; take the good soup," a voice was saying. "You've had it close."

Randall struggled to sit up. An old man was standing beside the bed on which he lay. "Where am I?" he asked.

"You're by the River Tay near the village of Stanley," the old man said. "And I am thinking you would be in heaven now, if I had not pulled you out of the wet. I have seen stronger men than you drowned dead when they tried to take a boat over yon waterfall. You have had a good sleep; now take some of the soup."

Randall took the bowl from him and drank without

using a spoon. "You are kind," he said at last. "I was beginning to think there was no kindness left in the world. I met a poacher on the river who was kind."

"You're talking like a loony. What is it that is wrong with you?"

"There are some people chasing me," Randall said. He held his head in his hands. "No," he said, "no, I won't mix you up in this. Is my camera lost?"

"It is standing on yon table, with your tobacco pouch and your money. The canoe will be in the sea by now."

"I've got to get to Perth. I'll leave the camera and come back for it later. May I use your shaving gear?"

"Aye, you may do that. It is raining hard enough to drown you right again, so I will lend you a cap and a mac."

It was dark by the time the bus upon which the old man had put Randall entered Perth. The town was strange to him; it looked drab and dingy. When the bus stopped in what seemed to be a central area, he got off. The driver gave him the directions to get to the police. It was still raining.

Was there someone following him? He felt sure that there was. He turned in at an alley and hid in a doorway, listening. He could hear no sounds but the whistle of a train. Going back to the street, he started to hurry toward the railway station. The waiting people looked up with hostility as he pushed by them. The loudspeaker system was announcing a train to Edinburgh. He followed the crowd going up a flight of steps and along a footbridge over the rails. He ran along the coaches until he found an empty compartment, opened it, and leaped in. It was an old-fashioned carriage with no corridor; the compartment extended completely across. He was sealed in, safe. The train jerked, moved, gathered speed.

Randall leaned back, his eyes closed, puzzling now about what to do when the train reached Edinburgh. If there really had been someone following him in Perth, there was sure to be someone to meet him at the other end. Even if there had not been, it was likely that his pursuers would be watching all trains coming into the Scottish capital. The train crept over the long railway bridge over the Firth of Forth, and passed through the suburbs of the city. As the train began to slow for Princes Street Station, Randall lowered the window and looked up and down the platform. He thought he saw a man in a green suit. He rushed to the other side of the compartment and opened the door. Someone on the rails of the adjacent line shouted; the shout moved past, away. He leaped, landed, stumbled, regained his footing and ran.

There was another platform ahead, and at the end of it a gate standing open and unguarded. More shouts rang out behind.

He raced through the station, with people looking
at him but not moving to intercept. Cabs stood in a
rank outside. He got in the first one.

"Take me to the police station!" he shouted.

The cab swung out into the nearly empty street.
Edinburgh Castle loomed dark over the city. Strings
of light shone down Princes Street, and the wet pavement glistened.

The driver pulled aside the glass which separated
them. "You want the buildings on High Street?" he
asked.

"Yes, anywhere, any police station," said Randall.

The cab turned and started up a hill. Looking
through the back window, Randall saw a large car leave
Princes Street and speed after them.

"Hurry! Hurry!" Randall shouted.

The car was pulling in front of them, forcing them
to stop. The cabby was blowing his horn, and a brightly
lighted tram was rattling its bell and slowing too.
Randall opened the door on the left-hand side and
stumbled out onto the cobbles. As he got to his feet, he
saw the tram creep past, still clanging indignantly. He
ran for it, caught the pole that stood at the entrance,
and pulled himself aboard. He ran swiftly up the curving steps at the rear to the upper deck. He heard the
conductor coming up behind him.

"What was all the racket back there?" the man asked.

"I didn't see," Randall said. "I guess some fool tried

to pass another car on the hill." He held out a two-shilling piece. "To the end of the line."

The conductor gave him his change and a ticket, and went back down the stairs. Randall turned in his seat to watch the road behind. They had turned right onto Princes Street, and then they turned down toward Leith Walk. The tram poked along, stopping occasionally to take on or discharge passengers. Far back, he saw the same big car running beside another tram. They must have spotted the number of the line he took. They were pulling alongside each one and looking over the passengers. His only hope was to get off before they got to this tram. As he started down the stairs, he saw the car pass the tram it had been checking and speed forward.

He leaped down at a brilliantly illuminated junction of three lines. Several people descended with him. Not looking behind, he hurried into the first street he saw, turned left, then right, and ran along a street that twisted and turned. The buildings were grubby and a lot of them looked like warehouses. This must be the Leith dock area. Behind him he heard the sound of several men running.

Ducking around a corner, he bumped heavily into a tall man in blue with a high-domed helmet.

"Now, lad, what's this?" the policeman said, grabbing his arm.

"A gun, a gun," Randall gasped. "Have you got a gun?"

"You know we don't carry guns," the policeman said. "But I'll give you a touch of the stick if you try any hanky-panky."

The sound of running steps was getting louder. With only a night stick to defend them, this man would be no good at all. Randall wrenched himself free and ran. The clump of heavy boots told him the policeman was joining the chase. A whistle squeaked, and another answered somewhere ahead. The road jogged, and he was running beside some sort of canal. There was a shot, and a bullet pinged off the railing near him.

Straight in front of him, where a bridge crossed the canal, a large black car was parked with its headlights on and its motor running. Randall stopped, panting, his breath whistling. The rattle of footsteps behind him grew louder. There was a blue-lighted sign over the windscreen of the car. The sign said *Police*. Someone in the car put a blinding light on Randall. Behind him another shot rang out, and the light moved away to probe the street back there. He ran toward the car. A shot was fired from the car.

"No, no!" he yelled. "Not me!" He pitched forward on his hands and knees and crawled toward the car. Another shot banged behind him. He heard the sound of people getting out of the car on the far side. He put his hand on the handle of the car door. Something hit him

The policeman joined the chase.

a glancing blow on the head, and rough hands seized him. He felt himself sliding into unconsciousness.

"The film," he said. "The film in my pocket." Then he gave up. . . .

The room was crowded with policemen. "What's on the film?" a heavy-faced man was saying to him over and over again. "What's on the film? Where did you get it?"

"I don't know," Randall said. "A picture of some people. They tried to take it away from me. I took the picture at Loch Awe. They chased me over half of Scotland."

"Well, we'll be knowing in a minute," the inspector said. "The lab's developing it now. And we got two of the blokes who were chasing you."

"A man in green?" said Randall hopefully.

"Aye, one of them has a green suit on," the inspector said.

A door opened and a man wearing a white apron burst into the room, waving two photographic prints, one still wet with developing fluid. "Chief," he said. "Look at this! And compare it with this other picture we got from Scotland Yard. Look at this bundle of innocent tourists."

The police gathered about the man. One of them whistled. "It's Chambers and Mace and the rest of the bunch. I thought they were supposed to be in North Africa."

"But that chap in green, the one we've got downstairs," the inspector said, "where have I seen him before?"

"Let's see," said another. "Wait a bit. It's Mac . . . Mac-something. The yachting fellow who gets his pictures in the papers."

"The gold," the inspector said, "the gold that someone has been buying from all the fences in London! They must be pooling it in the Highlands with the idea of moving it out on this bloke's boat."

"And here we've been checking every ship that goes out of Leith, and all the airplanes from Prestwick!"

The inspector said, "All right, get cracking." He turned from the group and said to Randall. "No wonder they chased you. This picture you took of the yachtsman out hobnobbing with Chambers' gang of smugglers gives us the answer to something that has been puzzling us for months."

Randall blinked at the inspector, still not understanding all that had been said.

"This is a brave lad," the inspector was saying. "What he needs is a soft bed and a pretty lassie to stroke his brow. He's still all of a piece, but he's fair battered. Angus, take our American chum around to the Royal Infirmary, and tell them to treat him as a Prince of the Realm."

Randall let himself be led away. At that moment all that mattered was that he had completed his dead run and come off winner. When his curiosity came back to him, he would pick up the pieces. He would see what had become of his car, pay for the canoe he'd lost and square his bill at the hotel. He would go back to see the old man who had pulled him out of the water. He would take a few more innocent pictures. And then—

Well, then he might even be able to find the lanky poacher in order to toss a few drams of whisky with him, and perhaps do a little legal fishing with him.

G. K. CHESTERTON

The Blast of the Book

Professor Openshaw always lost his temper, with a loud bang, if anybody called him a Spiritualist; or a believer in Spiritualism. This, however, did not exhaust his explosive elements; for he also lost his temper if anybody called him a disbeliever in Spiritualism. It was his pride to have given his whole life to investigating Psychic Phenomena; it was also his pride never to have given a hint of whether he thought they were really psychic or merely phenomenal. He enjoyed nothing so much as to sit in a circle of devout Spiritualists and give devastating descriptions of how he had exposed medium after medium and detected fraud after fraud: for indeed he was a man of much detective talent and insight, when once he had fixed his eye on an object, and he always fixed his eye on a medium, as a highly suspicious object. There was a story of his having spotted the same Spiritualistic mountebank under three different disguises: dressed as a woman, a white-bearded old man and a Brahmin of a rich chocolate brown. These recitals made the true believers rather restless, as indeed they were intended to do; but they could hardly complain, for no Spiritualist denies the existence of fraudulent mediums; only the Professor's flowing narrative might well seem to indicate that all mediums were fraudulent.

But woe to the simple-minded and innocent Materialist (and Materialists as a race are rather innocent and simple-minded) who, presuming on this narrative tendency, should advance the thesis that ghosts were against the laws of nature, or that such things were only old superstitions; or that it was all tosh, or, alternatively, bunk. Him would the Professor, suddenly reversing all his scientific batteries, sweep from the field with a cannonade of unquestionable cases and unexplained phenomena, of which the wretched rationalist had never heard in his life, giving all the dates and details, stating all the attempted and abandoned natural explanations; stating everything, indeed, except whether he, John Oliver Openshaw, did or did not believe in Spirits; and that neither Spiritualist nor Materialist could ever boast of finding out.

Professor Openshaw, a lean figure with palleonine hair and hypnotic blue eyes, stood exchanging a few words with Father Brown, who was a friend of his, on the steps outside the hotel where both had been breakfasting that morning and sleeping the night before. The

Professor had come back rather late from one of his grand experiments in general exasperation, and was still tingling with the fight that he always waged alone and against both sides.

"Oh, I don't mind you," he said laughing. "You don't believe in it even if it's true. But all these people are perpetually asking me what I'm trying to prove. They don't seem to understand that I'm a man of science. A man of science isn't trying to prove anything. He's trying to find out what will prove itself."

"But he hasn't found out yet," said Father Brown.

"Well, I have some little notions of my own, that are not quite so negative as most people think," answered the Professor, after an instant of frowning silence; "anyhow, I've begun to fancy that if there is something to be found, they're looking for it along the wrong line. It's all too theatrical; it's showing off, all their shiny ectoplasm and trumpets and voices and the rest; all on the model of old melodramas and mouldy historical novels about the Family Ghost. If they'd go to history instead of historical novels, I'm beginning to think they'd really find something. But not Apparitions."

"After all," said Father Brown, "Apparitions are only Appearances. I suppose you'd say the Family Ghost is only keeping up appearances."

The Professor's gaze, which had commonly a fine abstracted character, suddenly fixed and focussed itself as it did on a dubious medium. It had rather the air of a man screwing a strong magnifying-glass into his eye. Not that he thought the priest was in the least like a dubious medium; but he was startled into attention by his friend's thought following so closely on his own.

"Appearances!" he muttered, "crikey, but it's odd you should say that just now. The more I learn, the more I fancy they lose by merely looking for Appearances. Now if they'd look a little into Disappearances—"

"Yes," said Father Brown, "after all, the real fairy legends weren't so very much about the appearance of famous fairies; calling up Titania or exhibiting Oberon by moonlight. But there were no end of legends about people *disappearing*, because they were stolen by the fairies. Are you on the track of Kilmeny or Thomas the Rhymer?"

"I'm on the track of ordinary modern people you've read of in the newspapers," answered Openshaw. "You may well stare; but that's my game just now; and I've been on it for a long time. Frankly, I think a lot of psychic appearances could be explained away. It's the disappearances I can't explain, unless they're psychic. These people in the newspapers who vanish and are never found—if you knew the details as I do . . . and now only this morning I got confirmation; an extraordinary letter from an old missionary, quite a respectable old boy. He's coming to see me at my office this morning. Perhaps you'd lunch with me or something; and I'd tell the results—in confidence."

"Thanks; I will—unless," said Father Brown modestly, "the fairies have stolen me by then."

With that they parted and Openshaw walked round the corner to a small office he rented in the neighbourhood; chiefly for the publication of a small periodical, of psychical and psychological notes of the driest and most agnostic sort. He had only one clerk, who sat at a desk in the outer office, totting up figures and facts for the purposes of the printed report; and the Professor paused to ask if Mr. Pringle had called. The clerk answered mechanically in the negative and went on mechanically adding up figures; and the Professor turned towards the inner room that was his study. "Oh, by the way, Berridge," he added, without turning round, "if Mr. Pringle comes, send him straight in to me. You needn't interrupt your work; I rather want those notes finished tonight if possible. You might leave them on my desk tomorrow, if I am late."

And he went into his private office, still brooding on the problem which the name of Pringle had raised; or rather, perhaps, had ratified and confirmed in his mind. Even the most perfectly balanced of agnostics is partially human; and it is possible that the missionary's letter seemed to have greater weight as promising to support his private and still tentative hypothesis. He sat down in his large and comfortable chair, opposite the engraving of Montaigne; and read once more the short letter from the Rev. Luke Pringle, making the appointment for that morning. No man knew better than Professor Openshaw the marks of the letter of the crank; the crowded details; the spidery handwriting; the unnecessary length and repetition. There were none of these things in this case; but a brief and businesslike typewritten statement that the writer had encountered some curious cases of Disappearance, which seemed to fall within the province of the Professor as a student of psychic problems. The Professor was favourably impressed; nor had he any unfavourable impression, in spite of a slight movement of surprise, when he looked up and saw that the Rev. Luke Pringle was already in the room.

"Your clerk told me I was to come straight in," said Mr. Pringle apologetically, but with a broad and rather agreeable grin. The grin was partly masked by masses of reddish-grey beard and whiskers; a perfect jungle of a beard, such as is sometimes grown by white men living in the jungles; but the eyes above the snub nose had nothing about them in the least wild or outlandish. Openshaw had instantly turned on them that concentrated spotlight or burning-glass of sceptical scrutiny which he turned on many men to see if they were mountebanks or maniacs; and, in this case, he had a rather unusual sense of reassurance. The wild beard might have belonged to a crank, but the eyes completely contradicted the beard; they were full of that quite frank and friendly laughter which is never found in the

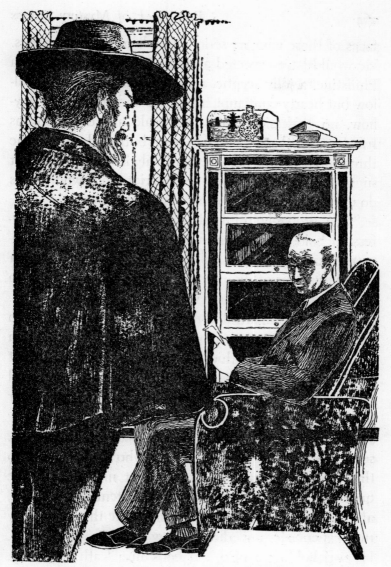

The wild beard might have belonged to a crank.

faces of those who are serious frauds or serious lunatics. He would have expected a man with those eyes to be a Philistine, a jolly sceptic, a man who shouted out shallow but hearty contempt for ghosts and spirits; but anyhow, no professional humbug could afford to look as frivolous as that. The man was buttoned up to the throat in a shabby old cape, and only his broad limp hat suggested the cleric; but missionaries from wild places do not always bother to dress like clerics.

"You probably think all this is another hoax, Professor," said Mr. Pringle, with a sort of abstract enjoyment, "and I hope you will forgive my laughing at your very natural air of disapproval. All the same, I've got to tell my story to somebody who knows, because it's true. And, all joking apart, it's tragic as well as true. Well, to cut it short, I was missionary in Nya-Nya, a station in West Africa, in the thick of the forests, where almost the only other white man was the officer in command of the district, Captain Wales; and he and I grew rather thick. Not that he liked missions; he was, if I may say so, thick in many ways; one of those square-headed, square-shouldered men of action who hardly need to think, let alone believe. That's what makes it all the queerer. One day he came back to his tent in the forest, after a short leave, and said he had gone through a jolly rum experience, and didn't know what to do about it. He was holding a rusty old book in a leather binding, and he put it down on a table beside his revolver and an old Arab sword he kept, probably as a curiosity. He said this book had belonged to a man on the boat he had just come off; and the man swore that nobody must open the book, or look inside it, or else they would be carried off by the devil, or disappear, or something. Wales said this was all nonsense, of course; and they had a quarrel; and the upshot seems to have been that this man, taunted with cowardice or superstition, actually did look into the book; and instantly dropped it; walked to the side of the boat—"

"One moment," said the Professor, who had made one or two notes. "Before you tell me anything else. Did this man tell Wales where he had got the book, or who it originally belonged to?"

"Yes," replied Pringle, now entirely grave. "It seems he said he was bringing it back to Dr. Hankey, the Oriental traveller now in England, to whom it originally belonged, and who had warned him of its strange properties. Well, Hankey is an able man and a rather crabbed and sneering sort of man; which makes it queerer still. But the point of Wales's story is much simpler. It is that the man who had looked into the book walked straight over the side of the ship, and was never seen again."

"Do you believe it yourself?" asked Openshaw after a pause.

"Well, I do," replied Pringle. "I believe it for two reasons. First, that Wales was an entirely unimaginative man; and he added one touch that only an imaginative man could have added. He said that the man walked straight over the side on a still and calm day; but there was no splash.''

The Professor looked at his notes for some seconds in silence; and then said: "And your other reason for believing it?''

"My other reason," answered the Rev. Luke Pringle, "is what I saw myself.''

There was another silence, until he continued in the same matter-of-fact way. Whatever he had, he had nothing of the eagerness with which the crank, or even the believer, tries to convince others.

"I told you that Wales put down the book on the table beside the sword. There was only one entrance to the tent; and it happened that I was standing in it, looking out into the forest, with my back to my companion. He was standing by the table grumbling and growling about the whole business; saying it was tomfoolery in the twentieth century to be frightened of opening a book; asking why the devil he shouldn't open it himself. Then some instinct stirred in me and I said that he had better not do that, it had better be returned to Dr. Hankey. 'What harm could it do?' he said restlessly. 'What harm did it do?' I answered obstinately. 'What happened to your friend on the boat?' He didn't answer; indeed I didn't know what he could answer; but I pressed my logical advantage in mere vanity. 'If it comes to that,' I said, 'what is your version of what really happened on the boat?' Still he didn't answer; and I looked round and saw that he wasn't there.

"The tent was empty. The book was lying on the table; open, but on its face, as if he had turned it downwards. But the sword was lying on the ground near the other side of the tent; and the canvas of the tent showed a great slash, as if somebody had hacked his way out with the sword. The gash in the tent gaped at me; but showed only the dark glimmer of the forest outside. And when I went across and looked through the rent I could not be certain whether the tangle of the tall plants and the undergrowth had been bent or broken; at least not farther than a few feet. I have never seen or heard of Captain Wales from that day.

"I wrapped the book up in brown paper, taking good care not to look at it; and I brought it back to England, intending at first to return it to Dr. Hankey. Then I saw some notes in your paper suggesting a hypothesis about such things; and I decided to stop on the way and put the matter before you, as you have a name for being balanced and having an open mind."

Professor Openshaw laid down his pen and looked steadily at the man on the other side of the table; concentrating in that single stare all his long experience of many entirely different types of humbug, and even some eccentric and extraordinary types of honest men. In the ordinary way, he would have begun with the healthy hypothesis that the story was a pack of lies. On the whole he did incline to assume that it was a pack of lies. And yet he could not fit the man into his story; if it were only that he could not see that sort of liar telling that sort of lie. The man was not trying to look honest on the surface, as most quacks and impostors do; somehow, it seemed all the other way; as if the man *was* honest, in spite of something else that was merely on the surface. He thought of a good man with one innocent delusion; but again the symptoms were not the same; there was even a sort of virile indifference; as if the man did not care much about his delusion, if it was a delusion.

"Mr. Pringle," he said sharply, like a barrister making a witness jump, "where is this book of yours now?"

The grin reappeared on the bearded face which had grown grave during the recital.

"I left it outside," said Mr. Pringle. "I mean in the outer office. It was a risk, perhaps; but the less risk of the two."

"What do you mean?" demanded the Professor. "Why didn't you bring it straight in here?"

"Because," answered the missionary, "I knew that as soon as you saw it, you'd open it—before you had heard the story. I thought it possible you might think twice about opening it—after you'd heard the story."

Then after a silence he added: "There was nobody

out there but your clerk; and he looked a stolid steady-going specimen, immersed in business calculations."

Openshaw laughed unaffectedly. "Oh, Babbage," he cried, "your magic tomes are safe enough with him, I assure you. His name's Berridge—but I often call him Babbage; because he's so exactly like a Calculating Machine. No human being, if you can call him a human being, would be less likely to open other people's brown paper parcels. Well, we may as well go and bring it in now; though I assure you I will consider seriously the course to be taken with it. Indeed, I tell you frankly," and he stared at the man again, "that I'm not quite sure whether we ought to open it here and now, or send it to this Dr. Hankey."

The two had passed together out of the inner into the outer office; and even as they did so, Mr. Pringle gave a cry and ran forward towards the clerk's desk. For the clerk's desk was there; but not the clerk. On the clerk's desk lay a faded old leather book, torn out of its brown-paper wrappings, and lying closed, but as if it had just been opened. The clerk's desk stood against the wide window that looked out into the street; and the window was shattered with a huge ragged hole in the glass; as if a human body had been shot through it into the world without. There was no other trace of Mr. Berridge.

Both the two men left in the office stood as still as statues; and then it was the Professor who slowly came to life. He looked even more judicial than he had ever

Mr. Pringle ran towards the clerk's desk.

looked in his life, as he slowly turned and held out his hand to the missionary.

"Mr. Pringle," he said, "I beg your pardon. I beg your pardon only for thoughts that I have had; and half-thoughts at that. But nobody could call himself a scientific man and not face a fact like this."

"I suppose," said Pringle doubtfully, "that we ought to make some inquiries. Can you ring up his house and find out if he has gone home?"

"I don't know that he's on the telephone," answered Openshaw, rather absently; "he lives somewhere up Hampstead way, I think. But I suppose somebody will inquire here, if his friends or family miss him."

"Could we furnish a description," asked the other, "if the police want it?"

"The police!" said the Professor, starting from his reverie. "A description. . . . Well, he looked awfully like everybody else, I'm afraid, except for goggles. One of those clean-shaven chaps. But the police . . . look here, what *are* we to do about this mad business?"

"I know what I ought to do," said the Rev. Mr. Pringle firmly, "I am going to take this book straight to the only original Dr. Hankey, and ask him what the devil it's all about. He lives not very far from here, and I'll come straight back and tell you what he says."

"Oh, very well," said the Professor at last, as he sat down rather wearily, perhaps relieved for the moment to be rid of the responsibility. But long after the brisk and ringing footsteps of the little missionary had died away down the street, the Professor sat in the same posture, staring into vacancy like a man in a trance.

He was still in the same seat and almost in the same attitude, when the same brisk footsteps were heard on the pavement without and the missionary entered, this time, as a glance assured him, with empty hands.

"Dr. Hankey," said Pringle gravely, "wants to keep the book for an hour and consider the point. Then he asks us both to call, and he will give us his decision. He specially desired, Professor, that you should accompany me on the second visit."

Openshaw continued to stare in silence; then he said, suddenly:

"Who the devil is Dr. Hankey?"

"You sound rather as if you meant he was the devil," said Pringle, smiling, "and I fancy some people have thought so. He had quite a reputation in your own line; but he gained it mostly in India, studying local magic and so on, so perhaps he's not so well known here. He is a yellow skinny little devil with a lame leg, and a doubtful temper; but he seems to have set up in an ordinary respectable practice in these parts, and I don't know anything definitely wrong about him—unless it's wrong to be the only person who can possibly know anything about all this crazy affair."

Professor Openshaw rose heavily and went to the telephone; he rang up Father Brown, changing the luncheon engagement to a dinner, that he might hold himself free for the expedition to the house of the Anglo-Indian doctor; after that he sat down again, lit a cigar and sank once more into his own unfathomable thoughts.

Father Brown went round to the restaurant appointed for dinner, and kicked his heels for some time in a vestibule full of mirrors and palms in pots; he had been informed of Openshaw's afternoon engagement, and, as the evening closed in dark and stormy round the glass and the green plants, guessed that it had produced something unexpected and unduly prolonged. He even wondered for a moment whether the Professor would turn up at all; but when the Professor eventually did, it was clear that his own more general guesses had been justified. For it was a very wild-eyed and even wild-haired Professor who eventually drove back with Mr. Pringle from the expedition to the north of London, where suburbs are still fringed with heathy wastes and scraps of common, looking more sombre under the rather thunderous sunset. Nevertheless, they had apparently found the house, standing a little apart though within hail of other houses; they had verified the brass-plate duly engraved: "J. D. Hankey, M.D., M.R.C.S." Only they did not find J. D. Hankey, M.D., M.R.C.S. They found only what a nightmare whisper had already subconsciously prepared them to find: a commonplace

Father Brown went round to the restaurant.

parlour with the accursed volume lying on the table, as if it had just been read; and beyond, a back door burst open and a faint trail of footsteps that ran a little way up so steep a garden-path that it seemed that no lame man could have run up so lightly. But it was a lame man who had run; for those few steps there was the mis-shapen unequal mark of some sort of surgical boot; then two marks of that boot alone (as if the creature had hopped) and then nothing. There was nothing further to be learnt from Dr. J. D. Hankey, except that he had made his decision. He had read the oracle and received the doom.

When the two came into the entrance under the palms, Pringle put the book down suddenly on a small table, as if it burned his fingers. The priest glanced at it curiously; there was only some rude lettering on the front with a couplet:

> *They that looked into this book*
> *Them the Flying Terror took;*

and underneath, as he afterwards discovered, similar warnings in Greek, Latin and French. The other two had turned away with a natural impulsion towards drinks, after their exhaustion and bewilderment; and Openshaw had called to the waiter, who brought cock-tails on a tray.

"You will dine with us, I hope," said the Professor to the missionary; but Mr. Pringle amiably shook his head.

"If you'll forgive me," he said, "I'm going off to wrestle with this book and this business by myself somewhere. I suppose I couldn't use your office for an hour or so?"

"I suppose—I'm afraid it's locked," said Openshaw in some surprise.

"You forget there's a hole in the window." The Rev. Luke Pringle gave the very broadest of all his broad grins and vanished into the darkness without.

"A rather odd fellow, that, after all," said the Professor, frowning.

He was rather surprised to find Father Brown talking to the waiter who had brought the cocktails, apparently about the waiter's most private affairs; for there was some mention of a baby who was now out of danger. He commented on the fact with some surprise, wondering how the priest came to know the man; but the former only said, "Oh, I dine here every two or three months, and I've talked to him now and then."

The Professor, who himself dined there about five times a week, was conscious that he had never thought of talking to the man; but his thoughts were interrupted by a strident ringing and a summons to the telephone. The voice on the telephone said it was Pringle; it was rather a muffled voice, but it might well be muffled in all those bushes of beard and whisker. Its message was enough to establish identity.

"Professor," said the voice, "I can't stand it any

They verified the name on the brass plate.

longer. I'm going to look for myself. I'm speaking from your office and the book is in front of me. If anything happens to me, this is to say good-bye. No—it's no good trying to stop me. You wouldn't be in time, anyhow. I'm opening the book now. I . . ."

Openshaw thought he heard something like a sort of thrilling or shivering yet almost soundless crash; then he shouted the name of Pringle again and again; but he heard no more. He hung up the receiver, and, restored to a superb academic calm, rather like the calm of despair, went back and quietly took his seat at the dinner-table. Then, as coolly as if he were describing the failure of some small silly trick at a *séance*, he told the priest every detail of this monstrous mystery.

"Five men have now vanished in this impossible way," he said. "Every one is extraordinary; and yet the one case I simply can't get over is my clerk, Berridge. It's just because he was the quietest creature that he's the queerest case."

"Yes," replied Father Brown, "it was a queer thing for Berridge to do, anyway. He was awfully conscientious. He was always so jolly careful to keep all the office business separate from any fun of his own. Why, hardly anybody knew he was quite a humorist at home and—"

"Berridge!" cried the Professor. "What on earth are you talking about? Did you know him?"

"Oh, no," said Father Brown carelessly, "only as you say I know the waiter. I've often had to wait in your office, till you turned up; and of course I passed the time of day with poor Berridge. He was rather a card. I remember he once said he would like to collect valueless things, as collectors did the silly things they thought valuable. You know the old story about the woman who collected valueless things."

"I'm not sure I know what you're talking about," said Openshaw. "But even if my clerk was eccentric (and I never knew a man I should have thought less so), it wouldn't explain what happened to him; and it certainly wouldn't explain the others."

"What others?" asked the priest.

The Professor stared at him and spoke distinctly, as if to a child.

"My dear Father Brown, Five Men have disappeared."

"My dear Professor Openshaw, no men have disappeared."

Father Brown gazed back at his host with equal steadiness and spoke with equal distinctness. Nevertheless, the Professor required the words repeated, and they were repeated as distinctly.

"I say that no men have disappeared."

After a moment's silence, he added, "I suppose the hardest thing is to convince anybody that o plus o plus o = o. Men believe the oddest things if they are in a series; that is why Macbeth believed the three words of the three witches; though the first was something he knew himself; and the last something he could only bring about himself. But in your case the middle term is the weakest of all."

"What do you mean?"

"You saw nobody vanish. You did not see the man vanish from the boat. You did not see the man vanish from the tent. All that rests on the word of Mr. Pringle, which I will not discuss just now. But you'll admit this; you would never have taken his word yourself, *unless* you had seen it confirmed by your clerk's disappearance; just as Macbeth would never have believed he would be king, if he had not been confirmed in believing he would be Cawdor."

"That may be true," said the Professor, nodding slowly. "But *when* it was confirmed, I knew it was the truth. You say I saw nothing myself. But I did; I saw my own clerk disappear. Berridge did disappear."

"Berridge did not disappear," said Father Brown. "On the contrary."

"What the devil do you mean by 'on the contrary'?"

"I mean," said Father Brown, "that he never disappeared. He appeared."

Openshaw stared across at his friend, but the eyes had already altered in his head, as they did when they concentrated on a new presentation of a problem. The priest went on:

"He appeared in your study, disguised in a bushy red beard and buttoned up in a clumsy cape, and announced himself as the Rev. Luke Pringle. And you had never noticed your own clerk enough to know him again, when he was in so rough-and-ready a disguise."

"But surely," began the Professor.

"Could you describe him for the police?" asked Father Brown. "Not you. You probably knew he was clean-shaven and wore tinted glasses; and merely taking off those glasses was a better disguise than putting on anything else. You had never seen his eyes any more than his soul; jolly laughing eyes. He had planted his absurd book and all the properties; then he calmly smashed the window, put on the beard and cape and walked into your study; knowing that you had never looked at him in your life."

"But why should he play me such an insane trick?" demanded Openshaw.

"Why, *because* you had never looked at him in your life," said Father Brown; and his hand slightly curled and clinched, as if he might have struck the table, if he had been given to gesture. "You called him the Calculating Machine, because that was all you ever used him for. You never found out even what a stranger strolling into your office could find out, in five minutes' chat: that he was a character; that he was full of antics; that he had all sorts of views on you and your theories and your reputation for 'spotting' people. Can't you understand his itching to prove that you couldn't spot your own clerk? He has nonsense notions of all sorts.

About collecting useless things, for instance. Don't you
know the story of the woman who bought the two most
useless things; an old doctor's brass-plate and a wooden
leg? With those your ingenious clerk created the character of the remarkable Dr. Hankey; as easily as the
visionary Captain Wales. Planting them in his own
house—"

"Do you mean that place we visited beyond Hampstead was Berridge's own house?" asked Openshaw.

"Did *you* know his house—or even his address?" retorted the priest. "Look here, don't think I'm speaking
disrespectfully of you or your work. You are a great servant of truth and you know I could never be disrespect-
ful to that. You've seen through a lot of liars, when you
put your mind to it. But don't *only* look at liars. Do,
just occasionally, look at honest men—like the waiter."

"Where is Berridge now?" asked the Professor, after
a long silence.

"I haven't the least doubt," said Father Brown, "that
he is back in your office. In fact, he came back into
your office at the exact moment when the Rev. Luke
Pringle read the awful volume and faded into the void."

There was another long silence and then Professor
Openshaw laughed; with the laugh of a great man who
is great enough to look small. Then he said abruptly:

"I suppose I do deserve it; for not noticing the nearest helpers I have. But you must admit the accumulation

of incidents was rather formidable. Did you *never* feel just a momentary awe of the awful volume?"

"Oh that," said Father Brown. "I opened it as soon as I saw it lying there. It's all blank pages. You see, I am not superstitious."